Imperiled Young
Widows #2

A TREACHEROUS TREASURE

Imperiled Young Widows Book 2

Melanie Dickerson

GraceFaith Press

ISBN-13: 9798784672247
ASIN: B09NMNMZVN

Cover design by: Erin Dameron-Hill
Library of Congress Control Number: 2018675309
Printed in the United States of America

To Aaron
I have found the one
my soul loves

CONTENTS

A Treacherous Treasure

CHAPTER ONE

January, 1811, Derbyshire, England

Rebecca finished the tiny sock she'd been knitting as two tears dripped off her cheeks and onto her hand.

She took a deep breath then dabbed at her eyes with her handkerchief. She'd spent too much time crying. And these socks would warm the feet of the new baby that the Carter family had just welcomed into the world.

"Why do you torture yourself?" Rebecca's mother had said when she caught her crying a month after she lost her unborn child.

"I'm not torturing myself." Rebecca was still sad. Was that so strange?

"The doctor said you are well enough. You can try again."

Rebecca wanted to retort that she didn't want her child to have a father who was unfaithful to his family. But she said nothing. Her mother would only stare sadly at the floor and mumble something about hoping Arthur Heywood would change his ways.

A man who was unfaithful didn't change his ways, did he? Not when his whole life's aim was to make conquests of other men's wives.

Rebecca busied herself with gathering the things she would take to the Carter family. They'd had five children in seven years, and the poor mother was pale and sickly. Rebecca feared she wouldn't last the coming winter, so she was determined to bring her nourishing food as often as she could.

She went into the kitchen to gather the rest of the things, taking the servant girl Agatha with her to help carry the baskets.

The cold, crisp air and sunshine on the lane seemed to lift some of the heaviness in her chest. Then a brightly colored bird with a red face and yellow wing flew across their path.

"How pretty. Agatha, was that a goldfinch?" Rebecca asked.

"I believe it was, ma'am."

Rebecca took deep breaths as they walked along, forcing her mind not to linger on anything sad. It was a lovely day, cold but not too cold, a few bright white clouds in a blue sky.

"I wonder that they call it a goldfinch," she said, forcing herself to make conversation, which always took her mind off her troubles. "It only has one tiny spot of yellow on its wing and has that red cap."

"They should call it a redcap instead of a goldfinch." Agatha smiled up at her.

"I quite agree. Redcap is much more accurate."

When they arrived at the small home of the Carters, the mother greeted them at the door. She was quite thin, though she'd just given birth, and she held a small child of about two years old on her hip.

"Mrs. Heywood. How good of you to visit."

"We brought a few things for your larder." Rebecca held up a basket.

"You are so good." Mrs. Carter's eyes swam with tears. "Won't you come in?"

"Just for a moment."

Rebecca and Agatha went inside and sat on the only two upholstered chairs in the room, while Mrs. Carter sat on a stool and rocked her baby's cradle with her foot.

The sleeping baby's face started to crimp, his fists moving about. He was about the same age her baby would have been, if he or she had lived.

A pain went through her chest. She had to look away from the baby and blink back the tears that threatened.

Mrs. Carter's three older children stared up at her from the floor, the oldest only seven years old.

They talked for a few minutes about Mr. Carter's harvest that year, which had been "nothing out of the common way, but we're not complaining," Mrs. Carter said.

After a few more minutes, Rebecca stood up to go.

At the door, Rebecca said softly as she and Agatha were leaving, "Please send for me if you become ill." Rebecca let Agatha move far enough away that she couldn't hear what she was saying. "I can send some remedies. I know you and Mr. Carter don't have any near relations, so if you need help with the children, since they're so young, I will have a servant come and help look after you."

"That is very kind of you, ma'am. You're so good to us, better than we deserve."

Rebecca only smiled and took her leave.

She and Agatha had only managed to walk thirty feet from Mrs. Carter's door when she saw one of the grooms hurrying down the lane toward her.

"Is something the matter?" she asked.

"Yes, ma'am," he said, swallowing, as if trying to catch his breath. "I was sent to find you and bring you home." He never looked her in the eye and shifted his feet.

"What is it? Who sent for me?"

"Ma'am, I . . . I cannot say." He ran a hand down his face, not once but twice.

Rebecca prided herself on being patient with her servants, but she felt heat rise into her forehead. "I insist you tell me why I'm being sent for."

Even Agatha looked stunned at the man being less than forthcoming.

"Ma'am, it's Mr. Heywood. He . . . well, ma'am, he's been found . . ."

Her stomach sank as a terrible dread washed over her. "Found? What do you mean?"

"He was found in the woods. He's been shot dead."

~ ~ ~

Rebecca watched them bring Arthur's lifeless body into the drawing room and placed him on the table, the one where Arthur entertained other gentlemen, sitting around the table drinking and smoking

and playing cards. Now his head and torso just fit, his legs dangling off the edge at the knees.

"Mrs. Heywood, ma'am?" Adler, the butler, was standing next to her.

"Yes?"

"Shall we send for the constable and the coroner?"

He didn't want to send for a physician? But if Arthur was dead, there was no need for a physician. Her mind seemed sluggish, slow to comprehend what was happening.

"Yes, please send for the constable and coroner. Thank you." It took a great deal of effort just to speak the words. Her body felt numb, except for her aching head, as her thoughts whirled and tumbled, one on top of the other.

Her father's words echoed through her mind: "Some enraged husband will shoot him dead before he's forty years old."

Her father was right, it seemed.

She was a widow.

Deep inside, in her innermost being, the numbness dissipated as pity and empathy invaded her spirit, pity and empathy for the horror Arthur must have felt just before he was shot, once in the middle of his forehead.

Such things didn't happen in England, not to wealthy gentlemen.

Could it have been a duel? But the seconds—the duelers' friends who volunteered to be witnesses and to make sure no one broke the rules of the duel—should have been there to care for him and send for a physician, or someone. Could they have run away when Arthur

was shot through the head? That would not have been proper at all, especially so close to Arthur's home. As seconds, they should have stayed, should have carried the body home.

The servants stared down at Arthur's marred face, at the hole in his forehead. Surprisingly little blood was seen, but Rebecca did not go near. She was even glad for the menservants blocking her view.

Arthur's mother entered the room, still in her dressing gown. When she saw him lying there, she started screaming, "My beautiful boy!" She screamed incoherently, covering her mouth. She moaned, then leaned over him, touching his face. Finally, she fell on him, draping her upper body over his chest.

Rebecca fled from the room.

She covered her ears as she hurried to get away from Arthur's mother's moans and exclamations of grief.

Perhaps if the woman had grieved her son's adulterous behavior enough to confront him about it, rather than continuing to dote on him in the midst of his immature, immoral behavior . . . But Rebecca was cruel to think such things at a time like this.

When she was finally in her bedroom, the sobs came, wracking her body. She sobbed until she couldn't breathe, until she thought she would faint.

She lay across her bed, the tears still streaming from her eyes. She was a widow, with no children. Only twenty-two years old and her life was over.

Rebecca's parents had ten children to provide for, so when the young and wealthy Mr. Arthur Heywood made her an offer of marriage, she could hardly have refused. Besides that, he was handsome and said such

things that would turn any young girl's head.

So many times her mother had said, "Rebecca, you are the prettiest of your sisters. You must marry well. Your family is depending on you."

She was also the eldest daughter, having three older brothers who were going into the church, the army, and the law. They would likely never be rich, so it fell on Rebecca to raise her sisters' chances of marrying well.

When Arthur came to her on bended knee, professing undying devotion, she truly believed he loved her. In the few weeks before they were married, he'd complimented her on everything from her teeth to her hair to her embroidery. She had enjoyed the compliments, not seeing them as empty flattery. He'd said nothing, after all, about her good character.

There were moments when she had doubts about his character—when she overheard him talking with other men about gambling and drinking and women—but she ignored her doubts. After all, her mother was thrilled with the match she'd made, and her sisters all said he was very handsome.

How foolish she had been.

And now it was over. Arthur was gone.

This couldn't be happening. It must be a dream she'd soon wake from. But until she did wake from this dream, she had to be strong and do what needed to be done.

Many details would have to be dealt with, and even though Rebecca had heard a bit about what had to be done prior to a funeral—an undertaker or funeral furnisher had to be sent for, the house had to be draped in black cloth, mourners had to be hired—she did not know about all the arrangements that went along with the death of a family member. No one close to her had died since her grandparents when she was only a small child. But her mother would know what to do.

Rebecca rose from her bed and wrote a letter to her mother in London, begging her to come to her as soon as possible, even though Mother had only just left her a few weeks earlier, having stayed with Rebecca until she was physically recovered from losing her baby.

Mother was so calm, and she always knew what to do. But would she be able to come back so soon after her last visit?

She sent the letter by express courier while her mother-in-law's voice could still be heard screaming and sobbing over Arthur's body in the drawing room.

The constable arrived soon after. He'd brought with him one other man, and she watched them from the window.

The constable—Mr. Fogg was his name, if she remembered correctly—was tall with gray hair and a rather large belly. The man with him was probably the coroner, who was responsible for investigating murders and suspicious deaths.

They dismounted from their horses as one of the servants met them in front of the house. The three men walked toward the stables, probably to speak with whoever had found Arthur's body.

Rebecca moved away from the window, weary to her bones, even though it was barely noon. To escape her mother-in-law's grief, she went back up the stairs to her room, her legs aching with the effort.

It was certain to be a long day.

~ ~ ~

"I have sent word to the Justice of the Peace," the constable, Mr. Fogg, said. "This is the coroner, Mr. Pursglove."

Mr. Fogg was seated across from her, along with Mr. Pursglove, both staring intently at her. They had been wandering about the estate for an hour before coming into the house and asking for her.

The landowners of the county were responsible for taking a turn serving as the constable for one year at a time. But since most landowners would rather pay someone to take their year's duty, Mr. Fogg had held the office for a few years now. As constable, he was responsible for investigating crimes happening in the area.

The coroner answered to the Justice of the Peace, who would call him in to investigate possible murders, which was just one of the coroner's duties.

"Mrs. Heywood, did your husband have any enemies?"

"Not that I know of. That is . . ." Her face started to burn, and no doubt her cheeks were turning red. Why was this so difficult to say? It was not as if she had done anything wrong. But the shame was still there. "My husband was unfaithful to me with several women, most of whom had husbands."

By the looks on the men's faces, they already knew this. Of course. Everyone knew.

"Did he speak to you about anyone who wanted to kill him?" The constable was a large man with heavy jowls that hung down on either side of his mouth.

"No." He rarely spoke to her at all for the last few months, since she lost the baby. "Was my husband killed in a duel?"

The two men looked at each other. Finally, the

constable said, "We don't think so."

"You don't?"

"Near the body, we found a hole in the ground that seemed to have been dug with a shovel. We think whoever killed him planned to bury the body."

"I see." Rebecca saw no reason to alter her opinion that he'd been killed by the angry, jealous husband of one of Arthur's paramours.

The coroner, a thin man with a thick black moustache, began to speak.

"Mrs. Heywood, when did you last see your husband?"

"Yesterday, about five o'clock in the afternoon. He left with his gun and said he was going shooting."

"Alone?"

"Yes."

"Is that unusual?" The constable took up the questioning again.

"Somewhat. I don't know. I've only been married to him for two years."

"And he did not return?"

"Not that I know of. Sometimes he doesn't come home and I don't know where he is. That is not unusual, and I did not think it very strange when he did not return home."

The coroner cleared his throat. "He appeared to have been dead for a few hours. The time of death was probably sometime yesterday evening."

Rebecca took this in. Had he died immediately, or had he been on the ground for hours before succumbing? She rubbed her temple as her headache worsened.

"Why wasn't I told?" Her mother-in-law's voice came from down the hall. "I will hear what is said about my son." She came bustling into the room, wiping her nose with a handkerchief.

Rebecca felt her shoulders tense as Arthur's mother turned red, puffy eyes on her.

"What did they say?" she demanded, as if the men weren't in the room.

"Mrs. Heywood, please accept our condolences for the loss of your son," the constable said in his deep, gravelly voice. "The coroner was saying that he believes the time of death was yesterday evening, perhaps around six or seven o'clock."

Mrs. Heywood's expression slackened, as if she didn't know what to say. Rebecca had never seen that look on her face before.

The coroner said, "Would you like us to send for the midwives—there are two excellent ones hereabouts —to come and prepare the body?"

"I will not have a stranger touching my son's body." Mrs. Heywood's imperious tone sent a shiver across Rebecca's shoulders as Arthur's mother raised her chin. But a moment later, her face began to crimp up, and soon she was wailing again, that high-pitched sound that made Rebecca want to jump up and run away.

Rebecca folded her hands together in her lap and squeezed until her knuckles ached.

"My poor boy," she said between sobs, as the wailing dissipated. "My poor, poor boy." She held the handkerchief up to her nose.

The men looked uncomfortable. Women of polite society did not cry and wail, especially in the company of others. But Mrs. Heywood did as she pleased.

The coroner and the constable stared at the floor

and then each other. Finally, they stood up. "We must go. Mrs. Heywood." They nodded at Rebecca, then at her mother-in-law. "Mrs. Heywood."

They hurried from the room, no doubt relieved to get away from the display of raw emotion.

"And his father dead these three years." Tears streamed from Mrs. Heywood's eyes. "I don't know how he could have lived through seeing his son like this, murdered at the age of twenty-eight, his life cut short. I will never get over this, never."

She started to wail again.

Perhaps Rebecca should try to comfort her mother-in-law, but she doubted that her efforts to embrace the grieving woman would be well received. Instead, she went up to her room and spent the rest of the day crying, praying, writing to her mother and sisters, and avoiding Mrs. Heywood.

CHAPTER TWO

The next day Rebecca still did not feel hungry, but she knew her mother would tell her to eat something, even if it was only some dry bread.

Her eyes were still a bit puffy and red from crying, but she washed her face and went down to the breakfast room. And there sat Mrs. Heywood still in her dressing gown, her hair in disarray, in a way Rebecca had never seen before. She looked up at her and pressed her lips together, then looked away. Somehow Rebecca couldn't bring herself to greet her mother-in-law with the usual "Good morning," either.

Mrs. Heywood had treated Rebecca like an intruder ever since she married her precious only child. She'd seemed determined to let Rebecca know that she was not good enough for her son without ever saying so outright. But in a hundred little ways—her looks of contempt when Rebecca mentioned her family, her sneers and grunts whenever Rebecca said something about her own dress or hair or preferences of food—Rebecca's mother-in-law let her know that Rebecca was inferior and she disapproved of her.

All Mrs. Heywood's compliments were for her son and her dead husband. Although, one of the maidservants had let it slip once that Mrs. Heywood expressed nothing but contempt for her husband, until he died. After his death, her husband was suddenly a saint, the best man, the best husband and father, the best at shooting, the best at whatever was being talked of at the moment.

"Arthur was such a good son, so good to me," Mrs. Heywood said in her tearful voice.

There was no one else in the room so Rebecca had to assume she was speaking to her. But she couldn't truthfully agree, so she said nothing.

"When he was twelve years old and came home from school on holiday, he gave me a whole armful of flowers he picked." She started sobbing again.

"That was thoughtful of him."

He never gave Rebecca flowers, not once. Perhaps she should have married him when he was twelve.

"And I loved him so much and would have done anything for him." Mrs. Heywood dramatically sobbed after every few words. "And he loved me. He was the best son, and I doted on him, and now he's gone. Whatever shall I do?" The wailing started anew.

"And you." She pointed her finger at Rebecca, her sobs suddenly ceasing. "You changed him. I know you must have coerced him into changing his will so that you would inherit everything if he died. And now I shall be forced from my home, this home, where I raised my child! This home that he loved!" She paused to wail and then blow her nose, loudly, into her handkerchief. "He never stayed away from home so much before you came here to live. I know you must have treated him poorly to make him stay away so much. I blame you for every night he spent away from me, every unkind word he spoke to me. You don't know what you did to me."

The sobbing began again.

Rebecca's breaths were coming fast as she rose from her seat and hurried out of the room and out of the house, only pausing to grab a bonnet and a shawl.

She hurried across the yard toward the woods, not knowing, not caring where she went, as long as she escaped from that insufferable woman.

It was true that Mrs. Heywood doted on Arthur, and now that he was gone, she would have nothing to focus her energy on. Truly, Rebecca did feel pity for her. But the woman felt no pity for Rebecca, not when Rebecca cried for hours in her room because of Arthur's newest tryst with his paramour; not when Rebecca cried for days after she lost her unborn baby; and not now, when Rebecca had lost her husband. All of Mrs. Heywood's pity was for herself. And now her false accusations were like a knife into her heart, as she was actually blaming Rebecca for Arthur's dalliances.

As she entered the woods, she had to pause to catch her breath, but not because of the exertion of walking. She focused on breathing in and out, on the trees around her, on the cool air that was unusually warm for January.

When her racing heart and breathlessness had eased, she began walking again, a new feeling seeping into her consciousness. Was the anger toward her mother-in-law, along with the shock of Arthur's death, starting to fade? Although she was still horrified that Arthur had been murdered, and Mrs. Heywood's cruelty still stabbed at her, she was beginning to feel something else. Dare she identify it as relief?

All but pushed out by sorrow and horror, the relief remained, a tiny niggling at the corner of her thoughts. Relief was the shy mouse in the vast room of grief and pain.

Her breathing back to normal, Rebecca knew she should return to the house to retrieve her sturdier walking shoes, but she couldn't bear the thought of going back. If she heard her mother-in-law's voice right now she might lose her sanity.

She kept walking through the woods, the bushes and low branches catching at her skirts and brushing against her shoulders. Perhaps the quiet trees and fields would calm her whirling thoughts and give her a bit of peace.

~ ~ ~

Thomas Westbrook strode toward the stables and encountered his head groom, Telfer.

"I'll need my horse. Are all the animals well?"

"All's well," Telfer said, as he set to work saddling Thomas's favorite horse.

"Even with the pointer, Sally? She hasn't had her puppies?"

"Not yet, sir. She's getting around, but slowly. All's well."

A high-pitched whimpering sound seemed to be coming from behind the stable. He left Telfer and went to find the source of the noise. When he reached the back of the building, he didn't see anything. Then he heard it again, coming from a pile of brush.

As he neared the brush pile, he saw a dog, white with light brown spots. It raised big soulful eyes at him.

Thomas squatted to examine the dog more closely. He wasn't one of Thomas's hunting dogs. "What's the matter, boy? Are you lost?" Slowly, Thomas reached out to the dog, let him smell his hand, then patted his head.

The dog struggled to his feet, wagging his long, slender tail. But the wagging seemed to put him off balance and he wobbled.

The poor thing was malnourished and a bloody wound close to his ear had crusted over.

"Did you lose a fight, little one?" He stroked the dog's head and the poor thing crumpled, as if he didn't have the strength to stand any longer. "You stay here. Don't move, now."

Thomas started back toward the stable, calling "Telfer!"

"Yes, sir?"

"Fetch me a blanket."

"Yes, sir." The servant returned with one of the rough woolen blankets they used for the dogs and horses.

Thomas laid the blanket on the ground beside the dog, then carefully gathered the dog in his arms and placed him on the blanket. Then he scooped him up in the blanket and carried him into the stable to the area where his trained hunting dogs slept.

"Easy now, there you go." Thomas placed the dog on the hay and knelt beside him. He looked up at Telfer. "Fetch him some food, will you? I think he's lost."

"Of course, sir."

Thomas stayed beside the dog, talking quietly to

him, surveying the injury, until Telfer returned and gave the dog some food and water.

"I can wash him, sir. Your horse is ready."

"That horse doesn't like to wait once he's saddled, does he?" Thomas smiled at how impatient his horse could be.

"No, sir."

Thomas stayed with the stray dog a bit longer, petting him and talking softly to him. Had he been mistreated and cast out? Or was he simply lost? He would ask around and see if his tenants had lost a dog.

"Don't worry, boy," Thomas said softly. "We'll take care of you."

Thomas gave instructions not to let the other dogs mistreat the newcomer. "I think he just needs food and perhaps a good bath," Thomas said.

"Yes, sir. We'll do our best for him, and I believe he'll be good as new in a few days."

"Thank you, Telfer."

Thomas went on his ride, anxious to clear his head of the unwelcome thoughts about Arthur Heywood, the ones that had kept him from sleeping the night before. He wanted to clear his conscience about his unforgiveness toward his childhood friend, to finally feel as if he had forgiven the betrayals.

A country ride, alone on his favorite horse, nearly always helped him figure things out.

~ ~ ~

Rebecca kept walking, admiring the hardiness of the trees and bushes to survive winter's cold, trying to think of anything besides the pain and horror of the last twenty-four hours—and indeed, the last two years of betrayal and crushing disappointment. But gradually her mind wandered, like a stream meandering down to a larger river, back to her life since she married Arthur Heywood.

Her mother-in-law had never allowed her sisters or her mother to visit for any length of time without making snide remarks about not having one's house to one's self, even when they only stayed for a few days. But now the house was Rebecca's and she could do as she liked. And she wanted her sisters and her mother. She wanted their comfort, their compassionate voices, their embraces.

Certainly she would never receive those things from her mother-in-law, just as she'd never received them from her husband. When he was alive.

She still could hardly believe he was dead.

She'd loved him so very much. But married life had never been as she'd imagined it. And in the last year or so, she'd come to associate his very face and voice with pain, rejection, and an ache in her chest.

"You can't hurt me anymore," she whispered, imagining she was speaking directly to her husband, even as the tears began to fall. She sat down on a fallen tree trunk and let the sad thoughts and tears flow.

Why was she crying? For all the bitter disappointments the last two years had delivered, the discoveries of her husband's unfaithfulness, his cold looks and cold words to her. For these she cried, as well as for a man's life, wasted and cut short, her own husband, to whom she was pledged and bonded.

She had grieved that she would never feel loved by him, but now, gaining his love wasn't even possible.

After what seemed like half an hour, Rebecca stopped crying and dried her face with her handkerchief. A bird sang nearby, completely oblivious to her sadness. And why should anyone care? Most people would probably, silently anyway, congratulate her on being rid of a philandering husband, the same ones who felt only scorn for her before he was dead.

As she thought of what she would do now, she thought of all the people she could help. Her mother-in-law hated that she took food baskets to the poor, but would she continue to make hostile, barely-veiled remarks now that Rebecca was inheriting everything her mother-in-law once called hers?

Rebecca did not look forward to living with her mother-in-law now that Arthur was gone. But she couldn't cast her out either. Perhaps the woman would go live with her stodgy brother in Cornwall.

Rebecca only knew that she was bone weary of feeling rejected and betrayed by her husband, and rejected and despised by his mother.

Her mother-in-law had already mentioned Rebecca getting a new husband. But how could she ever marry again? The thought made her feel sick to her stomach.

She'd been so sure that Arthur loved her before they married. He'd even had his will changed so that, if he died, and if they had no son, Rebecca would inherit his entire estate. That proved he loved her, did it not? His mother would be provided for by a jointure his father had set up long ago, and to which Arthur had added a small annual sum. Mrs. Heywood would also be entitled to live in the cottage near the main house, the Dowager Cottage, in which Arthur's grandmother had resided until her death.

She could still see Arthur's face when he said the

doting and sweet things he used to say. But he had ceased to say those things to her, his love hardly lasting a few months into the marriage. His feelings had gradually shifted to indifference and then cold resentment. Resentment for what? She'd done nothing except love him. He resented her for existing, she supposed, and for being so uninteresting that he had to go and chase other men's wives.

She'd been reassured by more than one woman that it was not her fault that her husband strayed.

"They all do it," Lady Broadhurst told her. "It's in the nature of a man. He wants to think he is irresistible to every woman he sees. He wants to think he can conquer this or that man's wife, to make himself feel superior. It has nothing to do with the wife."

But Rebecca didn't possess such a universally dim view of men. Her father, after all, was not the sort of man to want to "conquer" other women in order to "feel superior" to other men. However, she did feel a strong aversion to marrying again. How could she ever trust another man enough to marry him?

She was better off alone. Now she was free to do what gave her joy, which was to spend time with her sisters and her mother, and to take gifts to the poor. Just a month ago she had learned that one of their tenants had a broken plough and couldn't afford a new one. Rebecca secretly had her servant purchase a new one and deliver it to them. Rebecca had rarely ever felt such excitement and joy, especially when the tenant's wife sent her a note of profound gratitude, saying she was sure Rebecca had been the source of the gift.

Why should Rebecca not do what gave her pleasure, now that she was a wealthy widow?

As she continued on her walk, she made note of the trees. Though they were not very beautiful this time of year, she liked the starkness of the limbs against the gray sky, and she could imagine them on the cusp of summer, when they were the most beautiful. On her walks, there were certain meadows where the wildflowers were breathtaking. Whether they were on the Heywood estate or the Westbrook estate that was adjacent, she wasn't sure. She'd never been told where the Heywood land ended and the Westbrook land began.

Wyghtworth was the neighboring estate belonging to Thomas Westbrook, a former lieutenant who had recently come back from the war when his father died. He was a gentlemanly young man, but Arthur had told her once to stay away from him, that there was bad blood between the two of them.

"Because of a woman you took from him?" Rebecca had asked. It was just a guess, and she said it partly to goad him, as she was still upset by the rumors circulating about his latest conquest.

Instead of getting angry, as she half expected, Arthur simply arched his eyebrows and said, "How did you know?"

At the time she didn't feel much of a reaction to his words, but the memory suddenly made her blood boil. How dare he be smug about something despicable that he had done? And how could she ever have been fooled into thinking he loved her, that he was at heart a good man? How could she have been so naïve and imperceptive?

She plucked a leaf from a hawthorn tree and shredded it between her fingers as she walked, taking deep breaths as painful memories flooded her thoughts one after another.

She'd tried to keep herself as resigned as possible about her marriage and her husband, resigned to the way things were, while still hoping that her husband would change his philandering ways. But now that all hope was gone, the pain was suddenly coming over her in waves.

But she would not let it. She would not let herself think about it. Someday when it was not so painful, then she would think about it. But now she had to survive the next few days, the funeral, the people expressing their condolences, the hypocrisy of society's death rituals. How she hated them. But she had to survive them without drawing attention to herself, so she must stuff her feelings as far down as possible, out of sight and out of mind.

Clouds were gathering overhead, but it didn't look like rain just yet, so she kept walking.

She filled her lungs with air, breathing in deeply and letting it out slowly, gazing around at the flowers as she walked through a meadow between two small groups of trees. Truly, it was a lovely place, the flowers, the weeds and grasses, the trees on either side. She let the breeze flow through her hair and closed her eyes, imagining she was happy and at peace, surrounded by people who cared about her, without a trouble in the world.

A bee buzzed by her ear, waking her from her daydream. She shook her head at her own foolishness and continued toward the stand of trees, unwilling to turn back.

Just as she was about to enter the tree line, she saw a man to her far right, bent over with a shovel, digging in the ground next to a large rock.

She stared but couldn't see his face, and he was turned with his back to her. Who could that be? And why was he digging? She shuddered as a picture came to mind of the coroner saying that they found where someone had been digging a hole next to her husband's body. They'd assumed he was digging a hole to hide her husband's body. Was that what this man was doing? No, no, her husband's body was at home, in the drawing room, awaiting his funeral and a Christian burial.

So, who was this, and what was he doing?

The man lifted his head and turned toward her. He stood motionless, staring back at her, but with the position of the sun, his face was shadowed and she still could not see his face.

"What are you doing there?" Rebecca called out, shading her eyes from the sun's glare. "If you are one of the servants—"

The man threw down his shovel and picked up a gun, a long one. He swung it around, pointing it at her. Then he fired, the gun jerking back in his hands as a loud boom sounded and sparks came from the gun's barrel.

Rebecca's heart slammed against her chest. She ran for the cover of the trees.

How dare that man fire a gun at her?

She ran as fast as she could. Was she about to be murdered just as Arthur was?

O God, save me, help me. It was all she could think, just, *God save me. God help me.* The words reverberated in her head even as her blood raced through her veins and she kept running.

Tree limbs clawed at her hair and her dress. Soon

she would reach the other side of the small wood and be in a clearing once again.

Should she try to hide here in the woods? Once she reached the clearing, he'd have another clear shot of her. And he might even have run around the lower side of the trees and be waiting on her on the other side. Oh, why had she not run the other way, toward home!

Her heart pounded so hard she could hardly breathe. Her chest hurt with the effort to force in the air, but she kept moving toward the tree line, but veering to the left, staying in the cover of the trees as long as she could.

Finally, she emerged into the open field, running through the rows of mounded dirt.

The sound of the gun firing behind her made her knees go weak. A shudder shook her whole body. He was shooting at her again.

She felt no searing pain and did not hear a repeat sound of the gun going off, so she kept running, still praying, *God, help me.*

She'd heard her husband talk of a gun that would repeat without having to stop to reload. If that man had that type of gun, he would surely kill her.

Suddenly, she saw a horse and rider ahead of her, coming toward her at a fast trot. Would he try to kill her too?

She recognized him as Thomas Westbrook and ran toward him.

CHAPTER THREE

Thomas heard a gunshot, and a flood of urgency swept over him.

The sound transported him to the battlefield. He was being shot at again. His heart thumped hard against his chest and sent the blood flowing to his head.

But he was not on the battlefield. He was on his own land in the quiet countryside. And the sound came from toward the Heywood estate.

If Arthur Heywood were still alive, he'd say it was his old childhood friend shooting at some birds, and very near Thomas's property line, if he heard the sound correctly. But it could not be Arthur. Indeed, why would anyone be shooting birds on his property, when he was just shot and killed two nights ago?

Another gunshot rang out. The feelings swept over him again, but he did not feel them as acutely this time.

He turned his horse in the direction of the sound

and urged him forward.

Thomas had set out on a quiet ride to sort out his emotions about Arthur Heywood's death—in truth, to ask God to help him forgive his former rival for his treachery of a few years before. He had not expected to hear gunshots or to have these heart-pounding memories flood his mind, taking over his self-control, at least to some extent, and forcing him to relive moments on the battlefield that hadn't affected him this much while they were happening.

He rode hard. Would he find the person who shot Arthur?

As his horse topped a ridge, he saw a woman running across a field, holding up her skirts, a look of fear on her face. As he drew near, he recognized Arthur Heywood's wife—now his widow.

And then he saw a man running behind her, holding a rifle, who suddenly stopped.

She had almost reached him when she said, "A man..." She bent forward, obviously trying to catch her breath.

Thomas came close to her and dismounted from his horse.

"Mrs. Heywood?"

"He's trying to kill me." She gasped, pressing her hand into her side.

"Who's trying to kill you?"

"The man behind me." She turned to look. "He was chasing me. He shot at me twice."

No one was there. The man must have moved back into the small stand of trees.

"Who was he?" Thomas reached into his saddlebag and extracted the pistol he had brought with him.

She took a step back, her eyes fastening on the gun in his hand. "I don't know, but he was chasing me. He shot at me."

"Don't be afraid. I saw the man." Thomas squinted past her, searching for the man.

"Is he there?" She clasped her hands together, as if making an effort to hold herself together.

"I don't see him, but I will go and find him."

"No, don't leave me." Her eyes were wide and she was clutching her hands to her chest.

"I won't leave you. You're safe now." He tried to sound soothing as she leaned toward him.

She suddenly sat down on the ground, sinking straight down, as if her knees had just collapsed underneath her. She reminded him of the poor little dog that had collapsed in front of him just minutes before, behind the stable.

"Mrs. Heywood, you are unwell. Let me help you onto my horse and take you home."

"I assure you I am well."

He held out a hand to her and she accepted it. He lifted her to her feet and, still holding onto her, he said, "Are you well enough to ride?"

"Yes, I thank you. Forgive me. I'm not accustomed to running for my life."

An ironic smile flitted over her lips, only for a moment, just before she drew in a deep breath and let it out.

"Who was the man? Did you know him?"

"No. That is, I didn't see him clearly, but he did not look familiar."

"What caused him to shoot at you?"

"I don't know. I was walking and saw a man. He

was digging in the ground with a shovel, and so I called out to him to ask what he was doing. He picked up a gun and started shooting at me."

"How very strange. And how terrifying for you. You have no idea what this man was doing there or why he was digging?"

"None. But when they found my husband's body," she paused for a moment to swallow, staring out across the field, "they found a hole where someone had been digging. The constable said they thought whoever . . . shot him had meant to bury him there."

Poor woman. "You have had two great shocks in as many days. Please allow me to express my condolences on the loss of your husband."

He might have a very low opinion of her late husband, but he had no reason to think ill of his wife. In fact, he'd heard from some of his tenants how she often called on the poor and took gifts of food and other practical help.

He wondered that Arthur and his mother allowed her to do so. He knew their dim view of charity and of helping their tenants. But they may have ignored the young woman to the point that she could do what she wanted.

"I thank you. It was a shock." She lifted a hand to push back a strand of hair that had fallen across her cheek, and her hand was shaking.

"Let me take you home."

"Thank you, and I shall send the grooms out to look for this man who was trespassing."

"Don't send your grooms. They might get shot. I'll go look for him as soon as you're safely home. But you should send for the constable."

She nodded, but the look on her face and the way she wrapped her arms around herself, he could tell she was reliving the terror of a few moments before. He knew because he'd seen that look on the faces of his men after a battle.

Who was callous enough to shoot at a lady? Especially one as gentle as Mrs. Heywood? He would find the man who did this, Lord willing, and make sure he never bothered her again.

He helped her into the saddle of his horse and the dazed look dissipated. She gazed down at him.

"Thank you for coming to my aid. You probably saved my life."

"I'm grateful I happened to be about. I heard the gunshots and turned my horse in this direction and followed the sounds. I was curious as to who was shooting on my land."

"Is this your land? Forgive me for trespassing."

"Not at all. You may walk here any time you like. Your husband's—that is, your estate—ends just there at that copse of trees."

He led the horse at a slow walk across the field, his pistol in one hand and the reins in the other.

She still looked shaken, but she was amazingly calm for someone whose husband had been murdered the day before and who had just been shot at.

They were quiet on the way back, intermittently speaking of the weather and the wildflowers and trees. When they passed the stable, one of the grooms was standing outside and helping Mrs. Heywood down from the horse.

"We heard the gunshots," the servant said.

"Go and fetch the constable," Mrs. Heywood said.

"Tell him there has been more trouble."

He hurried away while another groom took charge of his horse. "I'll be back for him shortly," Thomas said.

He offered Mrs. Heywood his arm and she took it, leaning on him as they walked the rest of the way to the house.

"Is there anything you need? Any way I might be of service?" he asked as they neared the front steps. "The constable will be here soon. Perhaps I should stay and speak with him."

"Would you? I would be grateful to have you corroborate my story. Did you not say you saw the man who was chasing me?"

"I did."

"Please stay. You can have tea with me."

He couldn't imagine she was feeling up to having company, but she seemed earnest, and he did need to speak with the constable. It would seem strange if he had heard the shots and witnessed Mrs. Heywood being chased but did not stay to tell the constable what he'd seen.

"Very well, but if you need to go up to your room and rest—"

"No, I am well enough."

They went inside and she gazed into the drawing room as they walked past. Thomas caught a glimpse of Arthur's body lying on the table, and there was a servant sitting beside it, doing some kind of needlework.

Already the constant vigil had begun. He remembered when his father had died, someone had to be in the room with his body at every moment, day and night. It was one of the rituals of death and decorum, and it exhausted his mother, who felt she had to be the primary sitter.

Rebecca Heywood rang the bell. "Please bring the tea into the sitting room," she instructed the servant. "Is Mrs. Heywood downstairs?"

"No, mum, she's in her room."

Mrs. Rebecca Heywood's shoulders visibly relaxed, and they went into a sitting room.

"Are you certain you don't wish me to go so that you can lie down upstairs?"

"No, no. All I need is some tea, and the constable will be here quickly. He lives very near."

Soon the tea arrived. She held the cup in both hands, drained it, and poured herself another cup after less than a minute.

"Don't mind me," she said. "I grew up with a bunch of older brothers, one of ten children, and we were not so formal as my husband's family." She stared at the floor.

Was she remembering that her husband was now dead?

He hated to think negatively of the dead, but it was the truth that she had not suffered much of a loss. Still, he was her husband and she must feel as if she'd been dealt a blow. As she'd admitted, it had been a shock.

They drank the entire pot of tea, and her demeanor became less dazed. She suddenly sat up straighter.

"Forgive me. I should have offered you a glass of brandy. May I?"

"No thank you. I rarely indulge, especially this early in the day."

"Good. Oh, I mean . . . forgive me."

He did his best to hide his smile and changed the subject. "You said you were one of ten children?"

"Yes, my father was in business in London. I never lived outside the city until I married. But my father being in trade, I'm afraid my place in society was not very high, which was held against me by some." She smiled, but in an amused way. "I thought I was a very fortunate woman when I married, but life was not as I imagined it would be. And now . . ." She sighed and stared at the floor again.

He wanted to tell her he was sorry, that she had been wronged by her unfaithful husband, and that her status in society was unimportant compared to her worth as a human being of good character. But of course, he said none of those things.

"Forgive me," she said. "I shouldn't have said what I did. Sometimes I'm too honest and open, I'm afraid."

"Not at all. Honesty and openness are excellent traits, and you should not mind what some arrogant, cold-hearted people say or think."

"Thank you." She looked slightly embarrassed as her gaze flitted to the empty teapot in front of them. "And do you have siblings, Mr. Westbrook?"

"A younger brother and sister."

"And do they live at home with you?"

"They do. However, my brother is leaving soon. He will be studying for the church."

"And you are a lieutenant, I believe?"

"Was. I am recently back from the war, having sold my commission."

How strange it was to be in Arthur Heywood's house. It had been ten years since Thomas had set foot in the place. And now he was talking to Arthur's widow as if they were friends after he saved her life from a would-be murderer.

Events in life were sometimes stranger than a book of fiction.

They talked of many things, including their favorite books and authors, the sermon their rector preached on Sunday, and their favorite places in London, all while Arthur Heywood's body lay in the next room.

The time went by quickly and he was surprised when Mr. Fogg, the constable, arrived, as it didn't seem as if he'd had enough time.

As they all greeted each other, he noticed that Mr. Fogg had to wipe a dribble of sweat off his temples. In fact, he wiped his forehead and upper lip too. Strange, on this cool winter day.

"I came right away," Mr. Fogg said. "Are you hurt, Mrs. Heywood?"

"No."

He asked her several questions and she told him the whole story. When she mentioned Thomas and said she was "so relieved when I saw he had a gun and would protect me," he felt quite gratified.

"Has any effort been made to catch the man?"

"Not yet," she said.

"I don't mind going out and helping you look for him," Thomas said. "We don't want some madman running about the countryside shooting at people."

"Yes, and we need to bring him to justice. Murderers in Derbyshire, shooting gentlemen and ladies on their own property. I don't wish our county to have such a reputation."

Thomas stood to go with the constable, thinking how ironic it was that he should be searching for Arthur Heywood's killer, trying to bring him to justice.

"Take every precaution," Mrs. Heywood said, looking genuinely concerned.

Certainly, Arthur did not deserve this woman for his wife. What a terrible man he was, to leave this woman, his lawful wife, at home to chase after other women.

But today he was supposed to be forgiving Arthur and not holding a grudge against him. Obviously, he had more work to do.

CHAPTER FOUR

Rebecca stared out the window, watching the clouds roll in like her gloomy thoughts. But letting her mind go down that dark tunnel would only make her more susceptible to her mother-in-law's cruel words— she knew this from experience—so she tried to focus her thoughts on something more prudent and useful.

Someone would have to be summoned to help arrange things for the funeral. Rebecca knew that anyone with the wealth and social standing that the Heywoods enjoyed would have hired a funeral furnisher, if they were in London. But out here in the countryside, she did not imagine there was a funeral furnisher near enough. Would her mother-in-law know who to engage?

If she did not, Rebecca would speak to the housekeeper, Mrs. Atwater, or the butler, Mr. Adler.

Rebecca might also have to take over her mother-in-law's household duties of conferring with Mrs. Atwater and the cook, recording expenses and ensuring the necessities had been purchased for the week. After all, with the stipulations of Arthur's new will, Rebecca would be in charge of everything, including the house, land, and tenants. The responsibility for them would also fall to Rebecca.

Besides that, her mother-in-law had taken to her bed. But would she be offended by Rebecca taking over, especially if she did not *keep* to her bed? It could turn into a very awkward situation. Would Mrs. Heywood even accept that Rebecca was the new owner?

She caught sight of Mr. Westbrook and the constable striding across the lawn to the front door. Thanks be to God, they had not got themselves killed.

The men came inside.

"Won't you sit down? I can have some more tea brought."

"No, thank you, I will only stay for a minute," Mr. Fogg said. "I wanted to let you know that we found another hole, this time closer to Mr. Westbrook's property, which must have been where you saw the culprit this morning. What he is digging for, I can't imagine, but I think it best that you not go for any more solitary walks on the property until he is caught."

"Of course," Rebecca said.

"It's a very good thing Thomas Westbrook was nearby and had a gun, or you might have been killed." Mr. Fogg lowered his head, but the look coming from beneath his bushy eyebrows was strange, unreadable.

A shudder went through her. Truly, she might be lying beside Arthur now in the drawing room, and her mother-in-law would not mourn *her*, would she?

That thought made her want to laugh, which would be completely inappropriate in this moment.

"Thank you, Mr. Fogg. I am grateful for your help." Again, the laugh tried to bubble up and she had to press her hand to her mouth to stop it. What was wrong with her? She hadn't slept much the night before. Perhaps she was so tired she was becoming hysterical. She had once giggled uncontrollably when she had stayed up most of the night helping care for her little sister who was sick.

Truly, Rebecca sometimes wondered why she was so different from other people, who seemed so quiet and able to control their emotions perfectly well—Mrs. Heywood notwithstanding. Rebecca, on the other hand, was not only prone to laughter, but of speaking the truth out loud, even when it was inappropriate. And in polite society of 1811, the truth was often inappropriate.

"I would walk out with you," Mr. Westbrook said to the constable as he was leaving, "but I have a quick matter of business to discuss with Mrs. Heywood."

"Of course. Good day."

What matter of business could Mr. Westbrook have to discuss with her? Did he wish to buy her husband's property?

When Mr. Fogg had left, Mr. Westbrook glanced up and down the hallway, then came back into the room and said in a quiet voice, "Do you truly have no inkling as to why the man could have been digging on your husband's property?"

"No. None at all."

Mr. Westbrook came to stand closer to her, but not so close as to be improper, but the way he gazed into her eyes made her heartbeat stop and then lurch into motion again. When was the last time Arthur looked her in the eyes? She couldn't even remember.

"Had you never heard your husband tell of a treasure chest of gold doubloons buried somewhere on his property?"

It was a strange question, but there was something familiar about what he was asking. Then she remembered. "I did hear him speak of it once. But he told it as a tale his grandfather once entertained him with when he was a child. He did not think it was true, and yet he bade me not to tell anyone. Could it be?"

Mr. Westbrook raised his eyebrows. "It could, or at least it could be that someone thinks it's true."

"What should I do?" Rebecca whispered.

"If we could figure out why the person is digging where they are digging—did they have a reason for thinking the treasure was buried there? Hear a story about the treasure that indicated where it might be? We might be able to catch them in the act. Either way, tonight I can return to the spot where he was digging and try to catch him."

"Do you think that is prudent? He might shoot you."

"I will have my own guns. Besides, the constable won't do anything, and you need this person to be caught."

"But if any harm comes to you . . ." She didn't think she could bear it, but she didn't want to say that. Mr. Westbrook might get the wrong idea and think she had affectionate feelings for him. The truth was, she was far from feeling affection for any man. She might never feel anything for a man again.

"Do not worry. I survived the Peninsular War so I believe I will survive a treasure hunter."

"Very well. But do be careful."

"I will. And you can let me know if you think of anything your husband may have said about the treasure, where it might be buried, that sort of thing. I promise I will not steal it if I am the one to find it." He smiled.

"Oh, I have no notion that the treasure even exists." Rebecca sighed and shook her head. "But if it does, and if you find it, you should at least receive a reward."

"Any time a hidden treasure trove is found, the coroner must be notified, and an inquest will be called to decide to whom the treasure rightfully belongs, and I believe it will most likely belong to you. You will inherit Arthur Heywood's estate, will you not?"

"I believe so. There is no other heir than I know of."

"Then you can do as you wish with that pirate's treasure."

"Pirate's treasure indeed." She sighed again. What was the world coming to when a man was killed over a buried treasure that probably didn't even exist?

"What is this?"

The elder Mrs. Heywood was glaring imperiously back and forth from Rebecca to Mr. Westbrook with red, puffy eyes. She'd entered the room so quietly, neither of them had noticed.

Rebecca and Mr. Westbrook each took a half step back, away from each other.

To break the awkward silence, Rebecca said, "This is Thomas Westbrook."

"I know," her mother-in-law said with a cold stare. "I've known him since he was born. He and Arthur played together as children. Come to mourn with us and view the body? Or did you only come to pay a call to his widow?" She turned cold, accusing eyes on Rebecca.

She felt her stomach sink and her cheeks start to burn.

"Neither, madam," Mr. Westbrook said, looking calm and unfazed by her insinuations. "I apparently scared away the shooter who murdered your son. Mrs. Heywood and I were just informing the constable of what we saw."

"The constable was here? Why did you not send for me?" She sent another cold glare at Rebecca, then turned it back on Mr. Westbrook. "And you said you scared the murderer away? Why did you not capture him and bring him justice? Do you even want him caught?"

"I can see my presence is upsetting to you, and so I shall go. But I am sorry for your loss and you have my condolences."

He left while Arthur's mother's face grew redder.

"The nerve of that man coming here."

"Was there something amiss between him and Arthur?" Rebecca did her best to sound innocent, hoping Mrs. Heywood would give her more information.

"They did not speak to each other these last several years. And now you had to bring him into the house. Already on the hunt for a new husband, I suppose." She said this quietly, as if to herself.

Rebecca inhaled slowly and slowly let it out. *The woman is in mourning. God, help me be compassionate and not say anything unkind.*

"I have no interest in finding another husband."

"I should think not. But that man is not welcome in my house. Do you understand? He only wants to gloat over us."

It was a ridiculous accusation, given the facts of why Mr. Westbrook was there, but Rebecca knew it was pointless to argue. There was no reasoning with her.

"I am going to my room to rest." Rebecca fled her mother-in-law's presence before she could say anything else that would make her blood boil.

~ ~ ~

Thomas's mother wrote a note to Rebecca Heywood: *Please come to dinner tonight, if you are able. It would be our pleasure to give you a respite from the grief at home, and we are in great need of society ourselves. With all my compassion, Mrs. Anita Westbrook.*

Thomas gave express instructions not to give the note to anyone except the younger Mrs. Heywood.

The servant returned with a note from Rebecca Heywood, obviously hastily written on the back of his mother's note. *Thank you for your kind invitation. I accept. Mrs. Rebecca Heywood.*

Good. Now he could talk to her about the treasure. He shouldn't question whether there was another reason behind his rise in spirits when he saw that she had accepted. But surely he could be happy that his mother and Mrs. Rebecca Heywood could enjoy each other's company, as they were both in need of a friend to break the recent grief in both their lives, his father having just died six months ago.

Truthfully, he was surprised Rebecca Heywood was brave enough to accept the invitation. Her mother-in-law would punish her in some way, he was sure, if she discovered that Rebecca was going to the Westbrook home. Even though Mrs. Heywood had no reason to be angry with Thomas. Arthur must have either told her a lie about him, or Mrs. Heywood hated him because he had hated her precious son.

When Rebecca Heywood arrived for dinner, he watched how she would react to meeting his mother for the first time. She was not like most Englishwomen.

Mother stood and went straight to Rebecca Heywood, taking her hands in hers and looking her in the eye.

"You poor, dear child. May I?" Before Arthur's widow could answer, much less fathom what his mother was about to do, Mother hugged her, putting her arms around the young woman and patting her back.

Rebecca Heywood hugged his mother in return.

"My children tell me I'm too demonstrative, but I don't think so. And you have been through something terrible, just terrible, and I understand."

His mother took not only her hand, but her whole arm, as she led her to sit beside her on the sofa.

"My dear, this is my daughter Caroline and my son Benjamin. And you know my oldest, Thomas."

"We weren't formally introduced, but we are acquainted."

She smiled at his reference to how they met.

"I cannot imagine the shock and terror you must have felt, only one day after your husband's terrible accident. Well, it was no accident, but I am very sorry for what you have suffered. Most unusual and frightening. But we are here to take your mind off of all that."

"Please allow me to offer my condolences," Mrs. Heywood said shyly, "for your husband's passing. I was not allowed to call in person, even though we are such close neighbors."

"Do not fret yourself over that." Mother patted her hand. "I completely understand. Mrs. Heywood, Arthur's mother, doesn't speak to me since the falling out that happened between our sons, but I don't mind that. I am too close to heaven, as old as I am, to hold grudges."

"Of course. But I am very sorry."

"Yes, it was a very sorrowful time for us, but my Tom is in a better place with no sadness and no pain, and we shall all see him again."

"Yes, indeed."

"But it is very sad that we have never had you to dine before today, since we are such close neighbors. I am so glad you accepted my invitation. You have been married to Arthur how long? A year?"

"Two years." Rebecca Heywood appeared to blink back some tears that came into her eyes.

"Two years? Time goes by fast when you are as old as I am. I married my husband when I was older, you see, twenty-eight, and Thomas was born when I was thirty, so I am quite old." She grinned as if that was a good joke. "And now you can follow my example, as you have plenty of time to marry again and have children and a long and happy life. But you don't want to hear about that now, of course. In time . . ."

Caroline leaned forward, as if she was eager to stop her mother from talking, and said, "Mrs. Heywood, what do you do in your spare time? Do you like to read? Do you play and sing?"

"I do like to read, and I do play and sing, but not well."

"Oh, she plays and sings!" his mother exclaimed happily, looking at his sister. "We must hear you, for we love hearing our guests play and sing."

"She may not be up for that tonight, Mother," Thomas said, seeing the look of mild panic on Mrs. Heywood's face.

"That is all well and good. You don't have to play if you don't wish to."

"What is it you like to do?" Mrs. Heywood asked Caroline.

"I like to read, and I like to play and sing, but I dislike painting and drawing and embroidery. I was forced to do it by my tutor, but now I am quite finished with doing things I don't like." She grinned.

"Caroline is eighteen and very accomplished," his mother said.

"But she is not the most conventional eighteen-year-old," Thomas said.

"I do like to flout convention on occasion." His sister liked to imagine she was very unusual and even rebellious, but she was actually fairly quiet and mild. But he would not say that out loud.

Thomas only hoped Mrs. Heywood wouldn't mention the buried treasure in front of his family. His mother would be alarmed, and his brother and sister would want to help look for it. They'd be insulted if he told them it was too dangerous. Besides that, it wasn't buried on his property, it was on Mrs. Heywood's, and her mother-in-law . . . He was acquainted with how difficult she could be.

He had questions for her, and that was one reason he wanted her to come to dinner tonight, but somehow he had to find a way to be alone with her. The other reason he wanted her to come to dinner was to get her away from Mrs. Heywood and her spiteful accusations. The woman could not be pleasant to live with, even on a good day, and these were not good days.

He did feel sorry for Arthur's mother. He was sure she was genuinely sad and distraught over her son's death. But he felt more sorry for Rebecca Heywood.

CHAPTER FIVE

Rebecca probably shouldn't have accepted Mrs. Westbrook's invitation to dinner, but she was so desperate to be out of the house and away from Mrs. Heywood's oppressive, angry sorrow, she immediately wrote her acceptance on the back of the invitation and sent it back with the servant, hoping Mrs. Heywood wouldn't realize anyone had even been there.

She also had to sneak out of the house without her mother-in-law knowing she was leaving, unless she wanted to hear more of her wild accusations.

Fortunately for Rebecca, Mrs. Heywood had flown into a screaming fit about the time Rebecca went to her room to change her clothes. The screaming had ended in hysterical sobbing, which ended with the footman helping her to her room, as she appeared to collapse when the housekeeper was trying to console her. And there she had remained until Rebecca left for Wyghtworth, the Westbrooks' home.

She'd wanted to take the carriage, but Mrs. Heywood would certainly hear of it if she did, so she ended up taking her horse.

Though it would be dark on the way home, it was a short way to Wyghtworth. She would not encounter any murderers, as long as she stayed on the road. But even if she did, she could gallop away in a hurry.

And now, with Mrs. Westbrook treating her like a long-lost daughter, giving her all the compassion and warmth she longed for from her own mother, she was glad she came. It was worth all the wrath she might endure from Mrs. Heywood when she arrived back home.

Dinner was more comfortable than she might have imagined, with everyone treating her like a friend or family member instead of a stranger. She'd forgotten how that felt, having been much too long in the company of her mother-in-law. And while they ate and talked and smiled at each other's stories, she even forgot, for a few minutes here and there, that her husband had been murdered the day before.

She never would have thought such a thing was possible.

At one point, Benjamin said, "Thomas, you said you met Mrs. Heywood yesterday when she was taking a walk. What were you doing on the Heywood property?"

Thomas Westbrook glanced at Rebecca.

"Your brother was saving my life," Rebecca said. Perhaps it sounded dramatic, but it was no less true. "And it was I who was on your brother's estate, not the other way around."

His family members were all staring at Thomas Westbrook. He had not told them, obviously, that he had been the one to save her from the shooter.

"Mrs. Heywood was being chased by a man who was shooting at her," he said. "I heard gunshots and rode in that direction, and when the shooter saw me, he must have decided to run away."

"Oh my!" his sister Caroline exclaimed. "Thomas is a hero."

"He is indeed," Rebecca said.

"Not at all." Thomas shook his head.

"I believe I would be dead, or at least greatly injured now, if your brother had not been there."

"Oh, Thomas." His mother pressed a hand to her mouth, her eyes watery.

Thomas cleared his throat. "I am very thankful I was there at the right time to help Mrs. Heywood."

The table was quiet for a few moments. She dared to glance at Thomas Westbrook, but he was still not looking her way.

Caroline spoke up. "We are all thankful for that." She smiled at Rebecca.

"You are all so kind." Rebecca smiled back, but she still felt a bit numb, as if it were not real.

She already suspected that, even though Thomas had told his family that she'd been shot at, he had not told them about the buried treasure story, nor had he told them their theory that the treasure was the reason someone had shot and killed Arthur. She certainly was not about to mention it. She still remembered how adamant Arthur was that she never tell anyone.

She wondered at him telling her. But it was early in their marriage, the first month or so, when he was still treating her as if he cared for her.

After dinner, they retired to the music room. Caroline played a song, and when she was finished, she said, "There. Now you know what a poor musician I am."

"You did very well. I saw nothing remiss in your playing at all."

"Well, it is a simple song."

Benjamin said with a broad grin, "It's the only song she knows."

"It is not the only song I know," Caroline retorted. "Although I never practiced very much, and it is almost the only song I know well." Caroline conceded with an amused smile.

How refreshing to be around good-natured teasing, the kind she was used to from her own brothers and sisters, and to have made a new friend like Caroline, who was not too proud to admit her own faults.

"Will you play and sing for us?" Caroline asked.

"Only if you feel up to it, dear," Mrs. Westbrook said.

"I will play one." Rebecca got up and went to the pianoforte. She could not bring herself to sing, but she played a song that had been one of her favorites since before she met Arthur, which was associated with no bad memories.

They all applauded. "That was wonderful," Mrs. Westbrook said.

"You play very well," Caroline added.

"I liked to practice when I was younger."

"Only when you were younger?"

"I left the instrument to my younger sisters when they started to learn and I took up writing poetry."

"Truly?" Caroline's face lit up like a sunrise.

"Yes, but I haven't written any in a long time." Not since she was married.

As a wedding present, she had written a poem for Arthur. He'd laughed at it. She could still feel the pain and embarrassment at his reaction to reading the words that she had labored over for two weeks, expressing her love for him and her hopes that their union would be blessed and happy.

But with his laughter stuck in her mind, she hadn't been able to write anything since.

"I would love to read some of your poetry," Caroline said. "It is my opinion that people who play and sing well are also good at other artistic endeavors."

"Oh, yes," Mrs. Westbrook said. "Do you have any of your work memorized? You could recite some for us."

"No, no. My poetry is not very good."

"Why don't you let us be the judges?" Caroline said.

"I cannot. I'm sorry."

The dreadful feeling came over her again, of how unworthy Arthur had made her feel, not just about her poetry, but everything else as well. He'd never given her his approval nor been satisfied with her as a wife.

Perhaps Arthur was more like his mother than she ever realized.

"I wish you would."

"Caroline, she doesn't wish to recite her poetry tonight." Thomas's tone sounded like he was scolding her. Then he looked at Rebecca. "Perhaps another time."

Her heart swelled in gratitude. Was Thomas Westbrook really as good and kind as he seemed?

She'd been fooled before.

After she played one more song and they talked for a while longer, Rebecca said, "I should be going."

"Going?" Mrs. Westbrook said. "But you came on

horseback, did you not? You cannot think we will allow you to ride home after dark."

"No, indeed," Caroline said.

"I agree," Thomas said.

"You must stay the night," Mrs. Westbrook said.

"I'm so sorry, but I cannot." What would her mother-in-law say if she never came home? Her son did it often and was never scolded, but if Rebecca did it, she could just imagine the accusations she would throw at her.

"Mrs. Westbrook would wonder where you are," Thomas said. "I will take her home in the carriage," he said.

"I am sorry you have to go to so much trouble," she said.

"It is no trouble."

He was so stoic, she wondered how he felt about having to escort her home.

A few minutes later, Thomas Westbrook was handing her into his carriage. The prospect of speaking to him alone about the buried treasure, even if it was only for a few minutes, made her feel a bit less sad about having to go back to the place where she'd experienced so much sorrow.

~ ~ ~

Thomas spoke as soon as he heard the noise of the carriage wheels on the road.

"I will go out tonight, back to the place where the man was digging, and see if I can catch him in the act."

"I wish I could go with you." Mrs. Heywood sighed as she twisted her hands together in her lap.

Of course, she knew she couldn't. There were many reasons why, so he said nothing. Then he asked,

"Do you have any ideas about where you can search for information about the treasure, old letters, perhaps?"

"I will search in the library. I don't think anyone has used it since Arthur's grandfather was alive. I am sure to find some old letters in there."

"You may not find anything. It could be a great deal of wasted time."

"I don't mind. I have nothing else to do until my mother and sisters come. But the problem could be searching the room in secret, for my mother-in-law will want to know what I am doing and will no doubt forbid me to be in the library."

"She cannot forbid you any part of the house. It belongs to you now."

"That is true, I suppose, but I am not accustomed to standing up to my mother-in-law."

He could well imagine. That woman was like a fire-breathing dragon. He couldn't help but feel sorry for Rebecca, but . . .

"You will have to start standing up to her. Perhaps if you do, she will find someone else to live with."

"That would be a blessing." He could see her half-frowning in the dark carriage. But after a brief silence, she said, "Forgive me. That was unkind. I'm afraid I have a bad habit of saying what I'm thinking, and it's often improper."

"I believe that is called honesty." But they both knew that speaking the truth was not a very acceptable practice in high society social circles.

"I don't wish to be unkind, but she is very difficult. I must remember that she is grieving. Perhaps God will give me the grace to ignore it." She sighed.

"I'm sure He will, but if you ever wish to have a

respite from her sharp tongue, you are always welcome at Wyghtworth. My mother and sister would enjoy your company very much."

Was it rude that he did not include himself in the people who would enjoy her company? But he didn't want to create a false impression, and there was no chance he could ever be interested in Arthur Heywood's first wife. That was not an affront to her, but the very idea of marrying someone who had formerly been married to Arthur was abhorrent.

The disturbing reality, however, was that he found her appealing, interesting, and intriguing, with her honesty, her warmth toward his mother and sister, and her gratitude toward him for helping her that morning.

These feelings, no doubt, would pass, every time he remembered that she had been married to Arthur Heywood.

"I'm sure you will heed the constable's warning, but I wanted to add my own hope you will refrain from going on any walks in the near future. Best to stay indoors until the man who shot at you is caught."

"I agree." She sighed again, no doubt remembering with whom she was sharing the indoors.

He helped her from the carriage and walked her to the front door of the house. The door was locked and they waited two full minutes for someone to answer the door. No doubt it was her mother-in-law's way of finding out what time she arrived, and of punishing her for being out.

His heart sank at the look on her face when she took her leave of him and went inside. The poor girl. No doubt she would pay for accepting an invitation to dine elsewhere, and especially from the Westbrooks.

CHAPTER SIX

Rebecca relieved the servant who had been keeping vigil beside Arthur's body. The poor girl might have sat there all night and Mrs. Heywood would have still expected her to carry out her full duties the next day. For that reason, Rebecca was glad to be able to sit with the body tonight.

And yet, she was contemplating doing something no relative of the deceased should ever do, which was to leave the body alone while she went to search Arthur's grandfather's library.

It was almost a superstition, this sitting with a dead body at all times until burial. Rebecca even wondered if she'd be able to leave it. But the ritual had arisen from the very real possibility that the deceased was not dead at all, but only in a deep sleep, and keeping vigil could prevent them from being buried alive.

When Rebecca was sure no one was stirring about the house this late, she got up and stared down at Arthur where he lay inside the black velvet-covered coffin. He was not covered in the shroud as of yet, so his face was fully visible. His body had been washed and dressed by two of the menservants, one of whom Mrs. Heywood was particularly fond of, and she had insisted that he be put in charge of preparing the body.

No amount of preparation could disguise the hole in Arthur's forehead where the bullet had entered. And there was certainly no way that Arthur was only in a deep sleep, as she'd heard the servants speak of the much larger hole in the back of his head where the bullet went out.

No, it was safe to leave his body alone.

Carrying a single candle in a candlestick, Rebecca slipped from the drawing room. She went up one flight of stairs and down the hall until she could see that the crack under her mother-in-law's door was dark.

She walked as soundlessly as possible in her thin slippers back down the stairs to the library. The door was closed. She half expected it to be locked, but when she turned the knob, it opened.

Rebecca went inside and closed the door most of the way, leaving a small crack. She still felt raw from everything that had happened, and leaving it partially open made her feel safer.

She glanced out the window, which was in the direction of where Thomas Westbrook would be watching for any digging that might be taking place.

The moon was full and was shining out of a mostly clear sky. Rebecca found herself listening for the sound of a gunshot, fearing Thomas would be shot as her husband had been.

Rebecca had liked coming into this room when

she and Arthur were first married, but only to choose a book from the shelves. One day when she had been perusing the shelves, she looked up to find Mrs. Heywood standing in the open doorway staring at her. The look on her face was so disapproving, Rebecca instantly felt as if she was doing something wrong.

"What are you doing in here?" Mrs. Heywood asked.

"I was looking for a book."

"A book?" She looked as if Rebecca had said she was looking for a scorpion. She had never seen her mother-in-law with a book in her hands.

There was an awkward silence and then she said, "I was looking for a book to read while I—"

"I had an aunt who read books constantly," Mrs. Heywood interrupted her. "She died a spinster, living off the charity of her siblings. I don't suppose that will happen to you, now that you've married my son." She raised her head so that she was looking down her nose at Rebecca. "This was Arthur's grandfather's favorite room. See that you don't disturb anything."

"Of course. I was only looking at the books." Feeling like a scolded child, Rebecca had taken her book and fled the room.

Remembering that encounter and how it had made her feel, Rebecca's blood began to boil, sending heat up her neck and into her face. If she could do it over again, she would tell Mrs. Heywood that she had every right to be in any room of the house that she pleased, and no one could make her feel as if she was some kind of intruder. This was her home just as much as it was anyone else's. And now it was solely hers.

She wouldn't dwell on that. She needed to focus

on finding something about that silly treasure for which Arthur had been murdered, and for which she very nearly had been killed. Perhaps she would even discover that the treasure did not exist. Or that Arthur's grandfather had spent it all building this house.

She started with the old desk that was sitting by the window, which had no shutters or curtains. As she went toward it, she only hoped no one was outside, or they would see her candle, and her in its light, snooping through someone's things who had been long dead.

She set her candle on the desk, which was a massive wooden thing full of drawers and cupboard doors, not fancy or decorated, but heavy and spacious. She opened a drawer and pulled out its contents, spreading the papers on the desk, along with a couple of old quill pens and an inkwell.

Only interested in the papers, she put the pens and inkwell back in the drawer and bent over the papers, holding them close to the candle.

One was a letter from his son. She perused it quickly but there was nothing of interest in it. Another appeared to be a list of items to bring back from the shops in London. A third was a letter that was still sealed, which had apparently gone unsent for many years, as the paper was yellowed. The address on the outside was to an M. Pipken in London.

Who was M. Pipken, and why did Arthur's grandfather never send the letter?

Rebecca stared at the wax seal. She wanted desperately to open it and read it, but she just couldn't bring herself to break the seal. It was someone else's letter, after all, and if she did open it, anyone in future might see what she had done.

But they would not know *she* had opened it. And there was no one alive to care, besides Mrs. Heywood.

She held it a moment longer, then put it back in the drawer.

The rest of the papers were equally as uninteresting as the shopping list and the letter from his son, so she put the papers back and closed the drawer, leaving the sealed letter on top.

She opened a cupboard door that looked large enough to hold three cigar boxes stacked on top of each other. But inside was only a small snuffbox sitting by itself.

Smokeless tobacco. Rebecca never understood why anyone would use it. Her brother told her it would give him a calm feeling when he used it, which wore off fairly quickly, forcing him to snuff more of it.

"Why do you do it, then, if you just have to do more?"

He just grinned and said, "It's the fashion, that's why."

She thought it quite foolish to do something simply because it was the fashion, but she said nothing.

She continued to look through the drawers and found some keys. She tucked them into the pocket on her dressing gown. Why not? After all, if she never needed them for anything, she could always put them back.

Another drawer looked like a letter from his wife, in which she asked him to speak to their son about his behavior, the son being Arthur's father. The writer never specified what kind of behavior he was to speak to him about, but apparently it was well-known, as she said, "No one will ever invite us to another dinner party or ball again if you do not at least urge him to be more discreet."

As the father, so the son?

Rebecca had never met Arthur's father, and Arthur rarely spoke of him, and she did not trust anything Mrs. Heywood said about him, which was only glowing praise.

She put the letter back, feeling the weight of sadness its contents had brought on. What caused a man like Arthur to ignore his wife? Even after she'd been told by multiple people that she was not to blame, she could never cast off the fear that it was her own fault, that she had done something wrong or was somehow inadequate.

It was a pain so deep and so strong, she wondered if she'd ever get over it.

A baby would have soothed that pain, she was convinced. If she could be a good mother, loving her child but not spoiling him, teaching him right from wrong, and always encouraging him in his positive endeavors, she could have felt as if she wasn't useless. And unloved.

The betrayed, unloved wife. That's what she wanted to expunge from her mind and her heart. *God, help me expunge it.* A child would have removed the curse of being unloved and unwanted, but God had not seen fit to give her a child. And now she had a lingering, very uncomfortable feeling of suspicion toward God. *Why, God? Why did you not allow my baby to live?* She had no answers, and it did not make sense to her why God would withhold a good thing such as a baby from her.

She continued to look for something of interest, something concerning the treasure. If she didn't find that information, she might have someone digging up her property for some time, shooting at anyone who saw them, and over a treasure that didn't exist.

At least she had not heard any gunshots tonight. Hopefully Thomas Westbrook was still alive.

As she continued to search through the large desk, memories of the man who had saved her life flitted through her mind.

She'd always thought Arthur was a very handsome man, with his ready smile and his reddish-blond hair and his squared-off jawline and chin. He looked very much like his grandfather, he claimed, who had been a sea captain in the navy and a close friend of the famous Admiral Horatio Nelson.

"Perhaps I should have made the navy my career," Arthur said once before they were married. Instead, he'd waited for his father to die so that he would be a landed gentleman in his own right.

By the time Rebecca had looked through the entire desk, her eyes were burning from the candle's smoke, and her candle was nearly spent. She should probably stop for the night and come back to it another time.

She opened the first cupboard door she'd looked into, just to make sure she hadn't missed anything. There was the snuffbox, alone inside.

She picked it up and examined it. It was not made of gold or even silver. It appeared to be made of tin, so it was not very valuable. She opened it, leaning away, as she hated the smell of the powdery tobacco. But when she looked inside, there was no snuff, but there was something.

She turned the snuffbox upside down in her

hand. There on her palm was a shiny gold coin and a tiny, folder piece of paper no bigger than her thumbnail.

She held the coin closer to the light. Her heart started to beat double time. She turned the coin over and was soon convinced it was a gold doubloon.

She unfolded the tiny piece of paper, and inside was written *Romans 8*.

Was that referring to the Bible book of Romans, chapter eight? Or something else?

Rebecca put the tiny piece of paper and the gold doubloon back into the snuffbox and then placed it in her pocket with the keys she'd pilfered earlier. Next, she opened the drawer with the unsent, sealed letter to M. Pipken. She also put it in her pocket, then shut the drawer.

Her candle had dripped on the top of the desk in a few places. She found a letter opener and used it to carefully scrape the wax off the desk, trying not to scratch the wood. When she'd put everything back the way she had found them, except for the items she'd stowed in her pocket, she hurried out and shut the door, creeping back up to her room.

Once inside, she felt strangely excited, as if she had fooled her mother-in-law, although that was a childish sentiment. She hadn't fooled anyone. She'd only explored a room in the house she'd never explored before and had taken items belonging to a man who had been dead for twenty years.

She took the items out of her pocket, her excitement waning as a bit of guilt assailed her at how she had taken things that didn't belong to her. But it wasn't as if the owner would be angry or miss the items, she argued with herself. M. Pipken, whoever he was, was probably dead as well. And if that were so, there was no one to mind if she opened his letter.

She went and found her own letter opener. She used it to carefully pry the wax seal up from the paper. It was easier than she'd thought it would be.

With the seal removed, she opened the letter and began to read:

Dear Pipken,

Though I am still in good health, I thought I would send you these instructions in the event I might die unexpectedly.

I once told you the story of my sea-faring days, how I captured a few ships, which as everyone knows is how I made my fortune. Many of the ships I captured were pirate ships with crews who spent their days scuttling ships of every nation. There was one ship of Barbary corsairs that we raided, then we sank it to the bottom of the ocean, but not before we lifted four treasure chests full of gold doubloons.

Four chests of gold was more money than any of us could fathom. I gave three of the chests to my men to divide, and I kept the fourth for myself.

You might wonder why I shared so much with my men, when it was customary for the captain to keep whatever treasure was taken. But I wanted them to have a good share to ensure their silence, for I swore them all to secrecy.

I buried my chest of gold on my land. I told no one except my son, Geoffrey. But Geoffrey now says he doesn't believe the tale, that I would never have buried a treasure but would have spent it instead. Because of his disbelief, he probably told some people about the treasure that he shouldn't have.

When I die, I want to show Geoffrey that he was

wrong, and I don't want the treasure to stay buried, where it cannot do anyone any good. That is why I'm writing to you. I don't want to write down the instructions of how to find the gold in a letter, lest the wrong person see it. I need you to come to my home at your earliest convenience so I can impart this to you, and you in turn can tell Geoffrey.

You might wonder why I don't simply tell Geoffrey myself. But at the moment, he is sowing his wild oats, as people say, and if he were to find the gold now, he'd only ruin himself in revelry and dissipation. It is my hope that he will be of a more sober and mature mind when I do pass from this life.

Remember, at your earliest convenience, come for as long as you'd like to stay, and bring this letter with you. You are the only person I trust in this matter. The boy's mother cannot keep a secret.

Yours, R. Heywood

Rebecca's heart began to beat faster as she read the letter. There *was* a treasure! And since Arthur's grandfather had never sent the letter, then it was possible he never told anyone how to find it before he died.

But someone knew something about it, or else they would not be digging on the estate.

She could hardly wait to see the look on Thomas Westbrook's face when she showed him what she'd found.

She hid the items in a cloth purse, which she stowed in a drawer in her wardrobe. Then she hurried back downstairs to finish out the night's vigil with her husband's body.

CHAPTER SEVEN

Thomas went out, not long after he left Rebecca Heywood at her home, with a pistol and a rifle. He hid himself in the trees where he had a clear view of the place where the man had been digging when Rebecca Heywood happened upon him.

He propped himself up against a tree and memories started to flood his mind, of other times when he'd been propped against a tree with a rifle in his hand, waiting and watching for the enemy.

Those were days he wondered why he thought being an army officer was a good idea. Why would he ever want to shoot another human being? He'd been glad to sell his commission, and he would have done so even if his father hadn't died when he did.

He missed his father, even though they didn't see things the same way and often argued. His father had been the rock of the family, steady and unwavering in any situation. He'd wondered how his mother would endure life without him, but she had proven stronger than he imagined. She had become the steady one, no doubt for the sake of Benjamin and Caroline, who were both grief-stricken at the sudden loss of their father.

But Thomas was here, waiting for the digger, in order to prevent anyone else from getting killed by this person who thought they could steal a treasure that was hidden somewhere on the Heywood estate.

Never could he have thought he would be trying to defend the Heywood estate.

He was only doing what was right, and Arthur was no longer alive. Besides that, the estate was being inherited by Arthur's widow, and she was not to blame for her husband's betrayal. He had betrayed her more than anyone, and of this she seemed well aware.

It was true that society accepted adultery as almost a certainty, and definitely commonplace. Hardly a married man could be named who had never had a dalliance with another woman. Even his father had alluded to an affair with a woman, saying he had done something very foolish in the first few years of his marriage to Thomas's mother and had regretted it every day since.

"Learn a lesson from me," he said, "and watch yourself. Never stray. It's not worth your soul or the remorse you will feel later."

The confession had shaken Thomas, but he supposed it was a good reminder that no one was without sin, and no one was above being tempted. At least his father wasn't too proud to admit that, and it was indeed a good lesson for a young man like him who wanted for nothing and had a tendency toward pride.

He'd observed that same fault in many a young

man of similar status, who had all the wealth—and the doting parents—to make an idol out of pleasing themselves.

Arthur Heywood, for example.

Arthur had been a good-natured boy, but he'd succumbed to the idleness and lack of discipline of the young English gentleman, and he'd squandered his money and time on women. Thomas was of the opinion that Arthur had become addicted to the feeling of conquest that drove him to chase, and conquer, one woman after another. It was a game, and he was addicted to it just as other men were addicted to the gaming tables and often lost everything to this vice.

And his innocent wife was just one of his victims.

He must have sensed that he could never have her unless he married her, and so he did, knowing he'd need to have a child in order to keep Heywood House and estate in the Heywood family. Then he quickly tired of her and moved on to the next woman.

Perhaps it was terrible to think it, but . . . his wife was fortunate Arthur had not lived long. He would have continued to hurt and grieve her for the rest of their lives. And divorce was so uncommon and difficult as to be almost unthinkable.

Even so, it was a tragedy that he was murdered, since he'd never have the opportunity to repent of his sins and change. And though he'd heard people say, "Men don't change," he believed that they did. After all, his father had apparently started down the same path that Arthur had taken but had repented. He'd been a good husband to his mother, as she'd said many times, and there was a genuine affection between them that was mostly absent from the marriages he'd observed.

Thomas awoke to birds chirping. He opened his eyes and sat up, startled, his heart pumping fast.

No, he wasn't on the battlefield. He'd fallen asleep on the ground while waiting for the digger who had shot at Mrs. Heywood.

How embarrassing that he had fallen asleep while on watch. He was glad no one would ever know.

He stood up and went cautiously toward the hole that had been dug. It was undisturbed, looking just as it had the day before. The digger did not come back in the night.

He sighed and walked toward home. With any luck, he would return before any of his family knew he'd been gone.

~ ~ ~

A servant came to take Rebecca's place just before daybreak at Arthur's side in the drawing room.

Rebecca went up to bed and awoke a few hours later, immediately remembering that her husband had been shot and killed. She was no longer a wife but a childless widow.

As she lay in bed, a miry sadness seemed to hold her down, making it hard to rise. But then she remembered the dream she'd been having, about treasure chests and pirate ships, bringing to mind what she'd found the night before.

She got out of bed and dressed quickly before going downstairs to eat something. After not eating much since Arthur died, she was suddenly famished.

She hurried into the breakfast room—and found the windows draped in black cloth. And Mrs. Heywood was there in the semi-darkness, staring at her.

Mrs. Heywood was never up this early and rarely

even ate breakfast. But she was up today, and she was eating.

"Good morning, Mrs. Heywood," Rebecca said, moving to the sideboard to serve herself some food.

Mrs. Heywood made a quiet grunting sound, then said, "The local upholderer came yesterday evening while you were out. I have made all the arrangements with him for my son's funeral, which will be the day after tomorrow."

She might have asked her mother-in-law why she was having the funeral so quickly, but she didn't want to incite her ire.

The upholderer must be the person who furnished all the things, such as the shroud for the body, the black cloth for draping the house and the church, and did all the necessary hiring and arrangements for the funeral procession. It made sense, as there were a great deal of textiles involved, including the elaborate velvet cloth with which to cover the coffin, and that was the upholderer's business—textiles and upholstery.

"You will not be expected to attend the funeral, of course."

Her mother-in-law was referring to the current custom of the day in which women generally did not attend funerals or graveside committal services, especially women of polite society. But why should she not be allowed to attend her own husband's funeral, especially since this was the countryside, not London or some other large city where everyone had to be so fashionable? Perhaps her mother could tell her if it would be permissible for her to attend. But would her mother even arrive before the funeral?

"I doubt you would be able to tear yourself away

long enough to attend your husband's funeral, even if it were permissible. Perhaps you have plans with Thomas Westbrook again tonight and won't be able to hold vigil with your husband's body?"

Rebecca felt her cheeks start to burn. Of course, she would find out where Rebecca went last night.

"No. I have no plans, and I will be able to keep vigil tonight."

Mrs. Heywood made another sound in her throat. An awkward silence followed as Rebecca sat down with her food.

"You look as if you're going somewhere."

Rebecca merely shook her head. She'd felt famished only moments before, but as she tried to swallow her first bite of food, it was like a rock in her throat.

She forced herself to eat a few bites, but her stomach could only take a small amount before she started to feel sick. She put down her fork.

"The next time you wish to call on the Westbrooks, you don't have to sneak away. You can say plainly that you wish to see another man, while your husband lies dead."

"I wasn't going to see another man. It is not like that." She said the words softly, her stomach churning.

Her mother-in-law would ruin her reputation while her husband was hardly cold.

"It is strange that I find Thomas Westbrook in my house for the first time in years, having a private talk with you, then you go to his house the same evening to dine. But I'm sure you know what you're doing, calling on a man who betrayed your own husband when he is not even in his grave yet." Mrs. Heywood started to weep before she finished speaking and wailed into her handkerchief.

Thomas Westbrook betrayed Arthur? Hardly. It was the other way around, but you will believe what you want to believe.

Rebecca would never say that aloud. It would not be worth it.

For the first time, Rebecca's heart felt hard and cold at the sound of her mother-in-law's weeping. But she couldn't help but soften as her conscience reminded her that the woman's only child was gone. The woman might be cruel, and she might be manipulative, but her pain was undoubtedly real.

"I will keep vigil tonight." She wanted to say more, that she was sorry for her mother-in-law's pain. She cast about in her mind for something that wouldn't make Mrs. Heywood lash out. "I loved Arthur, and I know you did as well, and I am not interested in any other man. I know you are heartbroken, as am I. We must take comfort in God and in the hope of heaven."

"I am heartbroken." Her mother-in-law's voice was watery and strained. She looked up from her handkerchief. "But you can't understand how I feel. You've never had a child and can't know how much it hurts to lose one. A wife's loss is nothing compared to a mother's."

Rebecca swallowed, forcing herself not to let her mind go to the child she had lost before it had a chance to be born, which her mother-in-law had dismissed as "unfortunate, but you can try again." No, she would not let herself feel the anger that was swelling inside her.

"Yes. It's very unfortunate. Excuse me." Rebecca practically ran from the room.

Why had she ever married Arthur Heywood? It

was a mistake. *O God, it was such a mistake. Why did you let me do it?*

But the world would see her as blessed. Fortunate. She was rid of a husband who was unfaithful and neglectful, and now she had inherited his estate. But she did not feel blessed or fortunate. It was not an estate she wanted, but peace, a child, and her husband's love.

Now it seemed all her hopes were a sad joke.

~ ~ ~

Rebecca watched out her window as Mrs. Heywood left in the carriage.

Perhaps she was behaving like a child, "sneaking away" just as Mrs. Heywood had accused her, but Rebecca hardly cared. This was her chance to show Mr. Westbrook what she had found and to enlist his help in finding the treasure.

She hurried down and had the groom ready her horse. Mrs. Heywood would hear that she had gone to Wyghtworth again, but it couldn't be helped. She wasn't doing anything wrong, so why should she care what other people thought?

It was a simplistic way of looking at things, as she knew very well that a ruined reputation in a woman could change her life for the worse. Still, anyone who would listen to her mother-in-law's poisonous accusations was not her friend.

She stayed on the road instead of taking the quicker route across the countryside between the two houses, well aware that the man who had shot at her had not been caught, for if Mr. Westbrook had caught him the night before, he would have sent word to her.

She was greeted enthusiastically, just inside the door, by Caroline Westbrook.

"How good it is to see you!" She squeezed her hand and gave her a peck on the cheek. "I sent the servant to tell Mother you're here. She will be so pleased."

It felt good to be wanted, especially after the conversation she'd had with Mrs. Heywood that morning, but how would she be able to tell Thomas Westbrook what she had found without his sister and mother hearing?

She followed Caroline into the sitting room and her mother soon joined them. The time was passing quickly as Caroline and her mother talked and took Rebecca's mind off everything else but their fun and playful chatter. What a breath of fresh air the pair of them were after spending time with Mrs. Heywood. They laughed and smiled so often that Rebecca—for a few moments, at least—lost the dreadful, raw, exposed feeling she'd had since Arthur's body had been found.

Thomas Westbrook entered the room.

"Thomas, come and join us," his mother said. "I have just ordered tea."

He sat down and greeted Rebecca. He was looking a bit tired today. She wanted to ask him if he had stayed up all night and if he had found out anything about the digger, if the digging had continued, et cetera, but she dared not ask in front of his sister and mother.

"I would very much like to be with you tomorrow during the funeral," Caroline said, "since you said your mother and sisters will not be able to come until later. But I am assuming Mrs. Heywood will also be home. Do you think she would be offended by my presence?"

Rebecca thought for a moment. "I don't see how she could object to you being there. Neither she nor her son could have had any grudge against you. And I would be so grateful to have you. My mother-in-law has been hostile toward me, I'm afraid."

"Oh no," Mrs. Westbrook said. "Is it because you've been calling on us? I'm so sorry."

"I'm afraid she has never liked me. I was never good enough for her son, in her eyes." She bit her tongue. Why was she saying these things? She felt her cheeks starting to burn.

Mrs. Westbrook and Caroline both expressed their dismay, while she heard Thomas Westbrook mutter, "That's ridiculous."

"Well, Caroline and I shall both come and sit with you tomorrow," Mrs. Westbrook said, squeezing Rebecca's hand. "I shall stand in the place of your mother for the day."

"And I your sister," Caroline said.

"That is so very kind of you."

"But it's probably best if Thomas does not go to the funeral." Mrs. Westbrook sent a look her son's way.

"I agree," he said. "Your mother-in-law might take out her offended sensibilities on you if I were to attend the funeral services."

"Thank you for being so kind and understanding." She was relieved, for if Thomas Westbrook attended the funeral, her mother-in-law might very well create a public spectacle, with her wild accusations and unfounded hatred for Thomas Westbrook.

"Thomas, can you believe our dear Rebecca came here on horseback again?"

"I trust you did not encounter any strange men on the way?"

"No, I did not. Have you seen any more of the shooter?"

"I have not. I also ascertained that he has not done any more digging at the spot where you saw him."

"Perhaps we scared him away for good, although that doesn't seem likely."

"No. Were you able to discover anything about what he may have been trying to dig up?"

"I did discover some very interesting things about it." Did he want her to tell him in front of his sister and mother?

"You discovered something about why that man was digging on your property?" Caroline asked. "What is it?"

Rebecca's gaze met Thomas Westbrook's.

"Does Thomas not want you to tell me because he thinks I can't keep a secret? I will not tell anyone. I know this is very important and Mother and I won't tell a soul."

"Tell a soul about what?" Benjamin Westbrook came into the room looking mildly curious.

"It is your decision," Thomas said.

"I don't mind, as long as they won't tell." Perhaps it was unwise to tell so many people about the treasure, but the Westbrooks were good people and did not seem prone to gossip, so there could be no harm in it, could there?

Thomas Westbrook went to the door and closed it. He then came close to where they were seated. "You must all solemnly vow," he said quietly, glancing around and catching the eye of each of his family members, "not to breathe a word of this to anyone."

"Not to breathe a word of what?" Benjamin looked more curious now.

"Rebecca has discovered why someone was digging on her land," Caroline whispered excitedly.

"The man who shot at her? The one who killed Arthur Heywood?" He was leaning in.

In fact, they were all leaning toward Rebecca, forming a circle around her. She couldn't remember when she'd been the center of attention like this. But with the items in her purse, and with how much she'd been wanting to share them with Thomas Westbrook, she didn't mind.

"Yes, now say it," Thomas Westbrook ordered. "Say you will not breathe a word to anyone."

"I will not breathe a word to anyone." Caroline, Mrs. Westbrook, and even Benjamin all repeated the words almost simultaneously.

Rebecca opened the purse, which had been sitting in her lap, and pulled out the letter, handing it to Thomas Westbrook.

"I found this in Arthur's grandfather's desk. The library seemed undisturbed since he used it many years ago."

Thomas opened the letter and read it aloud, but in a low voice. There were a few gasps from Caroline and Mrs. Westbrook as he read.

"Isn't it incredible?" Rebecca was looking at Thomas Westbrook.

"It is an amazing confirmation." He was still staring down at the letter. "The paper is obviously old, and the ink looks old as well. Where did you say you found it?"

"In the desk Arthur's grandfather used to use. I was told the room was his grandfather's favorite and that he conducted all his business there. I found it among some other papers. And I also found this."

She took the ordinary-looking snuffbox from her purse and handed it to him.

He opened it and dumped the doubloon and the tiny piece of paper into his hand.

"Oh my!" Caroline exclaimed, the same time her brother Benjamin said, "Is that a gold doubloon?"

Thomas held it up, turning it over. "It does appear to be."

He gave the coin to Rebecca. She handed it to Benjamin, and Caroline joined him beside his chair and they put their heads together to examine it.

Thomas unfolded the tiny piece of paper and read, "Romans 8."

"What could it mean, do you think?"

"Bible book and chapter, I imagine. Was there a Bible in the room?"

"I didn't look, but I would think there'd be at least one. There are bookshelves lining all the walls."

"I would think if you look inside the Bible at Romans 8, you might just find something inside the pages."

"Why didn't I think of that?" Rebecca breathed. It seemed so obvious. Now she just wanted to hurry back and look for the Bible in that room.

"I'm thinking perhaps Arthur's grandfather hid those clues, and perhaps the whereabouts of the clues was what he didn't want to write down, and also what he wanted to tell this M. Pipken."

"Who do you think M. Pipken was?"

"Have you never heard the name?" Thomas asked.

"No, never."

"I think he may have been Mr. Heywood's solicitor," Mrs. Westbrook said. "I believe I recall the name, from when the grandmother was still alive."

"That would make sense, if he trusted his solicitor," Thomas said.

"We should go find that Bible," Benjamin said. "It could have the map showing where the treasure is buried."

They all started talking at once. "We can't go there, Mrs. Heywood hates us." "Mrs. Heywood won't allow us to plunder her house." "Thomas especially is unwelcome there."

"My mother-in-law had just left the house when I came here, but she could return at any time, and she might be furious—I'm sorry to say—if she were to find any of you looking around the grandfather's library. I don't even go in there when she might see me."

"Of course, my dear," Mrs. Westbrook said. "We understand."

"I'm sure I caused you quite a bit of trouble when she found me there yesterday." Thomas looked apologetic.

"And when you came here to dine," Mrs. Westbrook said, with a look of concern and compassion.

"It was worth it to make your acquaintance," Rebecca said with a gentle smile.

How kind they all were. Even Benjamin looked contrite. How long had it been since anyone had said a kind word to her in her own home?

"One happy thing that could come out of this," Caroline said, "is that Mrs. Heywood will go elsewhere to live."

"Caroline." Mrs. Westbrook gave a slight shake of her head at her daughter.

"She hasn't said she will leave," Rebecca said, "and

I cannot bear to force her out of her home. She's lived there for thirty years."

"It is your home now," Caroline said, "and if she cannot be respectful, then she should go."

"You would be within your rights," Thomas said. "The house belongs to you now."

"In all honesty, I have prayed that she will go live with her brother, or someone." It was a daily struggle to forgive the woman, so was it wrong to pray for her to find another home?

"Then I shall pray the same," Caroline declared.

"She does have a jointure, and the dowager cottage behind the main house has been willed to her for her lifetime." Truthfully, though, Rebecca was relatively certain the woman would never leave the main house, as she had alluded to a couple of times.

But the fact that Caroline would also be praying that Mrs. Heywood would go live elsewhere, the same thing that Rebecca was praying, was comforting.

CHAPTER EIGHT

Rebecca returned home with both well wishes and excited anticipatory words from the Westbrooks ringing in her head.

She hurried up the stairs. Thankfully, Mrs. Heywood had not returned home, so she went boldly into the library and started searching the bookshelves for a Bible.

After a few minutes she found a relatively small one and pulled it off the shelf. The top was dusty but its leather binding was in good condition.

As she carefully turned the pages, searching for the book of Romans, chapter eight, she noted that it did not look as if it had ever been opened. Many of the pages were stuck together, held by the gold leaf edges that she had to carefully pull apart.

She finally found the book of Romans. She turned to the eighth chapter but there was nothing there. It was just a normal page in the Bible.

She read the entire chapter, but there didn't seem to be any clues in the text itself. It was quite a delightful chapter, especially the last part, and she would go back and read it again later. But for now she flipped to the front of the Bible. Nothing there either, no inscription of any kind.

She sighed, feeling defeated. But perhaps there was another Bible in the room.

She continued to search, on table tops and on the bookshelves. When she had examined every book in the room, she started to go back through them again.

The sound of carriage wheels on the lane outside caught her ears.

She put the books back on the shelf, including the Bible, then hurried from the room, closing the door just moments before she heard Mrs. Heywood's strident voice below, barking an order at the servants.

Not wishing to see her mother-in-law, especially as her chest ached in her disappointment at not finding what she and her friends, the Westbrooks, had been so excited to discover, she hurried to her room and closed herself inside.

She had only been in her room for a few minutes when a servant came and summoned her. "Mrs. Heywood wishes to see you," the servant said.

With a heavy heart, Rebecca let the servant lead her to the breakfast room, which had to be lighted by candles due to the black cloth covering the window, even though it was the middle of the day.

Her mother-in-law sat at a writing desk, bent over and writing in a large book. Rebecca had rarely ever seen Mrs. Heywood write anything.

Mrs. Heywood placed a finger on the page of the

huge book she was writing in as soon as Rebecca walked in the room, a pen poised in her other hand.

"I was just writing Arthur Wendell Heywood's date of death." Her voice cracked and she made a whimpering sound, followed by a sniff as she dabbed at her nose with her handkerchief.

"Since there is no one else alive to care about the Heywood family line and family estate," Mrs. Heywood said, "I will be taking the family Bible and giving it to Arthur's cousin to pass down to his children. You certainly will not want it after you remarry and have children with some other man."

Rebecca's stomach twisted at her mother-in-law's words, then she suddenly realized what was niggling in the back of her mind. *Bible.* Mrs. Heywood had the family Bible.

Her heart pounded against her chest. She'd never seen the enormous book before. Did Mrs. Heywood keep it in her room? She said she was planning to take it and give it to someone else. Rebecca had to get a look inside it before she gave it away. But how?

Mrs. Heywood was writing in the front of the book. She wouldn't open it to Romans 8, surely.

"I never wrote down the date of his marriage to you," Mrs. Heywood went on. "And now I don't remember it. Do you remember?"

Of course she remembered the date of her wedding. And of course her mother-in-law only wished to insult her by saying such things. But she would go along with her.

"It was November 10th, eighteen—"

"Yes, I remember the year." Mrs. Heywood held her pen poised above the page for several moments.

Then she said, "No children came from the marriage, so why should it be significant enough to write down in the family Bible?"

She slammed the cover closed and slapped the pen down on the writing desk.

Rebecca wanted to turn on her heel and leave the room, but she also wanted to see what Mrs. Heywood would do with the Bible.

Mrs. Heywood stood. "I have made sure all the arrangements are being made for the funeral and burial. I have plenty of experience, having buried my husband three years ago. It must be convenient for you, not having to do anything. I have seen to all the arrangements for the funeral service, procession, and committal. And I suppose this estate will be bankrupt in a matter of a few years, sold off in pieces. You certainly have no experience with running an estate, any more than you have experience with arranging funerals."

"That is true. I have no experience with such things." Rebecca did her best to unclench her jaw and speak without any emotion, stating obvious facts. It was the way she had learned to deal with Mrs. Heywood when she was in a caustic mood such as this.

"Well, I suppose you will have your mother here in a day or two."

"Yes, in a day or two they should be here."

"And how many of your siblings will come with her?"

"I don't know. Perhaps three."

"Well, I'm sure they will enjoy taking over the estate now that its rightful owner is dead."

She covered her face with her handkerchief. A few moments later, she lifted her head and shook her handkerchief at Rebecca. "Why are you still here? Gloating over me in my grief. Go away. Get away from me."

Rebecca left the room but went down the hall to the sitting room, watching in the doorway. A few moments later she was rewarded with the sight of Mrs. Heywood leaving the breakfast room and walking the other way, and she did not have the Bible in her hands.

Rebecca tiptoed hurriedly down the hall to the breakfast room. There was the Bible where Mrs. Heywood had left it.

She ran over to it. Her heart beat furiously as she opened it up. She was not as careful as she'd been with the other Bible while she flipped the pages and found Romans, then turned the pages to find the eighth chapter. When she did, a loose piece of paper slipped from the page and fluttered onto the floor.

Rebecca snatched it up, not even looking to see what it was, and hid it in the folds of her dress.

She scurried up to her bedroom and locked the door.

The paper was folded into fourths. She unfolded it to find a drawing of some sort, with no words. Could it be just what they had been hoping for—a map of where the treasure was buried?

Rebecca spread it out on her bed. There were several crude drawings, probably symbols, and a black "X" at one corner of the paper. But she was having trouble recognizing anything.

There were triangles, wavy lines, parallel lines, and a large square, but Rebecca could make no sense of it.

Perhaps Thomas Westbrook would understand it. But was she bold enough to return to the Westbrooks' a second time that day, on the day before her husband's funeral?

Her husband's funeral. The words sent a pall over her and she refolded the paper and put it in a small box where she was keeping the letter and the snuffbox, then placed them in a drawer by her bed. It could wait a day or two.

Rebecca had a simple, early supper sent up to her room, where she ate alone. When that was done, with the sun going down, she went back down to the drawing room and sat beside her husband's coffin to hold vigil, relieving the hired sitter who was there, as she had promised Mrs. Heywood.

An uncomfortable weight settled on her. Was she so unfeeling that she could feel excited about a buried treasure when her husband had just been murdered? When he was not even in the grave yet? Perhaps Mrs. Heywood was correct in her accusations against her.

Tears stung her eyes as she remembered how much she had loved her husband. Arthur had been her whole world those first few months they were married, and though he had said and done things that hurt her, she'd been so in love that she had forgiven him immediately and barely remembered them. But it was not long before she heard the rumors of his unfaithfulness, of the other women. How much that had hurt, like a knife in the heart. And when the dalliances with other women had continued, even after she was pregnant with their child, even after she lost the baby, her broken heart had gone numb.

But she hadn't ceased to love him. She loved him still. How long might she have continued to love him, if he had lived? Five more years? Ten? How long before her heart ceased to love and forgive and grew completely cold to him?

And if he had stopped being unfaithful to her, if he learned to repent and turn from his philandering ways, could she have forgiven him? How could she trust him again after years of unfaithfulness?

But now she would never know. He was gone, and with him, all hope of reconciliation was gone, all hope that he would repent and learn to love Rebecca his wife and only Rebecca.

She had avoided looking at him, but now she stood and moved to the coffin, which sat on a low table that brought the body up to chest level. And she looked at Arthur, truly looked at him, at his pale face and blond hair, his lips, his chin, his hands, lying folded over his stomach. But something was different about his face. There was no life there, and he was not there. This was only his body, a shell that had housed his soul, his laugh, his thoughts. He was gone and only his shell was left.

They had shared some happy moments, but now when she looked at his lifeless face, she only remembered the pain.

She went back and lay down on the sofa, which was too short to accommodate the length of her legs, so even with bent knees, her feet hung off the side.

She might have considered attending the funeral if her mother had been there and could accompany her. After all, this was the countryside and people were less prone to observe all the fashionable rituals that seemed so rigid for the aristocrats, the dukes and earls and viscounts, who lived in London.

But her mother-in-law had already informed her she was not to attend.

Perhaps it was just as well. She might break down and cry, and that would be embarrassing. No one liked a public display of emotion.

She thought of something she hadn't thought of before. Would some of Arthur's women, his paramours, attend the funeral?

She shuddered. Yes, it was best she did not go.

She closed her eyes to rest them. If Mrs. Heywood heard of her sleeping instead of keeping vigil, she was certain to make some very contemptuous accusations. So she mustn't fall asleep.

Rebecca blinked, then sat up.

All the windows were covered in black cloth, but she heard voices in the other part of the house. It must be morning, but how late? Was Mrs. Heywood up?

Rebecca hastened to smooth out her skirt and press down her hair. Then she felt the drool that had dribbled from the corner of her mouth and pulled out her handkerchief. Had anyone seen her lying there, sleeping?

Rebecca shivered, feeling quite chilled. She rubbed her face and chose a book of poetry and read until a hired sitter arrived to relieve her.

Today was the day of the funeral. Her life was about to change forever, and she was not certain what that would look like.

CHAPTER NINE

The funeral was to be held at midnight, which was customary for wealthy families, and guests arrived all day. Arthur's uncles, his cousins, and even school friends were greeted by Mrs. Heywood and shown to a room. But none of Rebecca's family came.

She hadn't told anyone except her mother and sisters of her husband's death. She was so far away from London here, she didn't want to inconvenience her friends, many of whom were yet unmarried and had no means of traveling on their own. And her mother had written to say that she would be delayed at least a few days in coming because three of Rebecca's siblings were sick and her mother was feeling unwell herself.

Rebecca wrote back to urge her not to come until all were well.

She spent most of the day in the drawing room, receiving guests' condolences and wishing she could "sneak away," as her mother-in-law had called it, to Wyghtworth. But then her sense of guilt would remind her that she should give this day and all her thoughts to her dead husband. After all, he had been good enough to provide for her in his will.

She did finally go up to her room to rest late in the afternoon, and lay across her bed thinking of the map—if indeed it was a map. But the fact that it had been right there in the Bible, at Romans 8, made her shiver. It had to be related to the treasure somehow.

With so many people arriving and so much activity, as preparations were ongoing for the funeral procession and services, Rebecca was sure to be noticed leaving and traveling in the direction of Wyghtworth.

But would she be noticed if she walked?

The words rose up again: *Can you not give your husband one day?*

She should be mourning her husband's death, not thinking about sneaking away to confer about the map with Thomas Westbrook, her husband's rival.

"I'm sorry," she whispered, curling up on her side and remembering the small jabs Mrs. Heywood had spoken to their guests—*her* guests. She'd made Rebecca sound like a neglectful, unfeeling wife who could not even stay awake for one night of sitting vigil with her husband's body—this was how she let her know that she knew of her sleeping on the sofa that night.

But at least she didn't know about her going to his grandfather's library when she was supposed to be keeping vigil, or taking the map out of the family Bible.

How furious Mrs. Heywood would be if she knew. Rebecca almost laughed when she thought of it, but immediately sobered as she thought about the long day and night to come. For, Mrs. Heywood would follow the current trend—terrified as she was of being thought of as unfashionable—so that the funeral procession, funeral service, and committal service were all to be done just after midnight, well after dark.

How the tradition began of holding funerals after dark, Rebecca did not know, but she thought it the utmost inconvenience at best, and dangerous at worst. She'd heard of numerous funeral processions in London for some of the most aristocratic families that had been set upon by thieves as the relatives and the body of the deceased proceeded down the street to the church. It was one of the reasons ladies rarely attended funerals.

Another reason ladies rarely attended funerals, even of their closest relatives, was because they exhausted themselves with keeping vigil with their loved one's body. And of course, ladies' constitutions were so fragile, and they were so prone to losing control of themselves, they might actually show emotion by openly crying at the funeral, and that, of course, was not fashionable at all.

A woman could not cry or show open sadness and grief or she risked having the physician called, who would prescribe something that would keep her asleep all night and most of the day, so drowsy she could not show emotion of any kind. Or at worst, she might be declared insane and sent to an asylum where she'd never be heard from again.

She needed to stop this morbid thinking.

"God, please let Mother come soon." She felt so alone in this enormous house, with all of Mrs. Heywood's family there.

~ ~ ~

When the funeral procession finally left—a foolishly ostentatious funeral procession, with all the details and extra frivolities attended to, hired pages and bearers, dyed-black ostrich feathers on horses' heads as well as people's—Rebecca felt her heart sink to her toes. It was real. Her husband was dead. That man she thought she would love for the rest of her life, to whom she had given her loyalty, heart, and her body, was truly gone. She'd never see him again.

The ache in her chest was so bad, she wondered if she was dying. Would she die of a broken heart, as many widows had been known to do?

She turned to see Mrs. Heywood had fainted on the sofa.

All the men were in the funeral procession, so the women present—Arthur's aunt, cousin, and Mrs. Heywood's brother and sisters—fanned her face with their handkerchiefs.

It might not be fashionable to cry, but it was very fashionable to faint.

While everyone was gathered around Mrs. Heywood, Rebecca slipped away and went up to her room. "Thank you, God, that this day and night are almost over."

~ ~ ~

Thomas rode out, the day after Arthur Heywood's funeral, toward the hole beside a big rock, next to a copse of trees on the Heywood property, quite close to his own property line.

Thomas had been checking at least once or twice a day, but he had yet to catch anyone at the place where Rebecca Heywood had seen the strange man digging, nor had any more progress been made on the hole. They had either decided to abandon their digging for a while, or they had abandoned it for good. The latter seemed unlikely.

As he neared the hole, he dismounted and led his horse through the trees, where he could more easily observe without being seen. And as he crept as quietly as he could through the trees, he noticed movement.

He stopped and tied his horse to the nearest tree, took his pistol from his saddlebag, then moved forward.

A man was digging. He paused to wipe his brow with his sleeve.

He appeared to be a large man. Thomas crept closer, trying to get a better look at the man's face, but he was facing away from Thomas and his hiding place. Still, he looked strangely familiar.

Thomas watched him for several minutes. He was quite slow at digging, and he often stopped to wipe his face. At this pace, if there was a treasure buried there, it would take him many hours to unearth it.

Finally, the man put down his shovel, picked up a leather bag, and sat down on the large rock. He drew a cloth bundle out of the bag and unwrapped it and proceeded to eat. As he did, he looked around, turning his face so that it was in full view.

The man was familiar because he was the constable, Mr. Fogg.

Thomas eyed the rifle that lay on the ground next to the rock on which Mr. Fogg was seated. He could shoot him where he sat, in the arm or the leg perhaps, but how could he be sure the Justice of the Peace, or the coroner Pursglove, would believe Thomas over Fogg? And how convenient for the constable, as he had been investigating a murder that he himself had committed.

Thomas pondered his options as he watched the

man eat his bread and cheese.

He might walk out of the trees, his pistol aimed at Fogg, and demand that he tell Thomas what he was doing. But Fogg might refuse to tell him anything. And if taken before the assize, or in front of the Justice of the Peace, he could be found innocent, as there was no real evidence against him.

Thomas continued to watch the man, deciding to wait until he had some kind of real evidence against him. But he would need to warn Rebecca Heywood, and soon, that she must not trust the constable. Most likely he was the man who murdered her husband, as well as the man who had shot at her and chased her.

He chafed at the idea of letting the man go, of not confronting him and forcing him to confess what he had done. But since he needed evidence against him, he might just let Fogg carry out his intentions, for now, and see where it led.

~ ~ ~

Rebecca slept much of the day after Arthur's funeral, with Mrs. Heywood's guests staying in the house. But by the end of the week, her mother-in-law was accompanying her brother and his wife to their home in Kent, with no definite plans to return.

Truly, Rebecca would be left alone to manage the estate, having never been taught anything by her mother-in-law about its management. But if Mrs. Heywood could do it, so could she.

Rebecca came downstairs before dinner to make a show of being friendly and hospitable to Mrs. Heywood's guests before they took her away to Kent.

"Undoubtedly Arthur could not have suspected that he would die so young and without an heir," Mrs.

Heywood said to her brother's wife, Mrs. Millet, while Rebecca was expected to talk to Mrs. Millet's sister, who was almost completely deaf—and almost completely ignored by Mr. and Mrs. Millet.

"It is a shame," Mrs. Heywood went on, "that this fine estate should be left this way. Who knows what will become of it or who should get control of it? It will probably be sold off bit by bit, you know."

Mrs. Millet cleared her throat, then whispered something to Mrs. Heywood, cutting her eyes over at Rebecca.

Rebecca's cheeks burned.

She could no longer excuse her mother-in-law's rudeness as the product of her grief and strong feelings of pain and loss. And Rebecca was not sorry that she was leaving and going to live with her brother. Her only worry now was that she would not stay with them but would return to Heywood House.

She prayed for her mother to be able to leave London soon, the sooner the better, to come to her and help her. Her mother would advise her.

By the time Mrs. Heywood left in her brother's carriage, Rebecca actually cried a few tears watching them go, as she whispered, "Thank you, God, for the respite."

Selfish or not, she was thankful the house would be peaceful and quiet now.

The map in her drawer was all but forgotten the next two days, as Rebecca met with the servants and tried to resume the duties she'd assumed her mother-in-law had taken care of. But she was finding, much to her dismay, that the accounts were in great disorder, and the housekeeper and butler had been left to do as they liked with regard to keeping records of expenses.

Arthur had been in charge of recording business matters as pertained to their tenants and their farms, and he had not written anything in the ledgers in months.

As the mother, so the son.

After two days of trying to unravel the accounts, she began to suspect that the servants were taking a little extra money for themselves from the weekly market money.

"Oh, Mother, I wish you were here," she whispered at least once a day. Could she confront the servants about taking a little extra for themselves? Certainly she couldn't without proof, and the account books were in too much disarray for that. Besides, the wages Mrs. Heywood was paying the servants was well below what her family paid theirs. They probably used their low wages as justification, if they were taking extra, and Rebecca wasn't sure she blamed them.

Finally, after not hearing from the Westbrooks since before the funeral, she received an invitation to dine at Wyghtworth.

Rebecca dressed carefully and even had the servant help her with her hair.

Now that Mrs. Heywood was gone, the servants were beginning to treat her differently. The ones who had been very short and businesslike with her were suddenly smiling at her, nodding, and even giving her little compliments. The ones who seemed afraid all the time suddenly seemed much more at ease. And the butler and housekeeper gave her more deference, though they did treat her, sometimes, as if they thought her too young and inexperienced to know what she was doing.

They were mostly right.

But she was determined to change that. She would not fulfill her mother-in-law's prophecy that she would allow the estate to go to ruin with mismanagement.

Too busy to think very much about her mother-in-law's petty remarks, they nevertheless invaded her thoughts from time to time. But now she was going to dine with the Westbrooks. At least there she knew she would be treated kindly.

At the last minute, she remembered to get the map out of the drawer and take it with her.

She took the carriage to the Westbrooks' for the first time, no longer afraid of inciting Mrs. Heywood's wrath. But one thing she did have to consider was expense. She'd never thought much about the upkeep of the horses and the carriages, for her husband had owned three carriages of various styles and sizes, but now that she knew all the particulars of these expenses, she had more to consider than just her own comfort and whether it might rain.

And the funeral expenses had been extraordinary, almost a year's income. Her mother-in-law had spared nothing to make her son's funeral a memorable event for the few men who had actually attended it. At least for that she had been given a full account of expenses by the upholderer, who had arranged for all the many fees and hirings and furnishings, taking quite a tidy sum for his trouble.

But these bills had to be paid, and as far as she could tell, they had already been sent to the solicitor and he was taking care of those.

Mrs. Westbrook and Caroline greeted her as if she

was an old friend, expressing their sympathy with a sincerity that she had not felt in the past week from all of the mourners and funeral attendees who had come to her house.

"My dear, you look tired," Mrs. Westbrook said. "Come and sit with us while we wait for Thomas and Benjamin to return from shooting."

The word "shooting" made her heart jump in her chest. Of course, she only meant that they had gone to shoot pheasants, or some such thing, but her mind had conjured up a picture of the man who had shot at her, then disappeared when Thomas Westbrook came with his gun.

The night before, she dreamed about someone shooting at her, forcing her to run away. But her legs had been so heavy, practically rooted to the ground, and she'd been so terrified she'd woken herself up in the middle of the night.

"Are you well?" Caroline asked.

"Let me get you a glass of wine," Mrs. Westbrook said.

"I am well, I thank you. I have been quite occupied."

"Oh, yes. How are you coming along now that Mrs. Heywood is gone and you have the complete run of the place?"

"Yes, we heard that Mrs. Heywood left for an extended visit with her brother," Caroline said. "Nothing happens in this small country society that we don't hear about."

Why hadn't Rebecca thought that she could ask Mrs. Westbrook for advice?

"Perhaps you can advise me on a few matters of

household management. I have been anxiously await-ing my mother's arrival, which has been delayed be-cause of sickness in the family."

"Oh, how egregious. Who is sick?"

"My younger brothers and sisters, but I have heard that they are all on the mend and my mother should be coming very soon. But you must be managing this estate, with Thomas's help when he is home."

"Oh yes, I do some of the duties, but Thomas does most of it, along with our butler, Johnson. I see to the kitchen and the pantry and supplies, but Thomas man-ages the tenants and the accounting books and ledgers and things. And I believe I hear him coming."

A few moments later, Thomas and Benjamin en-tered the room, obviously having dressed for dinner.

"There you are. I'm surprised you were able to clean up so fast." Caroline turned to Rebecca. "One hour ago, they were covered in mud."

"You should never doubt us, little sister," Benja-min said with a grin.

"We weren't quite *covered* in mud," Thomas said. "My sister likes to exaggerate."

Caroline huffed.

"Behave yourselves, my dears." Mrs. Westbrook's voice was soothing and soft. "Rebecca has had a very difficult week and we must do our best to make her feel at home."

"I assure you, I enjoy being here. I am from a large family of ten children, and an absence of good-natured discussions and even bickering is strange to me."

"We are very good at bickering and shall make you feel quite at home, then," Thomas Westbrook said with a kind smile.

"Thank you." Rebecca smiled back, but immediately felt guilty. Should she be smiling at a man as handsome as Thomas Westbrook? It felt wrong.

"Did you get a chance to look in the family Bible?" Benjamin Westbrook asked.

"I did." Rebecca felt her spirits rise as she reached into her small purse and took out the folded-up piece of paper. "I found this in the large family Bible stuck in between the pages just at Romans chapter eight."

She handed the paper to Thomas, and his brother and sister immediately stood from where they were seated and surrounded him, leaning close as Thomas unfolded it.

"It's a map!" Benjamin's face showed his excitement.

Thomas's brows lowered, his eyes squinting as he studied the paper.

"Yes, but what does it mean?" Rebecca asked. "I have not examined it very closely, but I noticed what appeared to be several symbols, but I could make no sense of what they represented. Do you understand it?"

Thomas was slow to speak, while Caroline pointed at the paper and said, "Look at that. It's a cross, or an 'X.' That must be where the treasure is buried."

Benjamin and Caroline discussed what the various symbols meant, then Thomas said quietly, "Remember, we need to keep this all quiet. No one is to hear of this map outside of the five of us."

"Yes, yes, of course," Caroline said. Benjamin also agreed.

"It is a helpful distraction, this treasure trove," Mrs. Westbrook said, smiling. "But I cannot imagine how you will find a chest buried in the ground after all this time, on so large an estate as it is."

"I've never known you to be pessimistic, Mother." Thomas gazed at his mother for a moment before going back to perusing the map.

"I am not being pessimistic. I am glad you young people have something interesting to put your minds to, but I cannot imagine it will be easy to find such a thing."

"Easy things are seldom worth having." Thomas said the words in a very straightforward manner.

"Listen to the words of the wise philosopher," Caroline said with a mocking smile.

Thomas shook his head as if at the antics of a child.

"I don't particularly want the treasure," Rebecca said. "I just want it found so that I don't have to worry about anyone being killed." Anyone else, she should say. She took a deep breath, forcing her mind not to think about Arthur, since that tended to bring on tears and sadness.

"That is what I want," Mrs. Westbrook declared. "This is England, a civilized country, and we will not rest until this evil man is caught."

"You are so kind." Rebecca's heart warmed inside her, so thankful to have found such kind and faithful friends.

CHAPTER TEN

Thomas's secret was burning inside him as he struggled to decide whether and when he should tell them he knew who the evil man was. Would it only frighten Rebecca and his mother?

He'd been going every day to the place where Mr. Fogg was digging, wondering if he would find the treasure there. The hole had become quite deep but there was no treasure, and though he considered each time whether he would confront the man, he had never encountered him again, only the evidence of his digging.

Now, looking at this map, he knew for certain that the constable was digging in the wrong place.

"What if these triangles are trees," Thomas said, drawing their attention to the map. "And these wavy marks are fields. And this square here is Heywood House."

"That makes sense," Benjamin mumbled.

"But what are these lines here?" Caroline asked.

"That is the lane leading up to the house."

"That means the 'X' is behind the house, not where that man was shooting at Mrs. Heywood," Benjamin said.

While everyone was silently taking this in, Thomas said, "This map is very helpful, but it only gives us a general location for the treasure, if I'm interpreting it correctly. I can't help thinking we're missing one more clue that would show us exactly where to dig."

"Could we be missing something in the letter?"

Rebecca Heywood was quite pretty when she raised her eyebrows in that hopeful way, with her dark blue eyes and her brown hair hanging in curls beside her cheeks.

"I didn't bring the letter with me," she said, "but I could examine it more closely."

"And the family Bible? Did you examine it closely?"

"Not particularly. I was in a hurry and was only looking for Romans eight. And now Mrs. Heywood has the Bible. Or at least, she said she was taking it with her. With the management of the estate and trying to understand my new duties, I forgot to look and see if she took it."

"Why don't you let us come tomorrow," Mother said, "and we will help you look, and also help you with your duties, your ledgers and books, if we are able."

"Yes," Thomas said. "Mother and I can help you with the management of the estate, and—"

"And I can help you look for clues," Caroline said.

"And I." Benjamin folded his arms across his chest and gave a side glare to Caroline.

"My brother and sister can help, if they can stop

quarreling." Thomas frowned at the two of them, but they hardly noticed.

"If you would not mind, I'd very much like to have your help, as soon as you are able to come."

"We will be there early tomorrow, then." Mother patted her hand.

Thomas was gratified by how kind his mother was to Rebecca Heywood. She obviously was in need of some kindness, after living with Arthur and his mother for the past two years.

The servant announced it was time for dinner.

Dining with Rebecca Heywood added something to their conversation that was quite enjoyable. Thomas was glad she lived so close, as she could come quite often. They all seemed to enjoy each other's company, and tonight they were even more at ease with each other than before. But Thomas didn't like keeping this secret from Rebecca Heywood.

He'd made up his mind to tell her that the constable was the culprit digging on her land. After all, she might be fooled into trusting him, and if he suspected she had seen him, he would surely kill her. He had to tell her.

He'd also determined to confront Mr. Fogg, but he was still deciding how to do it.

When dinner was over, Caroline played and sang one song then persuaded Rebecca Heywood to play and sing. He'd thought her playing was good, but hearing her sing for the first time, he was struck by how beautiful her voice was. And though some ladies' faces distorted when they sang, somehow Rebecca's looked even prettier, almost angelic, to match her voice.

But always his mind took him back to the fact

that she was Arthur Heywood's wife. She belonged to that man who had deliberately done all he could to harm Thomas, completely without cause, as Thomas had been his loyal friend since they were young children.

He wanted nothing to do with anything that belonged to Arthur, even rued the fact that his own land had to share a property line with Arthur's. He forgave him for all he had done, or at least he was trying to, but that didn't mean he could overlook the fact that Rebecca had been his wife.

Thomas was young, with a desirable estate. He could marry well, as well as he wished to, and he intended to marry a sweet, innocent girl who adored him.

He had no wish to marry anyone's widow, especially Arthur Heywood's.

And yet, he would not be petty about it. He could see Rebecca Heywood's worth. She was a good woman, as charitable to the poor as she was, and she was a good friend already to his mother and sister. He had no wish to see harm come to her, and he would protect her as best he could.

He let all these thoughts roam through his mind while she played and sang a second time, obviously delighting his mother, Caroline, and even Benjamin, whom he suspected might be forming a bit of an attachment to her. She certainly had his attention. He was young, only seventeen, a few years younger than Rebecca Heywood, but that was nothing. More unequal marriages were made every day. But he'd go back to his studies in a few weeks and forget about her, most likely.

When it was time for her to leave, Thomas escorted her to her carriage and helped her inside. The rest of his family had vanished.

"Thank you for a lovely evening."

"Thank you, Mrs. Heywood." He should probably say something about her playing and singing delighting them, as well as her stimulating conversation, but he didn't want her to think that he was developing an affection for her.

"I shall see you all tomorrow morning?"

"Yes, we shall be there early, Mother said."

She smiled and nodded, and he shut the carriage door. The driver drove on.

He should have ridden with her, to tell her that Mr. Fogg, the constable, was the culprit who was digging for the treasure. But if he was honest with himself, he was afraid to spend another moment with her, and especially alone.

Truly, he was worse than Benjamin.

Tomorrow. Tomorrow he would tell her.

~ ~ ~

Rebecca rose as soon as she awakened, getting dressed and preparing herself to greet the Westbrooks. How lovely to have friends who were willing to help her. "Thank you, God," she whispered.

They arrived almost earlier than she thought possible, and her heart fluttered when she heard Thomas Westbrook's voice speaking to the servant at the front door.

What was wrong with her? Was she developing a *tendre* for Thomas Westbrook? That was foolish, for he would never want her, his rival's widow, when he could have any beautiful, young woman of polite society. But she couldn't help thinking he was handsome and capable and interesting, could she? Those were merely facts, not feelings.

"We're not too early, are we?" Mrs. Westbrook said, taking Rebecca's hands in hers. "I rarely sleep past dawn."

"Not too early at all. I was waiting for you." Rebecca's spirits lifted at the sight of them. To be welcoming her own guests into her own home without fear of angering her mother-in-law was a new but wonderful pleasure.

Rebecca gave Benjamin and Caroline Arthur's grandfather's letter and told them the last place she'd seen the family Bible. Next, Thomas and his mother came with her to her desk in the little room she was using to conduct business and keep the accounts.

"I cannot quite understand these books," she said, showing them some of her mother-in-law's last entries.

Thomas sat at the desk and started poring over the ledgers, making notations on a separate sheet of paper as he did so. Meanwhile, Mrs. Westbrook explained what she needed to keep a record of and what was unnecessary, the questions she needed to ask the housekeeper and butler on a regular basis, and the things she needed to pay particular attention to, and how often to send the servants to the butcher and the market.

"Your advice is so helpful," Rebecca said after their long conversation.

"Come and I shall show you something." Thomas lifted his hand and waved her over.

Thomas had her sit at the desk while he leaned over her shoulder, pointing out some of Mrs. Heywood's notations and symbols and how there were gaps where she had not been recording some of the more important numbers.

"You can hire a steward to take care of the farm records if you wish, thus having him deal directly with the tenants, while you record all of the household expenses and supplies."

"That is what I did," Mrs. Westbrook said, "but now that our steward has gone to live in London, Thomas is dealing with the tenants and the farming records."

Should Rebecca trust someone else with the business of the farm and the tenants? She still was unsure which of her servants would prove loyal to her and whether or not her mother-in-law would return and somehow try to take back possession of the estate. Rebecca was finding it hard to believe that she would go so quietly and without a fight.

Afterward, Thomas explained to her the questions she needed to ask her grooms and other menservants, as well as what to require from her tenants, informing her of the things that were considered her responsibility and the responsibilities of her tenants.

"This is very helpful. Thank you both. I needed to understand all of this better. But perhaps I should have written it all down."

"You can make notes now, if you wish."

Just then, Benjamin and Caroline came rushing into the room.

"We found it!" Benjamin said.

"We did, we found something!" Caroline said, breathless.

"For heaven's sake, keep your voices down," Thomas said.

"We found this little notation on the back of the

letter." Caroline showed them some tiny writing.

"What does it say? You know I can't read that," Mrs. Westbrook said.

"It says 'E P H three twenty,'" Caroline said.

"For you non-clergy, that is Ephesians chapter three, verse twenty." Benjamin was carrying the large tome that Rebecca had last seen in the breakfast room.

"You found the Bible, then."

"Yes, but it was not where you said you last saw it," Benjamin said. "Forgive us, but we found it in what I believe was your mother-in-law's bedroom."

Rebecca lost her breath. They had invaded Arthur's mother's room?

"What were you thinking?" Thomas said quietly, but in a harsh tone. "Did any of the servants see you?"

"We were very careful," Caroline said.

"Careful? You're carrying around an enormous Bible," Thomas said.

"Don't you want to know what we found?" Benjamin glared at his brother.

"Inside the Bible, in Ephesians chapter three, we found this. It's another map." Caroline used the desk to spread out a piece of paper, about the same size as the other map.

As she and Thomas leaned down, their heads nearly collided.

Another "X" was drawn on this map, and it was between what appeared to be a drawing of a tree and a strange shape, more round than square.

"What is it?" Caroline asked.

Everyone seemed to be waiting for Thomas to speak.

"Does this mean there are two treasures?" Caroline asked.

"Or perhaps it's showing a closer view of where to find the treasure," Rebecca suggested.

"I think you are correct," Thomas said, glancing up at her.

"But a tree? There are so many trees behind the house," Rebecca said.

"We have to find this." He pointed to the rounded object.

"I think it's a rock," Benjamin said.

"That is my guess as well," Thomas said. "Do you recall seeing a large rock with this shape somewhere?"

Rebecca tried to think. "There are several rocks, and little rocky hills, beyond the house, if I remember correctly. I rarely go out there. Arthur told me there were many badgers living among the rocks, so I never went walking there, and I am not much for riding."

"Badgers aren't dangerous," Benjamin said. "We can scare them away."

"I can retrieve my gun from the carriage," Thomas said, "if it would make everyone feel safer."

They were still gazing at Rebecca.

"Yes, that would be safest. Thank you."

Thomas left as Benjamin and Caroline talked of the likelihood of finding treasure today.

Rebecca's eye was caught by the large Bible that Benjamin was still holding. What would Mrs. Heywood say if she could see it now, if she could know what had been found in it, and if she knew two Westbrooks had been in her own bedroom and had taken the Heywood family Bible?

Mrs. Westbrook saw her staring at the Bible and said, "Darlings, please return Mrs. Heywood's Bible to her room."

"But Mother, we have to make sure nothing else is hidden inside." Benjamin set the large tome on the desk and flipped through the book, and though he was probably being careful, Rebecca wished he would be just a bit more careful.

After a few minutes of searching its pages, Benjamin conceded that he did not think there were any more hidden maps or clues in the Bible, so he went to return it to where he'd found it, and Caroline went along as his lookout.

Thomas returned with his hand hidden under his arm under his coat, no doubt concealing his gun there. Benjamin and Caroline joined them and they set out to find the place indicated on the map.

As they walked through the structured garden behind the house, Rebecca hoped they looked like they were simply taking a walk, as she had told the housekeeper as they left. She wondered for the hundredth time since Mrs. Heywood left what the servants would tell their long-time mistress when she returned. For she had left many of her personal belongings, including much of her clothing.

Caroline slipped her arm through Rebecca's as they walked. "What shall you do with the treasure when you find it?"

"I don't know. I suppose I should invest it."

"Buy land," Benjamin said.

"Land? That is very uninteresting," Caroline said. "I think she should buy a house in London. Wouldn't that be a wonder, a woman owning the biggest house in London?"

"She could never own a house bigger than the

royal palaces in London."

"Well then, she could own the biggest house that was not a royal palace."

Mrs. Heywood had always complained about not having a house in London, although they often rented some very opulent rooms when they went there. Arthur and his mother spared no expense when it came to indulging themselves. But she should not think such thoughts, now that her husband was dead.

"I wouldn't need the biggest house," Rebecca said.

"But you would buy a house?" Caroline's smile was triumphant.

"Land, a grand estate that you could lease to someone else, would bring you a profit, and that's surely worth more than a house that would only cost money." Benjamin was adamant.

"Before you two help Rebecca spend her fortune," Mrs. Westbrook said, winking at her, "You should make sure you can find it."

"Someone may have already dug it up years ago," Rebecca said.

They walked on in silence for a few moments before the lively conversation started up again.

Truly, Rebecca knew she shouldn't spend money, even in her head, that she might never have, but there was something she wanted more than she wanted a house in London. She wanted to help her brothers and sisters in whatever way she could, to help her brothers make their fortunes, and to help her sisters be able to marry whomever they wished to. That would be the greatest luxury, knowing she had brought good fortune to her beloved siblings.

And then of course, she would want to help the

poor. Wouldn't it be wrong to not share a good portion of whatever treasure God provided to her?

They approached the rocky area where she imagined the map indicated as the spot where the treasure would be found.

"Are we looking for a large tree?" Caroline asked. "But the trees end where the rocky hills begin."

"I think we're looking for a large rock near a large tree," Benjamin said.

They wandered around looking at rocks, then going back to the trees and searching around them, then taking another look at the maps.

"Keep in mind," Thomas said, "these maps were drawn at least fifty years ago, and the chest was buried even longer ago than that, when Captain Heywood came home from the sea."

"How long do trees live?" Caroline asked.

It was a good question.

"I suppose it depends on the kind of tree it is," Mrs. Westbrook said. She had ceased to look and had seated herself on a rock overlooking a lovely little glen.

Caroline's brows were drawn together. "This is more difficult than I thought it would be."

"We just have to keep looking," Benjamin said. But even he had a look of mild frustration on his face.

"One thing we cannot do," Thomas said, with his usual sober expression, "is let anyone see us looking. No one can know we are searching for something out here, even if we don't tell them what we're searching for."

"We understand," Benjamin said with a slightly exasperated sigh. "We know someone else is looking for it as well."

They all seemed to glance at Rebecca, no doubt

remembering that she was shot at by that someone, and that her husband was murdered by them.

Thomas stared at her the longest. He looked as though he wanted to say something, but he ended up turning away and looking more closely at a rock. All the while, he had a pistol in his hand, pointing it at the ground while he went about searching.

Truly, he was a good man. He didn't draw attention to himself the way Arthur used to. He didn't say flirtatious or flattering things, and where Arthur was blond and had light-colored eyes, Thomas Westbrook's hair was dark brown and his eyes a deep blue. Arthur also never seemed to think of anyone who wasn't directly connected to him, but Thomas Westbrook had been kind to her when there was nothing for him to gain, disinterestedly protecting her and making sure she was safe.

Sometimes she wondered what she ever saw in her husband, why she'd been so foolish as to fall in love with him. He'd humiliated and betrayed her, over and over. But at least he'd left her his estate. Why he took the time to provide for her, she still didn't understand. It seemed to be the one loving thing he'd done for her.

She'd been pregnant with their child, so that must have contributed to his decision. She tried to remember exactly what he'd said when he told her he'd changed his will.

"I increased Mother's jointure, should I die, but I made sure you would inherit everything if I die before the baby is born." Strange that at his age, and given his unsteadfast nature, he would have been thinking about dying. Perhaps he also anticipated being shot by a jealous husband.

Then she remembered he'd said, "My solicitor said it was the wise thing to do and that he would take care of it. He brought me the papers and I signed them." The idea had been his solicitor's, apparently, and not his.

But it had been one of the times when she'd been buoyed by hope that he would change. She had hope that the new baby would be the catalyst to make him ashamed of his trysts with other women and would make him finally love her enough to stay home with her.

But that hope had ended in disappointment on top of disappointment.

She mentally shook herself. She couldn't let that pain invade her time with the Westbrooks.

They continued to search the rocks and trees for a while longer, until Mrs. Westbrook said she was beginning to feel tired.

"You may come and look out here any time you like," Rebecca told the three younger Westbrooks. "There is no one to care, but please do be careful."

"Yes, we need to bring a weapon when we do come." Thomas gave his brother and sister a pointed look.

"They should inform you they are coming, should they not?" Mrs. Westbrook said.

"There is no need. The less information written down or spoken, the better." Rebecca would feel horrible if anyone was harmed looking for the treasure.

Thomas nodded.

They all walked back to the house in companionable conversation. Truly, she couldn't remember a more enjoyable day, even though they hadn't found the treasure. But that sent a pang of guilt through her.

When would she stop feeling guilty for the moments when she did not feel sad?

CHAPTER ELEVEN

Thomas mentally harangued himself for not telling Rebecca Heywood who had shot at her and was digging for the treasure on her land. But how did one inform a woman the identity of her husband's murderer? It could not be done lightly or without first preparing her.

But he should have informed her. He should have hung back and told her when his family went to get into the carriage. But that had not seemed appropriate, telling her quickly with no notice. Besides, someone might have heard them.

Perhaps he should have told her when they were out looking for the treasure. He could have told his family at the same time—except that he wasn't sure he wanted to burden them with that knowledge.

But now it was the next morning and he was readying himself to go to confront both the constable, Mr. Fogg, and the Justice of the Peace, Mr. William

Strader. After all, it was the Justice of the Peace's responsibility to arrest Mr. Fogg and bind him over to await the assize, where he would be tried for murder.

Thomas would deal with this the proper way and keep his family and Mrs. Rebecca Heywood safe. Mr. Fogg should face judgment for his crimes.

Perhaps he should get Rebecca Heywood's permission first. After all, the treasure was her secret, and he would probably be forced to reveal it to the Justice of the Peace.

First, he went to make sure Fogg wasn't currently digging in his spot on the Heywood estate. He was not. Then he rode to Fogg's home.

When he knocked on the door, the servant who opened it told him the constable was not at home.

"Do you know when you expect him home?"

The servant did not.

Thomas got back on his horse and rode the short way to the home of the Justice of the Peace, Mr. Strader. Fortunately, both men lived less than ten miles from Heywood House and Wyghtworth.

Thomas was admitted to Mr. Strader's home and into a room lined with bookshelves. The JP was seated in front of a window, and when Thomas entered, he rose from his chair and came around from behind his desk to greet him.

"What brings you here on this fine day, Mr. Westbrook?" His words were friendly but his tone was gruff.

"I have a serious matter to discuss with you."

"You may speak freely."

"No doubt you have heard of the murder of Arthur Heywood on his own property, his body found near a hole that was being dug in the ground."

"Yes. Mr. Pursglove has been there to investigate. Do you have information about this suspicious death?"

"I believe I do. I found the man who has been digging on the Heywood property near my boundary line, who shot at Mrs. Heywood and no doubt is responsible for killing Arthur Heywood."

"Oh?" Mr. Strader crossed his arms over his chest, then stepped back, bumping into his desk.

"Yes."

"You say, you saw this person digging?"

"Yes. It was the constable, Mr. Fogg."

Thomas watched Mr. Strader's eyes. His expression didn't change at the shocking information.

"That is surprising, indeed."

In fact, Thomas could not tell that Mr. Strader was surprised at all. But perhaps he was good at hiding his feelings.

"I am sure you understand that I would like Mr. Fogg to be apprehended at once and bound over to the assize."

"I see." Mr. Strader stood staring at Thomas, a severe look on his face. "What evidence do you have?"

"I saw him digging near where the body was found. What other evidence do you need?"

"It is a serious matter to accuse a man of murder."

"It is indeed, and even more serious to commit a murder."

Mr. Strader raised his eyebrows.

"The man has already murdered my neighbor, shooting him in the forehead, and then he shot at the dead man's wife with a rifle. For everyone's safety, he should be apprehended at once." Thomas could feel his blood rising. "I understand you have a dilemma, Mr.

Strader, as no one wishes to believe in the corruption of the constable. But I saw him with my own eyes."

"How sure are you that it was Mr. Fogg? Did you call out to him? Speak to him?"

"I know it was Mr. Fogg, and no, I did not call out to him." Thomas resisted the urge to say something rude.

"How can you be sure it was him? Perhaps it was only someone who looked like him."

"I know what Mr. Fogg looks like. I saw him very recently, and I saw his face while he was digging with a shovel, the same hole he was digging when Mrs. Heywood happened upon him."

"And why did you not apprehend him yourself?"

"If you are unwilling to do your duty, I shall apprehend him myself."

Thomas's blood was boiling, but he stood his ground and gave the man stare for stare.

Had Thomas foolishly divulged what he knew to a man who would betray his office and the trust they all had in him? Had Fogg bribed him already?

After a short silence, Mr. Strader said, "I have every intention of doing my duty, Mr. Westbrook. But if you feel you or your neighbors are in danger, then you may apprehend the offender. I will certainly bring Mr. Fogg in to question him."

"I would like to be present when you question him."

Mr. Strader took his time in answering. Finally he said, "I shall permit it. We shall meet here, tomorrow at twelve noon."

"Very good. Thank you, Mr. Strader."

The man nodded and Thomas left, mounting his

horse and riding toward home.

The last thing Thomas had wanted when he came home from serving his country in its military was to face danger and treachery of this nature. He'd planned to live a quiet life, using his guns to shoot pheasants, not to defend himself and his neighbors.

But if a fight was what Fogg and Strader wanted, a fight was what they would get.

~ ~ ~

Rebecca was surprised when the servant announced that Mr. Thomas Westbrook had arrived, but she bade the servant show him in.

She couldn't help thinking he looked a bit agitated. "Are you well, Mr. Westbrook?"

"I am very well, thank you. But I am come to give you news of a very serious nature, I'm afraid."

"News?"

"Yes. I believe I know who shot at you. I caught the man digging in the place where you saw him."

"Oh. That is very good." Her heart fluttered a bit at the thought of the man who was wicked enough to look for treasure that was not his own and even kill for it.

"I would not burden you with it now, since the man has not been apprehended yet, but I wanted to make sure you were on your guard, should the man come here again."

"Again? Is this someone I know?"

"Indeed, it is the constable, Mr. Fogg."

"Mr. Fogg?"

"I saw him digging. It was Fogg, I am absolutely certain."

"That is shocking." Could the man who had

looked her in the eye, sitting in this very room, be the man who killed Arthur? A shiver snaked across her shoulders.

"I'm sorry to have to tell you, but I felt you ought to know, for your own safety."

"I thank you for telling me, and for catching him. I know you must have taken quite a bit of trouble to watch for him." Her voice was trailing off as the truth and shock set in.

"I regret I did not simply apprehend him while he was digging."

"Oh no, that would have been dangerous. He might have shot you."

Thomas Westbrook had a strange look on his face. "I have faced down men with guns before."

But she got the feeling he would not like to do so again. "I am sorry. I imagine you anticipated a quiet life after coming home."

"I shall do what must be done. A woman should be able to take a walk on her own property without being shot at. I detest men who terrorize other men, but how much worse to threaten a woman."

"I appreciate your chivalry, Mr. Westbrook, but cannot the Justice of the Peace simply arrest him and put him in jail?"

"That is what I was hoping. I spoke with Mr. Strader, the Justice of the Peace, this morning but he refused to arrest him until after the three of us meet. I am meeting with him and with Mr. Fogg tomorrow at noon, and I trust at that time that the constable will be taken and bound over to the assize."

"Shall you need me to come with you?"

"Not unless you can swear that the man who was

shooting at you was Mr. Fogg."

"Unfortunately I couldn't see him well enough. But it certainly could have been Mr. Fogg. He appeared to be the same size and build, although he was too far away for me to say with certainty. I suppose I'm of no use to you. Forgive me."

"There is nothing to forgive. I thank you for being willing."

Truly, this was unsettling. Mr. Fogg had been constable since before Rebecca had come there to live, and she'd never heard anything that would have disparaged his character. How could a man committed to uphold the law have so blatantly broken it? Everyone trusted him, which made it all the more vexatious.

"I am sorry this is upsetting your peace," she said, considering how Thomas must feel. "It is unfair that you must involve yourself in this dangerous matter."

"Do not trouble yourself. It is a privilege to defend my neighbors, if I am able. I would not be a man if I could not stand up to a troublemaker, thief, and murderer so close to my home. I am only annoyed that I allowed him to be at liberty all this time. I blame myself for not apprehending him when I caught him digging several days ago, but I was trying to wait and see if he would somehow leave evidence . . . It was foolish."

"You are too hard on yourself." Rebecca shook her head. "Please do not take on any blame, for I'm sure the Justice of the Peace—Mr. Strader, is it?—should have arrested Mr. Fogg as soon as you informed him of what you saw."

"Yes, that was my thought as well."

"This is all very unsettling." How could they be safe if they could not rely on their Justice of the Peace and constable? "I do hope there is no corruption on the part of the Justice of the Peace."

"I fear there may be." Mr. Westbrook's expression was very grim.

Truly, Rebecca had always thought that a man in Thomas Westbrook's position—wealthy landholder, from an old, well-respected family—was too powerful for any person to ever be able to harm him. But obviously, with her husband murdered, and with the local authorities unwilling to arrest the person Thomas Westbrook said was responsible, even he was not untouchable.

"I do not like the idea of you being here alone without means of protection," Thomas said.

For a moment, she was taken aback, but then she said, "I have menservants."

"But do you know how loyal they are to you? You have not been mistress of Heywood House long."

"That is true." Rebecca had been thinking these same thoughts, but she didn't want to appear cowardly. "I am sure they would not allow harm to come to me. Besides, my mother is coming for a visit and is expected to arrive tomorrow." *Finally*, Rebecca added silently. She was so ready to see her mother.

"Will your father or brothers be coming?"

"No, they are all too busy just now."

"I was hoping you might have a male member of your family come. I do fear for your safety, Mrs. Heywood."

"As long as I stay in the house, I should be safe, I think." But she was getting rather tired of not being able to even take a turn about her own grounds.

He sighed, a barely audible sound. "I don't like

this. I shall bring you a gun to keep beside you."

"I've never used a gun before. I don't know if I'd be able to shoot it."

"I shall teach you how to use it, just in case you need it."

"That is very kind of you." Her heart fluttered a bit, staring at his face. Was he so disinterested and yet concerned about her? She could hardly believe he would want to protect her so much that he would teach her how to use a gun.

But that was just the kind of person he seemed to be. He was kind to everyone. She remembered something his sister Caroline had said once, that he was "kind to everyone except me." She'd said it playfully, as if in jest, but Rebecca could easily believe the truth behind it, which was that he was kind to servants, tenants, and peers alike.

"There are guns here, in the house."

Thomas Westbrook gave her a questioning look.

"Would you teach me to shoot those, so as not to have part with one of your guns?" They belonged to her husband, but would that matter to him?

"If you wish. That should be just as effective."

She couldn't imagine Arthur ever teaching her to shoot his guns. He never allowed her to touch them. Thomas Westbrook was so different from her husband. And how sad that she couldn't imagine her husband being as concerned for her in this situation as Mr. Westbrook was.

Rebecca went up to her husband's bedroom to look for his guns, not wishing to send a servant on such an errand. She took the hunting rifle he'd had with him when he was shot, steeling herself against the strange sensation that crept along her spine. This was a practical decision, to take the gun. She needed it.

She also found one of his pistols and carried the both of them, along with the ammunition, down to where Thomas was waiting for her.

Rebecca called to a servant. "Please tell Adler that I will be shooting at the back of the house across the garden."

The servant's eyes went wide, but she scurried away to do as she was told.

Thomas Westbrook took the rifle from her and they walked out to the garden.

The first thing he did was check both guns to see if they were loaded.

"Did your husband always keep his guns loaded?" Thomas frowned.

"I don't know."

"Generally, I would say it's not safe to keep one's guns loaded in the house. But since there are no children in the home, and since this is a special circumstance, it's probably all right if you want to keep the pistol loaded and near you, perhaps in a drawer next to your bed, but not on a table where it might fall off."

Rebecca nodded.

"Many men have shot themselves unintentionally." His gaze was intense as he looked her in the eye.

"I will be careful."

He proceeded to show her how to unload and load the dueling pistol. "You only get one shot before you have to reload, so if someone is attacking you, make sure you shoot to kill."

Rebecca's stomach churned. Could she shoot someone? Perhaps, if they were truly trying to kill her, she could shoot them in self-defense. She hoped she could do it, for the sake of the people who loved her, and for her own sake, to save herself from an evil person. After all, she wouldn't want to disappoint Thomas Westbrook after he took time out to show her how to use a gun.

"An important rule is to never point the muzzle of a gun at anyone unless you're willing to shoot."

Rebecca nodded.

Next, he showed her how to look and see that the gun was loaded, then how to stand with her feet apart, knees slightly bent, and how to hold the gun with both hands just before firing.

Their hands touched repeatedly as he gently showed her where to place her fingers.

Why did his touch, so innocent, send her heart racing and make her feel as if she could barely breathe? She mustn't let it show, but his fingers brushing hers . . . She must be depraved to feel so much at so little provocation.

"Now, aim for that tree trunk at the edge of the garden. Get ready for the gun to kick back at you. Don't let it hit you in the face or the chest."

She concentrated on holding the gun correctly, stiffening her arms, locking her wrists and elbows in place to keep the gun from recoiling into her face or body, aiming as she squeezed the trigger.

The gun blasted so loud, her ears seemed to fill with the sound, as the gun kicked back so fast that she had no time to react. But she'd locked her elbows so that the gun did not come all the way back.

"Did I hit the tree?"

"You may have, but I didn't see any bark flying.

We'll check it later. Try again."

He let her load the gun this time, patiently giving her instructions. His voice was gentle, but deep and masculine. Its warm timbre made her heart flutter and shallowed her breathing.

"Now, remember to keep a firm hold, knowing that the gun will kick backward. You might also want to aim a bit high, because the bullet drops a bit the farther it travels."

Rebecca readied her stance, paying a bit more attention this time to aiming the gun. She squeezed off her shot and this time saw the bark fly from the tree.

"A hit. Very well done."

She shot the pistol two more times, hitting the tree both times.

"You are doing very well," Thomas said. "Now, shall we move on to the rifle?"

She almost protested, saying, "Must we? I was just starting to enjoy the pistol." Instead, she held her tongue and let him put the pistol aside.

He showed her how to load and unload the rifle and how to hold it. She was competent enough now that he didn't have to place her hands on the gun to show her how to hold it, but he stood very close as he instructed her, and once again, she felt a pleasant tingling sensation as he spoke, his voice low and deep.

As he showed her where to look in order to aim the gun, she felt his breath on her ear and had to control the delicious shiver that ran through her.

She was so thankful he couldn't read her thoughts and prayed he didn't know how appealing he was to her.

"Men always know when a woman finds him

attractive," Arthur had said to her once. But she'd assumed it was his pride and arrogance that made him think that. He probably thought every woman was in love with him as soon as he smiled and said some flattering words to her. And perhaps he was right. It certainly seemed to be so.

But Thomas Westbrook never seemed to have that kind of arrogance. She'd never flirted with him, and he'd never flirted with her. They both seemed quite aware of the fact that she was the wife—now widow—of the man he rightfully despised.

She set the stock of the gun against her shoulder, as he instructed her, and aimed the gun at the tree trunk.

She squeezed the trigger and the gun slammed her shoulder like a hammer. She gasped.

"Are you hurt?" Thomas asked, taking the gun from her shaking hands.

Rebecca rubbed her shoulder. "That hurt worse than I expected."

"I should have warned you to hold the gun firmly."

"I must have expected my shoulder to keep the gun from kicking. I never expected it to kick my shoulder." She was sure to have a bruise.

"Forgive me."

"No, it is not your fault. Next time I will hold it more firmly."

"Do you want to try it again?"

The thought of shooting the gun again was not a pleasant one. "No, thank you. I think I can remember how."

"I am sorry you're hurt." He looked contrite.

"No, no, I am not injured." She tried to smile and look undaunted. She never liked thinking she was the same as other women, and society always portrayed women as frail and soft. Besides, she didn't want him to regret showing her how to shoot.

"I feel quite safe and secure, now that I know how to defend myself if necessary."

Thomas said, "I'm glad. That was my intent, to help you defend yourself. And now I think I should go. Remember not to trust Mr. Fogg or let him in the house."

"I won't."

"And I don't think you should trust Mr. Strader, the Justice of the Peace, either."

"I won't."

"Or Mr. Pursglove, for it was strange that he came here to investigate before Mr. Strader had a chance to request his presence. The Justice of the Peace is required to pay for his services and is the one who would request it, not the constable."

"So many suspicious things." Rebecca shook her head. How troubling that they could not trust their own authorities and officials!

"If you ever need anything, please do not hesitate to send for me. I will help you any way I'm able. And if you suspect any of your servants of disloyalty, I hope you will send them away. Mother can probably help you find better ones. She knows a great number of people."

"That is very kind and thoughtful. Thank you, and please thank your mother for me."

"What are neighbors for if not to help each other?"

"But you seem to be doing all the helping, and I all the receiving." Her heart swelled as she gazed up at him, but not only because he was so handsome. Arthur had treated this gentleman so badly, and yet Thomas Westbrook had been nothing but kind to her, this man who could be attending balls in London or Bath, receiving the attentions of every eligible maiden in fashionable society. Or he could be enjoying the quiet life of a country gentleman, shooting, smoking, and calling on friends, not trying to ensure his widowed neighbor was not being murdered for a fortune in buried doubloons.

The entire situation was ludicrous. Killed over pirate treasure, indeed! This was the nineteenth century, for heaven's sake.

But it was not a sensational novel by Mrs. Radcliffe, it was her life. And if not for Thomas Westbrook . . .

"I am very grateful to you," she said, as he carried the guns to her bedroom.

"I don't want to intrude," he said, stopping in the doorway and letting her have the guns one at a time.

She placed the pistol in the drawer of the table beside her bed. Then she took the rifle and laid it on the floor, also by her bed, but where she wouldn't trip over it.

"I shall be quite safe now." She smiled, trying to make light of the situation.

"You may send a servant for me any time, day or night."

The way he was looking down at her, not moving, just staring into her eyes, made her catch her breath. Could there be a better man in England than this one? And did she dare hope . . . that he might be developing feelings for her?

What was she thinking? Marriage hadn't exactly

worked out the first time. What if she made another mistake? But Thomas Westbrook was nothing like Arthur. He would make a wonderful husband.

Oh dear. Could she be falling in love with him? Her heart skipped and thumped wildly, but more from fear than anything else.

CHAPTER TWELVE

Thomas stared so long into Rebecca Heywood's eyes, he must be frightening her, for she looked like a scared rabbit all of a sudden.

How could he be thinking of Rebecca Heywood as a woman and not as Arthur Heywood's widow? He must remind himself of his vow to have nothing to do with Arthur or any woman who would fall in love with him. Ever again. Had he lost all pride? Had he forgotten how he swore never to have any sort of relationship with Arthur Heywood's widow?

But she was so lovely and gentle, so appreciative of his help, which he would have given if she had been any woman, whether old or young, with no expectations at all. It was his duty, after all, to help his neighbor, especially a widow who lived wholly unprotected, except for servants who might be easily bribed by Fogg or Strader.

He had to get hold of himself. Staring into her

blue eyes, glancing at her perfect lips . . . He was going mad, surely, because he wondered how it would feel, and how she would react, if he kissed her.

He couldn't seem to help himself.

He reminded her, "You may send for me any time, day or night."

"Thank you. You are very kind." Her voice sounded as if she was losing her breath.

She leaned away from him, which somehow broke the spell that was holding him in place. He stepped out of the doorway to let her pass.

She wasn't interested in him either. They were simply two disinterested neighbors. Rebecca Heywood was his sister's and his mother's friend, nothing more.

And he was sure now that his brother, who was at least four years her junior, held a *tendre* for her. Another good reason he should not entertain any thoughts of his own for her.

She led the way to the front door, while he told himself sternly, *You're only falling for her because she's the damsel in distress of the knights' tales you read as a boy. Stop being so easily manipulated by your fantasies of rescuing the frightened maiden. You're no knight, and she's no maiden.*

It was unkind, perhaps, but he needed to get his feelings under control.

"Good day, Mrs. Heywood."

He hurried away, praying for wisdom about how to tell his family that their local officials were all corrupt and not to be trusted.

~ ~ ~

The next day, Rebecca looked out the window and saw her mother and sister being helped from the carriage by the footman.

She ran down the stairs and out the front door before they had even made their way up the steps.

"My darling." Her mother made a solemn face as she took Rebecca's face in her hands, then embraced her. "How are you holding up?"

"I am well. Mrs. Heywood is away in Kent, so that helps."

Her mother shook her head, then whispered, "Don't let the servants hear you say things like that."

"I won't." But why did she have to be so careful in her own house? It seemed unfair, but her mother was right. She shouldn't speak ill of her mother-in-law, and especially in the hearing of the servants.

Next, she embraced her sister Margaret. "Where are Charlotte and Abigail?"

Margaret answered, "Charlotte didn't want to miss Kitty Alexander's coming out ball, and Abigail didn't want to see you sad. She's such a ninny."

"Margaret, that's unkind." Mother frowned at Margaret.

"Well, I think it unkind that Rebecca's sisters didn't want to come and keep her company and cheer her up. They're selfish, and you said so yourself."

"I don't think I said that, but . . ." Mother sighed. "Forgive us, Rebecca. We are glad to see you looking so well." She gave a wan smile as she patted Rebecca's cheek.

"And I am very glad you are both here."

Rebecca led them inside as the footmen carried in their trunks.

After they had changed their clothes and had come down to the sitting room, Rebecca said, "I have news that I did not write in my letters, but you must both promise to keep it secret and tell no one, except perhaps Father."

Mother sent an anxious look Margaret's way.

"I may only be twelve, but I can keep a secret," Rebecca's youngest sister declared.

Rebecca proceeded to tell them all that had been happening, even how she and Thomas Westbrook believed their local officials were not to be trusted and that the constable had been the one responsible for Arthur's murder.

Mother looked alarmed, but only for a moment. "Surely you cannot suspect your constable and your Justice of the Peace. I don't think they could be capable of such things."

"Mother, I know you always want to believe the best in everyone, but it seems quite likely. Even Mr. Westbrook thinks so."

"It's not that I want to believe the best in everyone, but it just seems too far-fetched." Mother shook her head, a bland look on her face. Mother was good-hearted and without guile, and she could never bring herself to believe bad things existed, not unless it was absolutely right in front of her and impossible to deny. She'd made Rebecca feel as though she was overly dramatic, suspicious, and hard-hearted. But she knew that it was her mother who refused to see evil.

"It is farfetched." She simply would not discuss it with her mother, but only with the Westbrooks, who had been there the entire time and therefore understood.

"Tell me all the news at home," Rebecca said. "How is Father and everyone who was sick?"

Mother seemed pleased to discuss in detail the recoveries of everyone who had been sick. She had yet to mention Arthur or his death or funeral, but Rebecca was grateful for that, for now. She knew the questions would come eventually.

Rebecca's thoughts wandered to Thomas and how his meeting was going with Mr. Strader and Mr. Fogg. She'd prayed quite a few times already for his safety and that God would protect him from evil men. Would he have any firearms with him? The more she had thought about it, the more she wished she had asked him to consider the dangers and not to go alone to this meeting.

"Rebecca, are you listening?" Mother shook her head at her.

"Of course. You were saying that John was better and Colin never got sick."

"You have had a very difficult few weeks, I am sure." Mother squeezed Rebecca's arm. "Why don't you tell us anything you didn't tell me in your letters. I'm sure you must have much to tell."

Rebecca had been looking forward to telling her mother how difficult life had been with Mrs. Heywood so loudly and openly mourning Arthur's death, and how she had verbally attacked Rebecca with one accusation after another. So she poured out her pain to her mother, with Margaret sitting nearby, listening and looking sad and angry by turns.

She told her mother how she'd been shot at, which she had not written in any of her letters, and Margaret suddenly said, "If I were a man, I would go right now and shoot that Mr. Fogg."

"Margaret!" Mother's eyes and mouth were

equally wide as she stared at her youngest daughter.

"I understand how you feel, Margaret," Rebecca said, "but we first have to make absolutely certain he is guilty, and he must be treated like anyone else who is caught doing something terrible. He will not get away with it, as Mr. Westbrook and I will make sure of."

"Yes, let Mr. Westbrook take care of it." Mother looked as if that was, of course, the end of the matter.

"It is not Mr. Westbrook's responsibility to take care of Rebecca," Margaret said, sitting up straight, her eyes fairly sparking, "but she is my family, and if I were older, I would show him he could not shoot at my sister."

Rebecca smiled. "Thank you, Margaret. I appreciate that."

But Mother was not smiling. "That is not a ladylike attitude at all, Margaret Harper. You astonish me, talking like that."

While Mother was not looking, Rebecca winked at her sister, who hid a laugh behind her hand.

"I am glad you have neighbors like Mr. Westbrook," Mother went on. "He sounds like a very good young man. Is he married, or attached to anyone?"

"Not that I know of." Rebecca and her sister exchanged amused grins.

"Well, then, he sounds like a very good marriage prospect."

"Mother, before you marry me off to him, you should know that he's not interested in me at all. For one thing, he and Arthur hated each other, so he is not likely to want to marry Arthur's widow. Besides that, Thomas Westbrook can have any woman he chooses, for he is the three most valuable things a bachelor can be: Young, handsome, and rich. And furthermore, I have no wish to marry again, at least not right away."

At some point in the future she did want to have a baby. She knew that she wanted children, but it was the husband she wasn't sure she wanted. After all, a husband could hurt you and betray you and ignore you. But if she had a child, she could give them all her love and receive theirs in return.

She could wait, however. There was no sense in rushing into marriage again. If there was one thing she had learned, it was that she could be completely sure about man's love for her . . . and she could be completely wrong.

~ ~ ~

Rebecca was glad when she received the invitation to dine at Wyghtworth. Now she could find out what happened earlier that day when Thomas Westbrook met with the Justice of the Peace and the constable.

She was just informing her mother and sister of their invitation to dine when a caller arrived.

"Mr. Gilbert Heywood," the servant announced.

It was the cousin her mother-in-law had mentioned, the one who came to the funeral but did not stay at the house. Rebecca only met him briefly.

"Show him in," Rebecca said, while she and her mother and Margaret fixed themselves so that they sat looking demure and proper.

Gilbert Heywood was quite young, she noticed, as he swept into the room with a rushed manner, which was nothing like Arthur's, but there was something about him—his coloring, his hair and eyes—that reminded her of Arthur, the characteristic Heywood pallor. And though he might be considered handsome, he was not as handsome as Arthur.

But she no longer thought Arthur terribly handsome. In fact, sometimes she wondered that she ever found him handsome at all. There was an unkindness in his eyes that she hadn't noticed until sometime after they were married. She found she preferred dark-haired men to blondes.

After the usual greetings, Rebecca said, "You live near here, do you not, Mr. Heywood?"

"About fifteen miles from here."

Mother said, "And how are you related to Mr. Arthur Heywood?"

"His grandfather and mine were brothers. My grandfather was the oldest son and inherited the family estate, and Arthur's grandfather went to sea and made his fortune. He built this estate himself with what he earned as a captain in the navy."

"I see." Mother smiled and nodded.

"I was very sorry to hear about my cousin Arthur's untimely death," he said, nodding and staring at the floor. "I hope the authorities have apprehended the scoundrel who killed him."

"Not yet," Rebecca said solemnly.

"Well, it is shocking indeed."

"Indeed." Mother nodded.

Thankfully, Margaret said nothing, but Rebecca could tell that she was listening to every word.

They talked on about other things, the state of the roads and the weather, typical topics of conversation with a stranger. But the longer they talked, the more Rebecca wondered why he was there.

"It is good that your family can come to visit you,"

Gilbert Heywood said. "I should think, having lived all your life in London, you would be anxious to go back there."

Rebecca thought a moment before speaking. "I rather like living in the country."

"Oh, I see." He looked strangely happy with her answer.

"But I'm sure I will want to take some time to visit my family once I have the affairs in order at Heywood House."

"Yes, of course." He fidgeted with his hands, then stood to his feet. "Thank you for allowing me this call. I hope you are able to call on me at Beaumont."

Rebecca smiled and nodded but did not agree to the call, as she had no intention of making it.

"He was friendly," Mother said. "Do you think he's wanting to court you?"

"I don't know. I only met him once. He could not have been on very good terms with Arthur, for I never heard him mention him."

They speculated on why he had come to call on her until they returned to the happier discussion of what to wear to dine at the Westbrooks' that night. Rebecca described each of the family members in detail.

"They all sound like lovely people. How good that you can depend upon your neighbors."

"Is Thomas or Benjamin Westbrook handsome?" Margaret asked with an eager smile.

Rebecca could see Mother watching her with shrewd eyes.

"Mother has met them both, I daresay. What do you think, Mother?"

"They are both handsome, eligible gentlemen."

Mother was still gazing at Rebecca.

"They are both handsome," Rebecca agreed. "Margaret, you are not too young to begin to practice flirting. Benjamin Westbrook could be just the right age for you in six or seven years."

"Really?" Mother asked.

"He is about seventeen now, I think."

"That is only five years older than me!" Margaret looked quite excited at the prospect of flirting.

"But Rebecca, should you be encouraging her to flirt, at her age? Twelve is too young, surely."

"Perhaps, but since she is not able to attend balls for at least two or three more years, this could be one of her only chances." Rebecca winked at her sister, who winked back.

"You two always were the most ill-behaved of my daughters." Mother sighed.

Rebecca and Margaret both laughed, then stifled the sound to keep from being scolded. Then they began a game of chess while Mother went upstairs to lie down.

"Rebecca, do you like Thomas Westbrook?" Margaret asked.

"He has become a good friend, but he is not interested in me and I cannot be interested in him. It is too soon after my husband's death."

"How can you know that he's not interested in you? He's spent a great deal of time with you."

She hadn't even told her mother and sister about him teaching her to shoot.

"I can tell. He and Arthur were not friends. They seemed to be enemies, and besides that, he can marry any woman he wants. He wouldn't want a widow."

"I don't see why not." Margaret studied Rebecca's

face. "You are still very young and pretty."

"Why, thank you, sister. You are very young and pretty as well."

Very soon they were tickling each other and giggling hysterically. How lovely to be with family again.

CHAPTER THIRTEEN

Thomas was alone in the drawing room drinking his second brandy when he heard the carriage coming. He watched out the window as Benjamin and Caroline went to greet them and to help Rebecca and her mother and sister out of the carriage, as excited as if they were old friends who hadn't been to visit in weeks.

Mother had confirmed his suspicions that Benjamin was developing feelings for Rebecca Heywood. But surely he knew that a seventeen-year-old, especially one who was not an heir, could have little to offer a widow like Rebecca. But a seventeen-year-old did not always use the best judgment, as he knew from experience.

When he was seventeen, he'd been in love with Priscilla Dewberry and had even asked her to marry him, vowing to love her until he died. He'd been so foolish then, so innocent and wide-eyed. It was almost unbearable to remember.

Priscilla had seemed equally eager to marry him,

and he'd believed she loved him. But when Arthur discovered their engagement . . .

Thomas had himself told Arthur of it. Arthur had teased him, making a snide comment about him being eager to marry, too young to know what he wanted, getting engaged when he should be having fun, "sampling the wares," as he put it.

Then, a few weeks later at a ball, Thomas could still remember the way his childhood friend had looked, that sneaky, malicious grin on his face when he saw them together. Soon, Arthur was asking Priscilla to dance, and by the end of the ball, Thomas could see that her attitude toward him had changed.

The next day, when Thomas went to confront Arthur, he had been even more snide, saying he would prove to Thomas that he was making a mistake, that he should be thinking about how many women he could bed, not getting engaged.

And then, a couple of weeks later, the rumors started that Arthur was courting Priscilla. She broke off her engagement to Thomas in a letter, and then, a few months after that, Priscilla disappeared.

The rumors were that she was pregnant with Arthur's baby and had gone away to have the child in secret, since Arthur no longer wanted anything to do with her.

Furious, Thomas went to Arthur's home and the confrontation turned into a shouting match, then an actual fight with fists, resulting in Arthur's nose and lip dripping blood and Arthur's mother screaming that she would have Thomas thrown in jail and tried in the King's Court for attempted murder.

Needless to say, their friendship was over, with

Mrs. Heywood vowing quite loudly to have him horse-whipped if he ever showed his face on their property again.

And now Arthur's widow was dining again at their home, his mother, sister, and brother all happy to spend time with the widow of the man who had changed the course of Thomas's life.

Of course, he had come to realize that Arthur had done him a favor. Though he was sorry for Priscilla and had secretly, anonymously, sent her money, he was glad he had not married a woman who might have been unfaithful to him after marriage. To be rejected before marriage was bad, but rejection and betrayal after marriage would have been infinitely worse.

How strange to think that Benjamin was the same age that Thomas had been then.

They all came inside where Mother was waiting for them. Thomas could hear her from the drawing room as she exclaimed her rapture at seeing Rebecca and meeting her mother and sister.

He could hardly blame his family for wanting to spend time with Arthur's widow. Thomas had spent more time with Rebecca than anyone, and he'd come to enjoy nearly everything about her—her smile, her gentle voice, the way he never did anything she didn't thank him for. He had been quite generous with her, but it was only because her life was in danger because of that ridiculous treasure that may or may not be buried on her property. Arthur's property.

Thomas might not be seventeen anymore, but the pain of what Arthur and Priscilla had done was still fresh, when he allowed himself to think about it. Priscilla had rejected him, but Arthur had deliberately led her astray and then abandoned her, knowing he was hurting Thomas by doing so. But someone as cold and heartless as Arthur could never know just how much it had hurt.

He did believe that Rebecca had much more maturity and fortitude than other young women her age. Perhaps that was one reason why—besides the fact that his family loved her—he had let Fogg and Strader know he suspected them of murdering Arthur Heywood and shooting at Rebecca. He also made it perfectly clear that if they harmed Arthur's widow, they would have to answer to him.

But he absolutely did not want to forget that she had loved and chosen Arthur Heywood over every other man.

He probably shouldn't have had that second drink.

Once he was sure they had settled into the sitting room, Thomas came and greeted them all and sat down as far away from Rebecca Heywood as he could get. But that was almost worse, for he had a very good view of her, right in his line of vision. And she looked lovely, the way she was smiling happily, everyone else talking while she looked on. Then her eye caught his, and he could have sworn he could read her thoughts, and that she was wishing to ask him what had happened earlier that day when he confronted Fogg and Strader.

He still had not told his family where he had gone that morning, so he would tell them all at once.

The conversation quickly moved to the buried treasure that had become such a contentious problem, as they speculated on whether it would ever be found and how soon the would-be thief would be caught and brought to justice. Truly, they did not know how much danger they were all in, and as the only adult male between the two households, he'd have to be the one to protect them.

Where had his quiet life gone? The quiet life he'd so looked forward to when he was in the army and on the Continent, being shot at by the French? That life had been a daydream that faded as soon as he saw Arthur's widow running toward him, being chased by a man with a gun.

As they proceeded into dinner, he noticed his mother had paired Benjamin up with Rebecca.

"You have been awfully quiet all day," Mother whispered to him. "Has something happened?"

"Not exactly. I will tell you where I went this morning, but after dinner, when no servants are around."

Mother raised her brows in that concerned way of hers, and he patted her hand.

Dinner was pleasant, up until he began to notice that Benjamin appeared to be trying to flirt with Rebecca, and she seemed to look uncomfortable, holding herself stiffly and avoiding eye contact with his little brother.

His heart constricted. As painful as it was to see her rejecting Benjamin, he also could see that she did not wish to cause him pain, but she was not interested in him as a suitor.

Better to tell him honestly than to draw out his pain. If she didn't speak the truth to him, Thomas would have to do it. He was not looking forward to that.

~ ~ ~

Rebecca felt that sinking in her stomach. Benjamin, who was the sweetest young man, funny and good-hearted, was trying to flirt with her.

O God, what should I do?

She would rather disappear through the floor than hurt him or make him feel rejected. But she also couldn't let him think she felt affection for him when she didn't. Besides, he was five years younger than she, and she only thought of Benjamin as Thomas's younger brother.

"Darling? Mrs. Westbrook asked you a question." Mother was staring at her. Indeed, everyone was staring at her.

"Forgive me. I'm afraid my mind was drifting away." She shook her head, as if to laugh at herself. "What did you ask?"

"I was wondering if you'd had any more trouble with the accounting ledgers."

"Thank you for asking, but I have been managing very well after you and Mr. Westbrook came and showed me the mistakes and gave me advice."

"You are a very quick learner," Mrs. Westbrook said. "Isn't she, Thomas?"

"She is indeed." Thomas did not even glance her way.

Was he angry with her? He had been strangely quiet all evening, but she had caught him staring when Benjamin was saying something flirtatious. He must realize she had no feelings for his little brother. He'd probably hate her for breaking his heart.

But she would speak to Benjamin right away, if she could get a quick word with him when no one was listening, and tell him that she was a widow who had no wish to remarry, that he would find a young woman his own age.

The conversation went to other things, and Margaret was giving her opinion to Caroline on what to look for in a suitor. Expressions ranged from impressed to amused as Margaret said, "And don't marry a man just for his wealth, because if he's wealthy but old and ugly, you will still have to look at him, and if he's handsome but poor, you will grow tired of his face when there's no money to buy a new dress."

Mrs. Westbrook said, "That is very wise, child. But what do you advise Caroline? What should she look for?"

Caroline was smiling and wide-eyed as she turned her attention on Margaret.

"She should look for the man who has everything, because she is worth a good man who is handsome, wealthy, and most importantly, possesses good character and ideals."

Caroline nodded at Margaret and said, "I shall only marry a good man who has all the qualities I wish for. And you must do the same."

Margaret looked much older than her twelve years as she said, "Of course."

Everyone was obviously entertained by her, and Rebecca was proud that her sister had listened to her, for she had counseled Margaret and her other sisters with very similar advice, although Margaret added the "wealthy" stipulation.

Rebecca prayed her sisters would be wiser than she had been.

But how could she have known that Arthur would stop loving her and be unfaithful?

She should have known. She should have paid

attention to the warning bells when she heard him bragging about his conquests to one of his friends. She should have listened to her doubts on their wedding day when she saw him staring at a pretty young woman walking by the church. But she had married him anyway, and it had been a mistake.

If she could make such a terrible mistake once, might she not do it again?

Her stomach sank. She thought Thomas Westbrook was such a good man, and probably he was. But what if he changed after he married? Or what if he wasn't as good as he seemed? She didn't trust her own judgment.

But it felt wrong, at the same time, to think these thoughts when he had been so kind and protective of her. And on that topic . . . she was desperate to know what had happened when he confronted the coroner and the Justice of the Peace.

When dinner was over, they all moved to the drawing room.

"Thomas, did you invite your friend Andrew Lisle to dinner? I'm surprised he didn't stay."

"I invited him, but he needed to get back home for a previous engagement. And since you mentioned Andrew, I shall tell you all where he and I went this morning."

Finally. Now she would get to hear about his meeting.

"I hope you don't mind, Mrs. Heywood," he said, looking at Rebecca, "but I enlisted my friend Andrew Lisle to go with me, in case there was trouble. Andrew Lisle is a friend and was a fellow lieutenant in the Peninsular War, and I trust him. He tells no tales."

"I'm glad you had someone there with you. I was worried for your safety."

Everyone seemed to be looking sharply at her, especially Benjamin, as they realized she was the only person there who knew where he'd gone that morning.

"Lisle and I did not exactly intimidate them into confessing to any wrongdoing, even when I said I saw Fogg with my own eyes digging on your property. He adamantly denied it and said it must have been someone who looked like him. But they did tell us something interesting."

She could only imagine how much courage it must have taken to confront a murderer.

"They said that your cousin, Gilbert Heywood, wanted to purchase the estate from you and would be making you an offer soon."

Rebecca stared at him. "That is strange."

"That's the man who called on us today," Margaret said.

"Yes, but he did not make me an offer, nor did he even mention that he wished to buy the estate."

"Fogg and Strader were insinuating that Arthur's cousin, Gilbert Heywood, was the man who was trying to get at whatever was buried on the estate, if indeed there is anything."

Mother looked aghast, her mouth open and her hand over her chest.

"He did behave a bit strangely, as if he wanted to say something but changed his mind. But I wouldn't have imagined he was a thief or a murderer."

"And he very well may not be," Thomas said. "Fogg is the culprit, and I believe Strader is also an accomplice, and possibly Pursglove the coroner as well.

Gilbert Heywood may also be a partner, but if so, that is a large number of men amongst whom to divide the treasure."

It was a large number of men to be wanting to take something from her. They'd already taken her sense of safety.

"The treasure rightfully belongs to the man's descendants, I should think," Rebecca said, thinking aloud.

"I would think the treasure belongs to you," Benjamin said, looking at her. "You are the owner of the property where it is buried. The person who buried it never claimed it, so it is rightfully yours."

"It is possible the authorities would decide to give the treasure to Captain Heywood's descendants, but not if the descendants are willing to commit murder to obtain it." Thomas's gaze shifted to Rebecca's mother. "I don't wish to frighten anyone. We will be vigilant, now that we know there are ruthless men about, trying to steal what doesn't belong to them. And we will also be more likely to find the treasure, since we are the ones who possess the maps, and they are obviously digging in the wrong place."

"What else did the Justice of the Peace and the constable say?" Rebecca asked.

"Nothing of consequence, and I was careful not to reveal anything. I downplayed the existence of the treasure, saying it probably had been dug up long ago, if it had ever been buried at all. Hopefully they will begin to doubt its existence and stop searching for it."

"Where and how did they even hear of it?" Rebecca was again musing aloud.

"I believe I know." Thomas's lips twisted in an ironical way. "The JP, Strader, has a grandfather by the name of Pipken."

"The solicitor."

"Yes. Captain Heywood might have told him of the treasure's existence, even if he was never able to send the letter explaining how to find it."

"And Pipken would have told his son or grandson."

"Exactly."

Benjamin and Caroline discussed the possibility that Gilbert Heywood was involved, and that he only wanted the estate so that he could find the treasure.

"Keep in mind," Thomas interjected, "Gilbert Heywood may have no idea about the treasure. He may only want to keep the estate in the family. Don't condemn a man before any evidence has been found against him."

Caroline and Benjamin were both quiet.

"It is all very upsetting. Rebecca," Mother said, "I think you must come back to London with us before something terrible happens."

But her mother's suggestion made her spirit sink inside her.

"Rebecca? You know you ought to return to London with us, don't you? You see the wisdom in that, surely."

"I don't wish to go to London."

"But you are not safe here. Villains are about, doing terrible things, committing crimes. You will be safer in London, until this all is resolved."

"I understand why you feel that way, Mother, but I don't want them to see me running away like a scared rabbit. I want to help find the treasure and take away their reason for shooting at me and digging up my property. It's my home and I wish to defend it."

Now that she was keeping the books, taking charge of the duties of a landholder and homeowner, she didn't want anyone chasing her away. Besides, if she left, who would take care of the household and her tenants?

"But Rebecca." Mother looked quite anxious.

"Don't worry, Mother. I shall be well. I know how to shoot a gun, I have staff who will defend me—"

"And we shall be nearby," Benjamin said stoutly. "Thomas and I will make certain no one harms Mrs. Heywood."

"She can stay the night here," Mrs. Westbrook said, "if there seems to be danger about."

"This is England, after all," Margaret said, crossing her arms as if the thought of someone harming them made her angry.

"That is right." Mrs. Westbrook patted Margaret's shoulder. "There is nothing to worry about."

Thomas was very quiet as they discussed the situation, the level of danger, and how they would respond. But his expression was serious.

She wanted to ask him if he thought Gilbert Heywood was behind the digging and Arthur's murder, but Thomas had already warned Benjamin not to condemn the man, as they had no evidence against him. He was a gentleman, after all, and it was difficult for Rebecca to think of him doing something so desperate as to dig for treasure and murder his own cousin for something that might not exist.

Besides that, Gilbert Heywood had his own estate. Captain Heywood had built this house and bought this land and it was not as grand as the original family estate. And he had not offered to buy Heywood House, in spite of what Fogg and Strader had told Thomas.

Another thing she didn't understand was why she did not want to go back to London with her mother, where she'd be away from all of this conflict and danger. She would need to examine her feelings and motives when she was alone and had more time, but she wondered if it had more to do with the thrill of the hunt for the treasure, the powerful feeling that she could use a gun to defend herself, or her growing feelings for Thomas Westbrook.

Well, she was not so ridiculous as to fall in love, especially so quickly. No, she had surely learned that to be alone was far better than to be married to someone who did not even care for her.

Not that Thomas Westbrook had ever given any indication that he wished to marry her.

"I think we could all benefit from a bit of music," Mrs. Westbrook said after the discussion had waned and everyone seemed a bit tense and worried.

Rebecca was glad to change the atmosphere of the evening, so she volunteered to play. Indeed, it was a relief to let her fingers go flying over the keys and to lift her voice in song. And she had the gratification of seeing everyone's faces transformed by smiles, or at least more relaxed expressions.

She played two more songs before suggesting Margaret play something she'd been learning. And though she was only twelve, she was a better player and singer than many an adult woman Rebecca had heard.

"I am very impressed with your talent," Mrs. Westbrook said as soon as Margaret had played her song. "You are quite the prodigy, I imagine, and make your family very proud."

"My brothers aren't proud of me for anything," Margaret declared, "but my mother and sisters, at least, appreciate my playing and singing."

"I should imagine so."

Everyone was smiling, and the more serious topics seemed forgotten.

When they began to declare that it was getting late and they must be getting back, Mrs. Westbrook began urging them not to go home in the dark.

"You might as well stay and go home in the light," she said.

"I believe we must go back," Rebecca said. "We don't wish to inconvenience you, and we are not afraid of the dark."

After a few more protestations, Thomas and Benjamin walked them out to the carriage.

As soon Thomas had handed in Mother and Margaret, he turned to Rebecca and said, "Have you thought any more about the loyalty of your servants? Have you questioned or tested them in any way?"

"No." She hadn't thought about how she might test them.

He nodded and stepped back, letting Benjamin, who was standing quite close, hand her into the carriage.

As the carriage started down the lane, she glanced back to see the sober look on Thomas's face. Was he concerned for her? Or was he thinking of his younger brother's feelings once he learned Rebecca had no interest in marrying him?

She sighed. Even though she no longer had to worry about her husband being unfaithful, she'd never had so many, nor such a variety, of troubles to think about.

CHAPTER FOURTEEN

Thomas couldn't sleep that night. Finally, he rose from his bed, not long before the sun would be coming up, dressed himself, and went for a walk, taking his rifle with him.

Along with all the other things that had been happening, his mind was occupied with the conversation that had followed the departure of Rebecca and her mother and sister.

"Rebecca is such a lovely girl," Mother had started out saying. "It's a shame she had to marry who she did."

"But we might not know her if she hadn't," Caroline pointed out.

Everyone agreed that was true.

"I worry for her, in that house all alone when her mother is gone." Mother shook her head, clicking her tongue against her teeth.

"She's better off alone than with Mrs. Heywood," Caroline said. "She told me that Mrs. Heywood blamed her for Arthur being away at night. Can you imagine? Everyone knows why the man was away, especially at night, and it had nothing to do with Rebecca."

"Caroline." Mother looked aghast.

"Mother, I'm not ignorant of what Arthur Heywood did. Everyone talked about it."

"I hope you did not gossip about it."

"No, but I couldn't help hearing the rumors."

Mother shook her head. "It is a sad thing."

"But it all turned out well for her," Benjamin said. "She's wealthy now, in her own right. He's dead and she was able to inherit the estate. Now she can marry whomever she wishes and be happy."

Everyone stared at him.

"What? It's true."

"No woman wants to see her husband murdered," Mother said, "even if he was a bad husband. She hopes and prays for him, begging God to change him, and sometimes God does."

Thomas shifted his feet as he stood propped against the mantlepiece with a glass of brandy. Of course, his mother was thinking of how her own husband had been less than faithful to her but had changed his ways. Caroline and Benjamin did not know about that, and he hoped she wouldn't tell them.

"I still say she is fortunate he died. God worked it all out in her favor."

"Perhaps, but that is a cold way of looking at it," Mother said.

"He only says that because he's in love with Rebecca." Caroline smirked.

Benjamin turned on his sister. "What if I am? She is a good woman, and I could never do better than Rebecca Heywood."

An uncomfortable silence settled over the room.

"But is she in love with you?" Caroline asked. "She's older, she's been married, she even lost a baby. I don't think she would even want a husband right now."

Mother looked as if she wanted to talk about something happier.

"So, you don't think she could fall in love with me? Is that what you're thinking?"

"Benjamin, you're so young, only seventeen years old."

"You are very young, Benjamin," Mother said with compassion in her voice.

"And I get the feeling that Rebecca is still mourning, still almost in shock from her husband getting killed and then getting shot at herself." Caroline's arms were crossed over her chest and she spoke as one who was giving counsel to someone younger, which she was, but their little brother was not one to like being talked down to, especially by his sister.

"You just don't want me to take your friend away. That's how selfish you are, Caroline."

Caroline chuckled. "As if you could take her away. She's more likely to fall in love with Thomas than with you—forgive me for saying so."

"I will not forgive you." Benjamin's cheeks turned red. He turned to Thomas. "Is that how it is? You and Rebecca have formed an attachment? I suppose I should have known." He turned and stomped toward the door.

"No, Benjamin. There is no attachment between us." But was that the truth? He stopped himself from saying anything else. What was the usefulness of arguing about it? No one knew Rebecca's feelings. Thomas wasn't even sure of his own.

"There is no harm in liking her," Mother said. "She is a good woman, and she may return your feelings, in time."

"In time, yes. That is true," Caroline said.

"I don't need you to patronize me," he said, addressing his sister. "And yes, I shall continue to admire her, and yes, she may return my feelings. Better someone like me, who understands her worth, than a bitter, cynical man who is still holding a grudge against all women."

The latter statement was aimed, of course, at Thomas, who said nothing as Benjamin left the room.

Was he bitter? And cynical? Or was that only Benjamin's anger talking? He wasn't still holding a grudge, was he? And even if he was, none of that had anything to do with the fact that he just didn't wish to marry a widow, and especially Arthur Heywood's widow.

But there it was. Obviously, he was still holding a grudge, but against Arthur, not all women. He liked women. He intended to marry one someday.

Perhaps Benjamin was more right than Thomas wanted to admit. Perhaps he was cynical and bitter.

He sighed as he walked, the dawn casting an eerie light on the misty field in front of him.

This was the exact spot where he had come upon Rebecca as she fled the man who had shot at her. The poor woman. She'd been so frightened, and rightfully so, but she had not dissolved into hysterics as he imagined most women would have done.

Benjamin had said he admired Rebecca and saw her worth. But Thomas knew more about her worth and her admirable qualities than his little brother could. She was brave and intelligent, learning how to run a household and keep the ledgers and receipts with hardly any help. She'd also endured abuse from her mother-in-law that would have sent most young women running back to their homes.

And she was lovely and kind. She'd been tested and had proven herself charitable and good. How many women could he say that about?

He found himself heading toward the dig site without even planning to. He had come there often enough. So he kept walking, the fog so thick when he neared the trees that he could barely tell it was dawn. His rifle was slung over his shoulder, loaded and ready.

No one was there, but the hole was noticeably deeper, so deep Thomas had to lie down on his stomach and peer over the edge to see to the bottom. But nothing was there.

He stood up and, with a little niggling sensation at the back of his neck, he walked toward Heywood House.

If the men were certain they were digging in the wrong place, wouldn't they resort to more desperate measures to find the treasure?

He was not far from Heywood House. He could already hear the grooms stirring outside the stables, no doubt fetching feed and water for the horses. But he stayed in the cover of the trees behind the carriage house as he moved toward the back of the house.

As he approached the garden that he knew would lead to the rocky area farther back, he saw a man lurking in the bushes at the other side. Was it one of the servants? A gardener, perhaps? Thomas watched from the shadows of the trees as the man stared hard at the back of the house. He stayed crouched behind a hedge-row, until finally he turned around and, bent low so as to be mostly hidden from the house, started creeping around the outer edge of the garden toward the back of the property.

Thomas followed him, keeping to the edge of the wood.

When they were out of sight of the house, the man stood up and began walking and looking around, examining certain rocks and trees.

The man was too thin to be Fogg, and he did not look like Strader or, indeed, anyone Thomas knew, although he couldn't be certain, since he had yet to see him except from a distance of at least a hundred feet.

The man moved around, examining the area, even making notes on a piece of paper he took out of his pocket with a small pencil. Finally, when the man turned and started back the way he had come, Thomas stepped out of the trees, pulled his rifle off his shoulder, and pointed it slightly above the man's head.

The man froze.

"Good morning," Thomas said. "Misty morning, isn't it? I would like you to tell me who you are and what you're doing here."

The man's eyes narrowed and he held his hand palm out, as if to fend Thomas off.

"I am lost. It seems I wandered off my trail."

"What trail would that be? And you didn't say your name."

"My name is Adam Ledbetter. I was walking . . . that is, I'm one of Mrs. Heywood's tenant farmers."

"Tenant farmer, eh? How's your crop looking so far?"

"Excellent. The weather has been good so far."

He pointed the barrel of his gun just below the man's heart. "It's barely March and most crops hadn't even been planted yet. Now, you need to tell me who you really are and what you're doing here if you don't want a hole blown through your belly."

"Since when can a man be murdered for trespassing?"

"Since a few weeks ago when the owner of this place was murdered when he caught a trespasser."

The man's eyes were shifting from side to side. Suddenly, he turned and started running for a nearby stand of trees.

"Stop!" Thomas fired a warning shot well above the man's head.

The man ducked his head but kept running.

Thomas ran after him, but it was soon clear that while holding onto his firearm, Thomas couldn't outrun him. He just had to hope the man would trip and fall or otherwise make a mistake.

The man soon reached a denser forest that ran parallel to a stream and plunged into it, still running headlong.

Thomas followed him, but the man was getting farther away.

Running through the dense trees was much harder, so Thomas decided to run along the outside edge of the trees, hoping the man would come out at some point. But after finally getting to the end of the line of trees and looking all around at fallow fields, he saw no sign of the man.

He went into the trees, walking the whole way, but he still saw no one. The man must have taken off across a field while Thomas was running along the tree line.

Walking across all the fields and through trees, back the entire way he'd already run, he wondered if he should have shot the man in the leg. But it seemed wrong to shoot a man who obviously didn't have a gun. Besides that, the man hadn't done anything except walk around on Rebecca Heywood's property without permission. And yet, Thomas was certain the man was scouting for the treasure. The man knew it was there somewhere, and he was trying to see where they might dig next. But what had made him look there, where the treasure map had showed them to look?

He gripped his rifle tighter. Something had to be done. But what?

He hated this helpless feeling, like he knew he needed to keep Rebecca Heywood safe but he wasn't sure how. It was worse than being in a war, when he was determined to protect himself and his men from the enemy. At least then he had a plan and he could shoot at anyone who threatened. And at least the French were openly hostile, none of this sneaking around and scheming behind their backs, pretending to be friend when they were actually foe.

Finally, he came to the house. His boots were muddy, but after rubbing them on a fallen tree and then on the grass, they shouldn't make too much of a mess, so he knocked on the door.

Then he realized how early it was. Ladies and gentlemen were not awake at this hour of the morning. But a servant answered.

"Forgive me. I know Mrs. Heywood won't be up at this hour, but—"

"Is that Mr. Westbrook?" Rebecca's voice called from behind the servant. She hurried to the door. "Let him in."

Rebecca Heywood was fully dressed, and she led him into the sitting room. "I couldn't sleep and I got up to attend to the ledgers. Then I looked out the window and saw a man. A few minutes later, I heard a gunshot."

She waved her hand, asking him to sit.

"I'll only be a moment," he said, and remained standing. "Yes, I saw the same man. I couldn't sleep either and I went for a walk and ended up here. I followed the man and asked him who he was. He said he was a tenant of yours, an Adam Ledbetter."

"I don't have a tenant by that name."

"I suspected as much. When he turned and ran, I shot in the air. He kept running and I ran after him. Forgive me, but I lost him."

"No need to apologize. I am grateful to you for trying to find out who he was." She sighed, a troubled look on her face. "I'm sorry you've had to involve yourself in this."

"One good thing is that the man didn't have a gun."

"I am glad, since I wouldn't have wanted you to be in danger. You have been so kind."

She gave him a gentle smile, and his heart melted. He imagined taking her in his arms and holding her.

But then he immediately remembered Benjamin.

"I must go. I hope my boots weren't too muddy."

"Not at all. Thank you for coming by."

He stopped and turned back to her. "Please do be careful. This man may not have had a gun, but that doesn't mean the next one won't. You need to make sure you have a gun and are ready to defend yourself, especially if you venture out of doors."

"I will, thank you."

He nodded and left the house, retrieving his gun from just inside the front door as he went.

CHAPTER FIFTEEN

Caroline, Mrs. Westbrook, and Benjamin came to call every day that Rebecca and her mother and sister didn't call on them first. Thomas only came with them about half the time.

Rebecca's mother and sister were used to going for a walk on days when the weather was fine, but here, they only ventured out when either Benjamin or Thomas were with them.

About a week and a half into her mother's visit, Rebecca once again was obliged to receive Mr. Gilbert Heywood.

He was a bit fidgety as they sat—Rebecca, Mother, Margaret, and Mr. Heywood—together in the sitting room. He patted his knee with his hand, then put a hand on his hip, then pulled at his coat.

They spoke of the state of the roads between his home and theirs, the weather of late, and of their relatives' state of health.

"Mr. Heywood," Rebecca said, "I heard a rumor that you were thinking of making an offer to purchase Heywood House."

His brows went up, and his mouth fell open, and he seemed to freeze in place for a few moments. "As a matter of fact, Mrs. Heywood, I would like to purchase the Heywood House estate if you are interested in selling." He stared at her, his gaze no longer shifting around the room.

"I might possibly wish to sell it to you in the future, but at present, I have no plans to sell Heywood House nor any part of my late husband's estate."

"I see." His disappointment was palpable as his shoulders slumped and his brows fell.

"May I ask why you wish to acquire this estate when you already have one?"

"I simply wish to keep it in the Heywood family, to preserve the name and the inheritance. Someday I shall have children and I would like to leave them two intact estates instead of only one. And you and Arthur, of course, did not have any children." He cleared his throat. "Forgive me if I have said too much."

One of only a few times Rebecca confronted Arthur about his philandering, she asked him, "Why are most of your adulterous affairs with married women? Are you not afraid of their husbands?"

"If a man cannot keep his wife at home, then why should he care enough to harm me? And there are multiple reasons I like married women, but partly because, if a child comes from the affair, her husband will raise the child as his own and provide for it."

Rebecca had been disgusted by his answer, so much so that she never sought his love again. Two months later, he was dead.

"No, we did not have any children," she told her dead husband's cousin.

She couldn't fault him for his answer. Society prided itself on keeping inheritances intact and carrying on the family name. But could Gilbert Heywood be responsible for sending men here to search for the treasure? For bribing the Justice of the Peace and the constable into finding it for him?

There was no way to know.

Mother and Margaret were looking a bit frightened. No doubt they were thinking the same thoughts. But she would not falsely accuse the man, in the chance that he had no idea about the treasure.

"I have no wish to take something from the Heywood family, and that is why I say that someday I may be willing to sell it to you at a fair price."

"That is kind of you," Gilbert Heywood said. "I trust you will send word when you do decide to do so."

"I will."

He stood slowly and awkwardly. "I thank you again, Mrs. Heywood, and I wish you good health and happiness." He bowed and retreated.

When he was gone, Margaret said, in her usual straightforward way, "Somehow I can't imagine him stealing a treasure or shooting anyone."

Rebecca's thoughts exactly. But she had once thought her husband loved her, so appearances were sometimes deceiving.

~ ~ ~

The next time Thomas Westbrook's family came to call on her, he came with them, and Rebecca informed them of Gilbert Heywood's declaration and wish to purchase Heywood House.

"That makes him seem all the more guilty," Thomas said, "because how else would Strader and Fogg know of his intention to purchase the estate?"

"Perhaps they guessed as much," Rebecca said. "Or perhaps they heard a rumor that he wished to purchase it for his heirs."

"He doesn't have any heirs."

"No, but he intends to have heirs, someday."

"It seems quite coincidental."

"You may be right, but I do not wish to accuse him if he is innocent. He seemed quite sincere in wanting it for his heirs, and to keep it in the Heywood family."

"Neither do I wish to accuse an innocent man, but you must see the possibility that he wants the estate so he can get at the treasure."

"The estate is surely of more value than one chest of gold."

"It depends on the size of the chest."

Rebecca imagined she saw an amused twinkle in Thomas's eye. She tried to turn her amusement into a frown. "That is true, of course."

"You shouldn't trust Gilbert Heywood," Benjamin interjected. "We don't want him to take the estate through some kind of trickery."

"Trickery?" Rebecca's stomach sank. Of course, Arthur's family would take the estate from her if they could. She already knew how angry it made her mother-in-law that she was inheriting the estate.

"As long as Arthur's last will was done legally and in order," Thomas said, "stating that you were to inherit, then no trickery should be able to change that."

"I just hope you will tell us if anyone tries to intimidate you into selling," Benjamin said.

"I will."

Benjamin was staring at her, an intense, almost pained look on his face. What could she say that would deter him from thinking of her the way he was obviously thinking?

"I am happy to live here quite alone, with occasional visits from my family, for a long time. I suppose it's no surprise to anyone that my marriage was not a happy one, and I am not eager to enter into another marriage for a very long time." She emphasized *very*.

There. That should give Benjamin the hint. But had she said too much and been too pointed in her remarks? Would his feelings be injured, knowing that she meant to put him off? She was often a little too honest and not very subtle.

Everyone was looking at her. Had she embarrassed Benjamin? Would his mother and Thomas hate her now? She felt her cheeks start to burn.

"Of course, dear," Mrs. Westbrook said gently. "No one blames you for wanting to live alone for a while. You have been through a painful trial, and it is no wonder you are not ready to make any sudden changes. Of course."

Rebecca could have been imagining it, but she felt a collective sigh as the tension in the room eased a bit. But when she finally dared to glance in Benjamin's direction, he was staring at the wall, a bit of heightened color in his cheeks.

She had hurt him. But it was better to hurt him now, while his feelings were new and hopefully not very strong, than later.

She certainly would not marry a man just to keep

from injuring his sensibilities.

She would marry again, someone good and kind, whose values were the same as hers, mostly because she still wanted children. A family. And when she had her children, she would not send them away to be raised by others, as was the custom of wealthy families. Even her own mother sent her children away to the country for a few years when they were still babies, Rebecca included, to be raised in the fresh air of a farm. Rebecca could still remember waking up to the sound of chickens and birds in the morning, and of Mrs. Withers, the farmer's wife, who wasn't affectionate or loving, telling her to get up and get dressed.

Rebecca wanted that voice to be hers when her babies awoke in the morning. She wanted to kiss their cheeks every day, to be the smiling face they saw every night when they closed their eyes. Her heart ached for that, to make sure her little girls and little boys knew, every minute of every day, that she loved them. Then she would be satisfied.

But now was not the time to think of that. She was young. She still had plenty of time to find a husband and have children. Besides, she would rather never have children than be married to someone like Arthur again. She could be her nieces' and nephews' favorite aunt, the best and most loving aunt who ever drew breath.

Caroline was staring at her with such concern and compassion, it made tears sting her eyes. She forced herself to smile.

"Are you well?" Caroline said.

"Yes, of course." She drew in a long, deep breath, trying to dispel the tears. How silly of her to lose herself in her thoughts, to the point of forgetting where she was. The others were talking amongst themselves, thankfully, and did not seem to notice.

"You will never need to marry, if you do not wish to," Caroline said softly, coming to sit beside her on the sofa. "My brothers and I will always be your neighbors and will look after you. I can only imagine how difficult it must be for you to think of marrying again. You will always have me for a friend, and when you're ready, I'm sure you will be adored by the man you marry, for you will marry an equally virtuous man who could hardly help himself."

"Thank you, Caroline. You are so kind and understanding." The tears swimming in her eyes made Caroline's face blurry. "And you shall marry a wonderful man as well. Never settle for someone who is simply handsome. But I know you are much too clever to make that mistake."

She took a few more breaths and got her emotions under control while Caroline talked of the treasure. And Rebecca said a silent prayer that Benjamin would not be hurt or angry, but that he would redirect his affections elsewhere. *God, send him a good and kind woman his own age to marry.*

Thomas seemed to avoid looking at her the rest of the visit. Was he embarrassed by her eyes obviously tearing up? Or was he offended on his brother's behalf by her obvious attempt to put him off? There was no way to know. She couldn't read his thoughts, but her own thoughts about him thinking ill of her was enough to make her feel quite low when they left, and she went up to her room to lie down.

"I just need an hour to rest," she told her mother

and Margaret. But Margaret, who was far too clever for her age, gave her a shrewd look but, thankfully, said nothing.

~ ~ ~

Rebecca gazed out the window the next day at the sunny garden, which looked so inviting.

"Let us go for a walk."

Mother and Margaret looked up at her from their breakfast plates.

"I thought it was too dangerous for us to go out alone," Margaret said in her challenging way.

"I will take a gun."

Mother gasped. "Whatever do you mean? A gun?"

"I shall take a loaded pistol to make sure we are safe on our walk. I know how to use it."

"Guns are dangerous. What if you mistakenly shoot one of us?"

"I know how to be careful. I won't shoot one of us. Besides, I need to practice shooting."

"Oh my." Mother laid a hand over her heart. "Oh dear. This does not sound safe."

"You will be perfectly safe. I am tired of staying inside out of fear. And we need some fresh air and sunshine, so go get some walking clothes on and meet me downstairs in half an hour."

Margaret said, "I agree with Rebecca. If anyone comes trying to harm us, Rebecca will shoot him." She smiled gleefully.

"Let us hope I don't have to shoot anyone. The most likely scenario is that we will not encounter anyone dangerous, but it is best to be prepared." She made sure to look confident as she winked at her little sister.

They were ready and waiting for her half an hour

later.

"You walk ahead," Mother said, frowning at Arthur's pistol in Rebecca's hand.

Rebecca kept the dueling pistol pointed at the ground as she walked slightly ahead of Mother and Margaret. They took their time moving through the garden, and she tried not to think about the man who had been there a few days before, or the fact that Gilbert Heywood wanted this place, or that if she didn't sell it to him and sold it to someone else, the Heywood name would eventually become disassociated with this estate.

She would think, instead, about the way the hedgerows smelled, the faint scent of flowers in the air as the first flowering bushes came into bloom. She would think of how crisp the air felt, with the promise of warmer weather whispered in the slight breeze. She would enjoy the blue sky above and the budding leaves on the trees. The long, dark winter was over and life was springing up everywhere. The world felt new and alive, and she felt new and alive with it. She was taking control of her own life by learning how to run the estate efficiently and with accuracy in her accounting for expenses and income. She was taking control of her own safety by her willingness to use a gun, while refusing to live as a prisoner in her own home.

The birds sang as if they were genuinely happy, and the wind caressed her cheek and playfully tossed her skirt against her calves. This was her home, and she would enjoy it.

After they'd taken their walk, including a turn around the rocky area where it had been suggested the map showed the treasure was buried, they went back toward the house.

As they neared the back door, Rebecca heard some faint noises from the front of the house and got an uneasy feeling in the pit of her stomach. Was someone there? If so, they were making more noise than a caller would normally make.

They went inside, with Rebecca still walking in the lead, and as she cautiously made her way through the first floor, she saw a familiar figure coming toward her.

"Rebecca? Is that you?" Mrs. Heywood's unmistakable tone matched the silhouette. "Is that a gun?" She cried out, as though frightened, but the cry sounded so fake, it turned Rebecca's stomach.

"She won't shoot you," Margaret said, with a slightly disgusted tone in her voice, as she and Mother walked in behind Rebecca.

"Oh my! Oh, my heart! Oh, my nerves!" Mrs. Heywood started to fan her face with a handkerchief. "To be so greeted in the home where I lived for thirty years!"

"We didn't know you were coming." Rebecca purposely kept her voice quiet and devoid of emotion. "If we had known, we could have greeted you properly." Then she went straight to the stairs and up to her room to put away the gun.

Meanwhile, her mother-in-law was gasping dramatically below. "Oh, my nerves! My heart is running away! My nerves! Oh!"

She should have known Mrs. Heywood would return, but the crushing disappointment told her that she'd hoped she wouldn't. Arthur had made sure to provide for her, increasing her jointure and reiterating her right to live in the two-story cottage about a hundred feet from the main house. Well, if she lived in the cottage, perhaps Rebecca wouldn't have to see her too often.

Seeing her at all was too often.

Her stomach churned and her head hurt. The last thing she wanted was to see Mrs. Heywood at all. Her cruel remarks still jumped into Rebecca's thoughts daily, reminding her how much her husband's mother had hated and resented her, when Rebecca had tried so hard, especially in the beginning, to make the woman like her.

"God, forgive me, but I wish her back with her brother, miles and miles from here."

She placed the gun back in the drawer beside her bed and went downstairs to be polite—and to take the snide and sometimes vague verbal beating she would surely have to endure.

CHAPTER SIXTEEN

"It is so kind of you to visit your daughter out here in the country," Mrs. Heywood said, as they were dining that night, "as I'm sure you must have many duties and responsibilities in town with your twelve other children."

"Nine other children."

"What?"

"I have nine other children, not twelve, and I—"

"I only had the one child, but he was the light of my life. A better child you never saw. And he doted on me as much as I doted on him." She sniffed and dabbed at her eyes.

Rebecca stared down at her plate. *Don't react*, she counseled herself. This is her way of getting sympathy, so let her have it, but you don't have to say anything.

Mother, of course, made the appropriate remarks of condolence and compassion, and an awkward silence ensued, which was soon broken by Mrs. Heywood's voice.

"Arthur was so good and liked by everyone. I don't know who could have shot him. Only someone who was jealous of him." She made the last statement with anger in her voice. "Jealous people are never satisfied, and they took my beautiful boy away from me. He was my only child. How could anyone be so cruel? No one but a mother could ever feel this much pain."

Rebecca forced her own thoughts and feelings down, pushing them away as she focused her gaze on the food on her plate, and let her thoughts run to the last time she'd seen Thomas Westbrook, as well as the first time she'd seen him—it must have been at least a year ago—at a ball dancing with Penelope, the young widow of the Earl of Hampstead. She'd had a fleeting thought, even then, of how handsome Lieutenant Westbrook was and how he and Penelope made a handsome couple on the dance floor. She never imagined then that she would soon be the young widow, and that she would now be wishing she could attend a ball and dance with Lieutenant Westbrook.

How shameless was she? But no one could read her thoughts, at least.

"Rebecca, Mrs. Heywood asked you a question," Mother's soft voice came to her.

"Forgive me, I didn't hear."

Her eyes met Mrs. Heywood's cold, hard stare. "Sometimes I don't know where your mind goes when I'm talking to you."

She seemed to be waiting for an answer, but Rebecca said nothing.

"I asked if they had caught Arthur's murderer. You do remember that he was murdered? Surely there is someone who cares enough to be searching for the evil person who shot my son—your husband. Have they caught him?"

Her voice was hard and angry and there was no evidence of the sorrow she'd displayed just moments before.

"I don't believe so."

"You don't believe so?"

"I have heard nothing from the authorities." She was not about to tell her about all the things Thomas Westbrook had discovered—that the constable was the man who was digging on their property, that there was a pirate's treasure buried somewhere around there, and that she had found the map showing where. She would tell her none of that. She did not trust the woman in the slightest, and especially since she hated Thomas so much.

"Well. I should think you would try to find out something, put forth the effort, but . . ." She shrugged her shoulder.

Once again, there was silence.

What would the servants think of Mrs. Heywood casting doubt upon her love for Arthur? They were listening, of course. The ones serving dinner were in the very room with them.

The rest of dinner progressed in much the same way, and thankfully, when the meal was over, Mrs. Heywood went straight up to her room with a bottle of Madeira.

"Rebecca, why don't you sing something for us?" Mother was smiling as they retired to the sitting room.

"Margaret can sing for us tonight," Rebecca said. "I don't feel much like singing."

"Dear, I understand why the things Mrs. Heywood says would wound you, but I think she only says those kinds of things because she is mourning. He was her only child, after all."

"She said those kinds of things before Arthur died. But it doesn't matter why she says them, it's still difficult to hear her say things that are so untrue, to have her misunderstand my feelings and my motives, and for her to have so little concern for me, especially when I've tried so hard to be kind and understanding with her."

"I think she is petty and cruel, like Elinor's sister-in-law Fanny in the new novel I brought you, *Sense and Sensibility*."

"I shall have to read it." Rebecca smiled at her little sister. What a wise soul Margaret was, even though she was so young. She had already been praying that Margaret and their other sisters would never make the same mistake in marriage that Rebecca had made.

Margaret played and sang, and in the middle of her third song, a servant came and said that Mrs. Heywood had a headache and asked that they stop playing the pianoforte and making so much noise so that she could sleep.

Rebecca wanted to send the servant back upstairs to ask her former mother-in-law when she planned to move out to the cottage behind the house.

She wanted to. But she didn't.

~ ~ ~

The next day, Thomas had no reason not to go with his family to call on Rebecca, so he went, still feeling the coolness in Benjamin's demeanor toward him, and also feeling his brother's low spirits. But better that

Rebecca Heywood injure his feelings and put him on his guard now than later.

When they were informed by a conscientious servant, at the door, that Mrs. Heywood—not Rebecca Heywood, but Arthur's mother—was home, Thomas exchanged glances with his mother.

"I had better go, I think. But you all can stay, if you wish."

"You can stay too," Mother whispered. "Rebecca is the lady of the house, not *her*."

"I don't want to cause any trouble for Rebecca, so I'll go." He turned and walked back through the woods and fields to Wyghtworth, leaving the carriage for them.

How unfair for Rebecca, to have to deal with that woman's sharp tongue and cruel accusations. He had heard enough to know, and could well imagine, that that was how Arthur's mother treated her—with contempt and a complete lack of empathy.

If you married her, she could live at Wyghtworth, away from Mrs. Heywood.

The rebel thought seemed to appear in his mind out of nowhere.

It is Benjamin who is in love with Rebecca, not I, he argued. Besides that, she was Arthur's wife. Why would he marry Arthur's wife? The thought just didn't sit well with him.

How foolish would he be if he married a woman just so she wouldn't have to live with her cruel former mother-in-law? It was his nature, it seemed, to try to rescue and care for people, often people for whom it was not his responsibility to care. He wasn't sure why he cared so much and other people didn't.

But even he could see that it was idiocy to rescue a woman who was herself independently wealthy and could marry any number of men, almost anyone she wanted. She didn't need him to take care of her or rescue her. She could rescue herself. So why did he still wish to take her out of her situation, to protect her, to make her smile and laugh?

He would overcome this, and knowing that Benjamin cared for her would help.

~ ~ ~

Rebecca watched out the window as Thomas walked back across the yard, back toward his home.

He must have heard that Mrs. Heywood was back, and he of course did not want to cause trouble. But her heart sank at seeing him leave.

Why did Mrs. Heywood have to make her life sadder, more uncomfortable, and more disappointing? *God, it is too much to be borne.*

She sighed. There was nothing to do but go downstairs, receive her friends, and hope Mrs. Heywood would stay in her bedroom.

Just as Rebecca and the Westbrooks were seated and talking companionably, she heard Mrs. Heywood's strident voice in the corridor.

"We have callers?" She must have been speaking to a servant.

A few moments later, the woman entered the room, a sour look on her face.

"Good morning, Westbrooks," she said in a strained voice, as if it hurt her throat to speak.

Caroline, Mrs. Westbrook, and Benjamin greeted her politely, and Mother and Margaret nodded and said "Good morning" as well. But the atmosphere in the room changed so completely, it was like a black cloud had suddenly blotted out the bright sunlight.

Mrs. Heywood, Mrs. Westbrook, and Mother carried the conversation. Rebecca listened for a chance to say something, nervous that her former mother-in-law would say something rude, but she was surprisingly agreeable and friendly. She did mention Arthur a few times, but not in the heavy-handed ways she usually did, soliciting pity. Instead, she sounded quite calm, although a bit aggressive in her domination of the conversation.

It was so unfair that Thomas couldn't visit while Mrs. Heywood was there. He had been calling on her less often, and she wasn't sure why, but she missed him. It felt strange to admit that, but she did. She missed his contributions to their conversations, his steadiness, his rational reasoning, and also his intensity; he really seemed to care so much, about almost everything. It was a level of caring she'd never noticed in a man. In contrast, Arthur rarely seemed to care about anything.

Caroline, Mrs. Westbrook, and Benjamin stood to go. Had Mrs. Heywood said something to make them leave? But they did not look offended as they smiled and politely took their leave.

Rebecca walked them out to their carriage.

Mrs. Westbrook said quietly, "Thomas came with us, but he did not wish to upset Mrs. Heywood. That is why he didn't stay."

"I understand. And I hope Mrs. Heywood didn't say anything impolite."

"No, she was on her best behavior."

Caroline and then Mrs. Westbrook embraced her.

"I'm sorry she came back," Caroline whispered.

"I am sorry as well," she whispered back.

"We should look again for the spot where the treasure is buried." Benjamin wore the sheepish look he wore quite often lately. "Tomorrow, perhaps?"

"I would like to, but I'm not sure if that would be a good idea, with Mrs. Heywood here. She might wonder what we are doing, or might want to go with us. But if she leaves, to go calling or to town, I will send you word."

She hated the disappointment on his face, but it couldn't be helped.

When they departed, Rebecca went back inside, her heart heavy in her chest. At least she had her mother and sister to force Mrs. Heywood to behave with better manners than she would if they weren't there. But their visit was fast coming to an end.

~ ~ ~

Later that day an invitation arrived from Gilbert Heywood. It was for a ball at Beaumont, his estate about fifteen miles away. It included everyone in the household, but her mother and Margaret would be back home in London by then.

A few minutes later, she received a short note from Caroline Westbrook saying they had also received the invitation and they all planned to attend. That fact put a smile on her face.

The next day, Mrs. Heywood went to town to shop for fabric for a new frock. Rebecca immediately sent word to the Westbrooks that she was gone, if they wished to come and search for the treasure.

They all came, almost before she would have thought it possible.

Mother and Mrs. Westbrook stayed in the house

while the rest of them went on their search beyond the garden, with Thomas and Benjamin in the lead, both carrying pistols.

"I haven't been to a ball in so long," Caroline said, her voice breathy and excited. "I have never known Gilbert Heywood to give a ball. I imagine he is looking for a wife. He must be nearly thirty years old and has never been engaged."

"He wants Rebecca's estate," Margaret said in her forthright manner, "so he will want to marry my sister."

Benjamin's shoulders visibly stiffened.

"That is very possible." Caroline winked at Margaret. "I cannot imagine he could do better than your sister, but she may not wish to give up ownership of her home so quickly."

Rebecca could feel their eyes on her. "Marriage is the farthest thing from my mind," she said. "I'm still just hoping I can one day take a walk alone without being shot at, or without having to worry who wants my treasure." She shook her head. "But I am looking forward to dancing. A ball will be a good distraction."

"Oh yes!" Caroline clasped her hands. "I can hardly wait to hear music, to see people, and to dance!"

Rebecca loved her friend's enthusiasm.

"I wish Mother would let me go." Margaret's brows were lowered and her arms crossed. "You must remember all that happens and tell me everything. I want to know every last detail." She pointed her finger at Rebecca.

"You know I will tell you everything." Rebecca laughed. "Nothing terribly exciting will happen, I daresay."

Once they were out of sight of the house, they

took out the two maps and examined them, carefully noting the shape of the tree and the other object on the other side of the "X".

"Do you think they made the tree trunk crooked like that on purpose?" Rebecca asked.

"I think so," Thomas said. "And the rock seems to have been carefully drawn as well, with an exact shape. That they drew that shape this way is not coincidental. The person even corrected himself—see there?" He pointed to a smudge where they had tried to blot out a line. "I think we need to look for this exact tree and rock."

They discussed the map some more, talking about where they should begin looking.

"The map seems to show the treasure close to the garden, near where we're standing." Benjamin crossed his arms over his chest.

"We can split into two groups," Thomas said, "since Benjamin and I have the guns."

Benjamin immediately looked at Rebecca. She pretended not to notice.

"It looks to me like the treasure is this way, and farther away from the house." Thomas pointed slightly to the right. "Whoever agrees can go with me, and everyone else needs to stay with Benjamin."

Without looking at Benjamin, Rebecca started in the direction Thomas pointed. Margaret and Caroline stayed close to Benjamin.

"Don't lose sight of each other," Thomas said, falling into step beside Rebecca.

They moved into the tree line and slowly walked the edge, looking all around them. All was quiet until Rebecca broke the silence.

"Is it possible that the tree on the map might not still be standing?"

"Yes, it's quite possible, considering that this map was drawn fifty or so years ago. It will probably have died, and may even be rotted to nothing by now."

"I guess we should be focusing on finding the rock, then, not the tree."

"I agree."

"But how can we know how big the rock is?"

"I don't think we can know. I think we're looking for the shape, more than anything."

They were getting close to the rocky area. Rocks were embedded in the ground, some jutting above-ground, while some were almost completely hidden, with only a bit of gray showing. Others were sitting on top of the ground, and these were the ones Rebecca paid attention to, checking each one against her memory of the rock on the map.

"There are so many rocks here."

She turned to see Thomas squatting to examine a rock, then standing up again.

"I haven't found one yet that looks like the one on the map. But as you said, there are so many."

She kept looking, feeling a bit guilty as she thought of Benjamin looking with Caroline and Margaret. She prayed he didn't feel hurt by her going with his brother instead of him, but Rebecca did honestly think the map indicated that the treasure was farther this way.

"Who would have imagined that a map that seemed so precise could be so difficult to interpret?" Rebecca glanced over at Thomas. "But perhaps we're missing some more precise instructions."

"It certainly would have been helpful to have something saying, 'Walk fifty feet east from the back door, then walk ten feet to the south, then four feet east again.'"

"Exactly. That would be quite helpful." Rebecca sighed.

Suddenly, she saw a large rock several feet away and started toward it. It was big enough to sit on, too big to be moved without at least one mule or horse and much effort.

Her foot sank down. She tried to yank it up, but it was too deep and she fell, her ankle wrenching and twisting.

She pushed herself up with her hands, now on her hands and knees, and gasped in pain.

CHAPTER SEVENTEEN

"Are you all right?" Thomas was bent down beside her.

"Yes. Can you help me?"

He took hold of her under both arms and pulled her up. She was able to pull her foot out and stand, but when she put her weight on the injured foot, sharp pains shot up her leg from her ankle.

"Looks like you stepped in a badger's hole. That's a good way to break your ankle."

"I wouldn't have stepped in it if I had seen it."

The look on his face was a half frown, half smile, but it quickly vanished. "Of course, forgive me. Can you walk?" Thomas was still holding onto her.

"I don't know. I hope I didn't break a bone." She tried to take a step and almost went down again.

"Don't put any pressure on it. You can put your arm around me." He bent and put his arm around her back, and she held onto him.

She breathed in his scent—the smell of outdoors and a hint of warm, earthy, oil of bergamot cologne. She closed her eyes, her knees going weak for a moment at how good he smelled, and how good it felt to be this close to him, to feel his muscular arm and his warmth.

Her ankle did hurt, but she was almost glad.

He walked her over to the very rock she'd been moving toward and helped seat her on it.

"I can carry you back to the house, if you need me to." He was looking at her with concern.

His expression was so different from what she had come to expect from Arthur. Her husband had made her feel as if she was a burden. He resented it when she needed or wanted something from him, even when she was sick, after she lost the baby. He'd avoided her, and never once did he look at her with half the concern in Thomas's expression.

She'd told herself that that was just how men were. Men weren't meant to care for the sick or injured, or to show compassion. Men were hunters, fighters, and procreators. But was that true? Perhaps there were men who cared, who showed compassion and care for others, especially when they were sick or injured.

If Thomas Westbrook was everything he seemed to be, then Rebecca was even more convinced that she'd chosen the wrong man, that she'd married the wrong person and had cheated herself out of love and happiness.

She realized she hadn't answered him. "I am sure I can walk back, after I rest my ankle for a few minutes." She didn't want to be a burden, after all, to see his expression of concern change to resentment, to have him help her grudgingly. She wasn't sure she could bear it.

"I am no expert, but I heard a surgeon once say that if there is a great deal of bruising and swelling, there is a good chance that the bone is broken, but it's harder to tell with ankles."

"Was that when you were in the army?"

"Yes, in the Peninsular War. I carried a fellow officer to the surgeon's tent when he injured his ankle."

"Was it broken?"

"I don't know. I had to return to the battle, and I never saw him again." He stared off through the trees. "I hope he was sent home, but I never heard."

She desperately wished she could read his thoughts. "I can't imagine how difficult fighting in a battle must be."

"Some men seem to enjoy it, but I hated it." He looked down at his hands. "I did come to know several good men, men to whom I would give my right arm if they needed it. How does your ankle feel?"

He turned his eyes on her, that wistful look gone and the concern back in place.

"Maybe a bit better. I think I can walk on it."

"Don't put your weight on it. No sense prolonging the healing, and you know that Gilbert Heywood's ball is in a week."

She had forgotten about that.

"I have twisted my ankle before and it healed after a few days. Hopefully this will be the same."

He was staring hard at something. She looked down.

"What is it?"

"That rock you're sitting on. May I see the map?"

Rebecca took the folded paper from her pocket and handed it to him.

He looked from the map to the rock and back again.

"I was walking toward this rock when I stepped in the hole because I thought it might be the rock on the map. What do you think? Do I need to get up so you can see it better?"

"No, stay there. I think it is the rock. Now we just have to find the tree."

They looked around them, at all the trees. Rebecca stayed seated and spun around, trying to see all around her. Soon they were both looking at the same tree.

A twisted, crooked tree stood about five feet from the rock, but it looked old and dead, bearing no leaves and very few branches. The only reason they hadn't seen it immediately was because there was a smaller tree growing between it and the rock.

"This is it." Rebecca's heart beat faster.

"I think you're right. And if it is, this tree is growing right on top of the treasure chest."

"How difficult will it be to dig it up?"

"Not that difficult."

Would Thomas and Benjamin dig it up? Would they find the treasure chest there?

"We have to tell the others. This is very exciting, but . . . I can't ask the servants to dig it up because they might tell someone, and we'll have more people out here, possibly shooting at us again."

"Benjamin and I can help. That is, if you wish it."

"Oh yes, of course. That is so kind of you. And I would be happy to share the treasure with you, since you helped me find it."

"That will not be necessary. The treasure is on

your property, so it is yours, and my family and I have enjoyed helping you search for it."

"It might not even still be here. Someone else may have dug it up long ago."

"That is possible, of course. Come, let us get you home, and then I will tell the others about what we found." He tried to hand her the map.

"No, you keep it. You can use it to show Benjamin and Caroline and Margaret."

He put it in his pocket. Then he bent and slipped his arm around her and helped her to her feet. "Don't walk on it," he said.

Rebecca leaned against him and put very little pressure on her injured foot, limping heavily.

"If you will allow it, I think you need to let me carry you."

"Very well." She was rather enjoying how he seemed to want to help her, and she didn't want to make her ankle worse, as she was hoping to dance with him seven days from now.

He bent and slipped his free arm under her knees and lifted her in his arms.

She hadn't been carried since she was a very young child. She felt awkward, not quite sure where to place her hands, and ended up leaving one in her lap and her other on his shoulder.

Thomas seemed to walk carefully, minding where he stepped, but without any strain, as if her weight was insignificant.

"I will send for Adams, my physician, unless you have someone else you prefer." His voice was so gentle and warm, it made her breath shallow.

"Thank you," was all she could manage to say.

Surprisingly, they made it all the way to the house without Benjamin, Caroline, and Margaret seeing them. She could tell he was starting to get winded.

"Put me in the drawing room," she said, as it was the nearest room.

"Very well." He placed her on the sofa so that she was sitting up at one end, with her legs stretched out before her.

"Thank you," she said. "I'm sorry to be so much trouble to you."

"Not at all." He picked up a blanket nearby and spread it over her feet and legs. He knelt beside her and looked her in the eye. "It was my pleasure to be of service to you."

His words, and his tone, went straight to her heart. Could she be imagining this feeling, the idea that he was in love with her? Certainly, she was being foolish, but her heart was racing at the way he was looking at her. *O God, please bless this good man.*

Perhaps it was a strange thought-prayer, but she wanted Thomas Westbrook to have all the good things that he deserved.

"Are you always so very kind?" Her voice sounded breathless. Could he see how much he was affecting her?

He reached out and gently brushed his palm over her cheek. Her stomach turned inside out. Thomas made her feel so different from how Arthur made her feel. How dead she'd felt just a few weeks ago, but how very alive she felt at this moment.

"Rebecca, I . . ." He stopped and swallowed, then removed his hand as he leaned away from her. "Forgive me. I shall fetch your mother."

He stood up and walked away, while she sat wishing she could think of something to make him stay, to prolong the delicious moment when he touched her cheek and gazed into her eyes.

Her heart was beating so fast, she wondered if her mother would take one look at her and know that she'd been wishing Thomas Westbrook would kiss her.

She tried to slow her breathing, praying silently, *O God, help me calm myself before he comes back in the room.*

~ ~ ~

Thomas's pulse pounded in his temple as he realized how close he'd come to kissing Rebecca. Ah, those lovely lips. But he must be losing his mind. He hadn't meant to kiss her, or even touch her. Benjamin would be so hurt. What had happened to his vow to stay away from Arthur Heywood's widow?

He watched as her mother and his lamented over her swollen ankle as she lay on the sofa.

"Don't worry," Rebecca said in her sweet voice. "I will be well in a few days, I daresay."

"Oh, I hope so," his own mother said, "for it would be a shame to miss the ball at Beaumont."

"Shall I send for Adams?" Thomas asked when there was a slight pause in their conversation.

"Oh, no," Rebecca said, turning to look at him. "Please don't bother. If I'm not better in the morning, I'll send for him."

He nodded. "Very well. I'll go and find Benjamin and the ladies." He hurried away.

As he walked through the garden, he asked himself where this was leading. How did Rebecca feel about him? When he'd touched her face, she hadn't exactly pulled away. And he'd noticed how breathy her voice was. She seemed neither disgusted nor offended. On the contrary, she seemed just the opposite.

But what to do about Benjamin?

If he felt Benjamin had even a small chance at marrying Rebecca . . . Well, perhaps he did have a small chance, but very small. After having been married to someone as immature as Arthur, she surely wouldn't want to marry someone as young as Benjamin. Would she?

There was no way of knowing, of course, but he hadn't seen her show any interest in his younger brother. Rather, she seemed to try to put him off, gently but firmly letting him know that she was not interested in marrying.

That was what she'd said, wasn't it? Her face appeared in his mind as she had said, ". . . my marriage was not a happy one, and I am not eager to enter into another marriage for a very long time."

Arthur had no doubt made her miserable. But had she said those words for Benjamin's benefit? Or for his as well?

He almost wished he had kissed her so he could gauge her response.

He was surely losing his mind.

He caught sight of Caroline and Margaret just beyond the garden next to a stand of trees.

"I think we found it," he said as he drew near.

Caroline clasped her hands together, her eyes and her mouth opening wide. "You found the treasure?"

"I think we found the rock and the tree that were on the map, and therefore where the treasure is buried."

"Can we see?" Margaret asked excitedly.

Benjamin stepped out of the trees. "I saw you carrying Rebecca." His tone was sullen, as was his expression.

"She stepped in a hole and injured her ankle."

"Oh no!" Caroline cried. "Is she all right?"

"I think so. She didn't want me to send for the physician just yet, but she's resting, and Mother and her mother are with her."

"I hope she doesn't miss the ball," Margaret said. "Then I won't be able to hear who danced with whom."

Caroline nudged Margaret's shoulder. "I would tell you all about it, but you ought to be nice to your sister."

"I will." Margaret grinned.

Thomas let them follow him to the rock and the tree. He wanted to make sure he could find it again. As they drew near, he pointed at the ground.

"Take care," he said to Margaret. "That's the hole your sister stepped in."

When he showed them the rock and the tree, Caroline and Margaret took the map and examined it, chattering excitedly.

"It seems we found it just in time," Thomas said. "I doubt the tree would have stood much longer. It looks dead and starting to rot."

Benjamin hung back with his arms crossed. He was still sullen after seeing Thomas carrying Rebecca. But if he was in love with her, shouldn't he be more worried about her than angry with him?

For that matter, shouldn't Thomas care more about how Rebecca felt than whether Benjamin's feelings would be hurt if she chose Thomas? After all, Benjamin was only seventeen. He'd find his own love when the time was right. Obviously, he was a bit immature still for marriage.

"Are we going to dig it up?" Benjamin said, finally uncrossing his arms and kicking at the dead leaves where the treasure should be.

"We cannot let anyone else know, I wouldn't think," Margaret said. "It has to be us."

"Margaret and I will help," Caroline said, winking at Margaret.

Benjamin frowned at Caroline. "You wouldn't last five minutes with a shovel."

"That's five minutes you can rest." Caroline smirked.

"Ben and I can dig it up."

"I will help too." Margaret lifted her chin and crossed her arms.

"It is hard work," Thomas said, trying his best to look serious and respectful as he gazed down at Rebecca's little sister.

"I don't want to be left out of retrieving this treasure. I want to be there when it's found."

"Very well." Thomas nodded.

"We won't let the men leave us out, will we?" Caroline said.

"But we have to do this all secretly," Benjamin said, glaring at Caroline and then Margaret. "You cannot tell anyone, and you cannot let anyone suspect why you are coming out in the woods, or they might follow you."

"We are not imbeciles," Caroline retorted.

"No one said you were an imbecile," Benjamin said, rolling his eyes.

"We all need to take care not to invite suspicion," Thomas said, trying to head off the inevitable argument. "That means we don't let the servants see us leaving at the same time, and we'll keep the shovel hidden in the woods rather than taking it back and forth."

They all nodded.

"Mrs. Heywood could return at any time, so we cannot go back to Heywood House."

"Even me?" Margaret asked.

"Of course you may go back."

She looked relieved.

"So we will go home and get a shovel?" Caroline asked.

"Yes."

"I'll go with you," Margaret said.

"It's a great deal of walking, there and back here," Benjamin said.

"You better go and tell your mother where you'll be," Thomas said. "Then you can meet us back at the spot where the treasure is buried, if your mother gives you permission."

Margaret clasped her hands together, a huge smile on her face.

They parted and Thomas couldn't help wishing Rebecca could be with them, but she would still be hobbled by her injured ankle.

CHAPTER EIGHTEEN

Rebecca was still on the sofa when Mrs. Heywood returned from her outing. Mrs. Westbrook had just left in the carriage, having been told by Margaret that Caroline, Benjamin, and Thomas would not return to Heywood House, but would walk home.

Her former mother-in-law greeted Mother but ignored Rebecca, perhaps because of the way she was seated on the sofa, which caused her back to face the doorway. She didn't even ask why they were in the drawing room instead of the sitting room. Instead, thankfully, she moved past the doorway and up the stairs, a footman following her and carrying several packages.

As it grew late and the sun was going down, Mother said, "It will be time for dinner soon and Margaret is still not home. Perhaps I should go and try to find her."

"No, Mother, please don't," Rebecca whispered.

"It's not safe for you to walk alone, and you might get lost in the dark."

"I could send a servant, the footman or groom, to look for her."

"You will only draw suspicion. Besides, Margaret is safe, as she is with Thomas, Benjamin, and Caroline. They will not let anything happen to her and will make sure she gets home safely."

"Very well. I suppose you are right."

Mother, who was generally very calm and seldom seemed distressed by anything, paced in front of the windows facing the back garden.

A servant came in and stoked the fire and lit the candles. Soon afterward, darkness descended over the windows. Should Rebecca allow her mother to send a servant to look for Margaret? Might it not seem suspicious that she was not home, if indeed anyone realized she was not there? She was still a child, after all.

They both heard the back door open. Mother went scurrying into the hallway, and Rebecca heard them whispering. Moments later, Margaret and her mother came in.

"We found it," Margaret whispered, her eyes and her smile equally wide with excitement. "Benjamin and Thomas dug up the little tree, then dug down about two feet and there it was, a wooden chest."

Rebecca's heart leapt inside her. "Did you open it? What was inside?"

"We decided not to open it. It was so dark, we couldn't see. Benjamin and Thomas could only feel the wooden chest. They said it was about three feet this way and two feet this way." Margaret used her hands to show the size of the chest. "We don't know how deep it is yet. Oh, Rebecca, isn't it wonderful? You're going to be so rich." Margaret laid her hands over her chest, sighed dramatically, and fell down on a chair.

"Don't sit there, dearest. You might get dirt on the upholstery." Mother waved her hand to tell her to get up.

"They even let me help dig. Benjamin and Thomas are such gentlemen, and they treat me as if I'm a lady. I think I may grow up and marry Benjamin. What do you think of that?"

"I think that sounds very good, if he makes you happy and you are both in love with each other." Rebecca couldn't help smiling.

"You told me yesterday that you weren't planning to marry at all," Mother said. "You said you would just live with Rebecca and me and do as you pleased, not as some husband wants you to do."

"A woman can change her mind." Margaret said, arching her eyebrows as she slowly left the room to change for dinner.

"Margaret is in love with Benjamin."

"She could do worse." Mother smiled.

Rebecca laughed. How quickly people changed their minds sometimes.

~ ~ ~

Rebecca awoke the next morning and her ankle already felt somewhat better and barely looked swollen at all.

The footman had helped her up the stairs after dinner the evening before. She'd worried that she might not be able to go to the ball, and certainly wouldn't be able to dance. But this morning her heart felt quite light and hopeful. Would they discover the contents of the mysterious pirate treasure buried in the woods?

Margaret was fully dressed and had eaten her breakfast when Rebecca went downstairs.

"This just arrived for you." A servant handed her a folded piece of paper.

The writing on the outside had Rebecca's name in Mrs. Westbrook's handwriting style, but inside, the note was obviously written by Thomas, and was signed simply with a *T*.

I don't feel comfortable opening the parcel without your presence. When your ankle is healed, we shall proceed. In the meantime, rest, and Caroline and Mother shall visit you soon.

Rebecca handed the note to Margaret to allow her to read it.

"Oh, but Rebecca!" Margaret slumped in her chair. "That is so unfair."

"It's not unfair, it's just disappointing. But I'm heartily sorry."

"What can it hurt for us to open it, just to see—"

"Margaret, *sh.*" Rebecca gave her a look and pressed her finger to her own lips.

Margaret frowned and crossed her arms, her brows lowering into a scowl.

"You will be happy to know that my ankle is feeling much better."

"Oh!" Margaret's expression transformed immediately. "Write him back right now and say that your ankle is better."

"I don't want to make it worse, and it's not healed. I only said it was better."

"I will help you walk," Margaret said. "You can lean on me and I can get you a walking stick."

Rebecca laughed. "You are so determined sometimes. But give me one more day to heal. Will you do that?"

Margaret huffed out a breath. But before she could say anything else, Mrs. Heywood entered the room.

"Heal?" Mrs. Heywood's mouth hung open as she placed her hand over her heart. "Are you sick? There is no contagion in the house, I hope?"

"No." Rebecca resisted the urge to roll her eyes. "I injured my ankle."

"How did you injure your ankle? Have you been running down stairs again?"

Rebecca wasn't sure what she was speaking of. "No, I went for a walk and stepped in a hole."

"A hole? Where? The gardeners are letting the badgers dig holes in the garden?"

"No, all is well. I went for a walk in the woods. I shall be well, I dare—"

"In the woods? What were you doing in the woods?" Mrs. Heywood's mouth was open again, then spread into an amused, incredulous smile.

The servant entered the room to bring Mrs. Heywood's breakfast and his gaze moved from Mrs. Heywood to Rebecca, a shrewd look in his eyes. Or was she only imagining it?

"As I said, I went for a walk. I have enjoyed many good walks on our grounds." Rebecca refolded her serviette and laid it across her lap, as if the conversation was boring her.

Mrs. Heywood made a little sound in her throat, as if to dismiss the subject, and began to talk of the good weather. "For March, the roads are very serviceable. I believe I may go out again tomorrow, call on some friends in town, visit some shops. I am sure your mother wouldn't care to shop in our little town, since she has the London shops, or I would invite her to go with me."

Rebecca made no reply, while Margaret sat staring into her tea cup, no doubt thinking of the treasure.

Had Thomas and Benjamin covered up the chest? She hadn't thought to ask Margaret, but surely they wouldn't leave it uncovered for anyone walking by to see. But there was no reason for anyone to be walking in her woods. Still, they all knew there were treasure hunters about.

"I think I shall speak with the constable about what he is doing to catch poor Arthur's murderer. Someone should be doing something, asking questions, pushing the authorities to take action. A good man has been murdered, a gentleman of good standing in the community, loved by all. I should think they would have done something by now to catch the evil man who destroyed my life forever." She sniffed, taking out her handkerchief from where she had stuffed it in her sleeve. "I don't believe anyone has ever suffered a more terrible wrong."

Rebecca stared down at her plate lest Mrs. Heywood read her thoughts. How could the woman think no one had ever suffered more than she had? But she said nothing, and as soon as she was finished eating, she and Margaret excused themselves, and Margaret helped her up to her room, insisting Rebecca lean on her shoulder.

"I want to go make sure no one has been there to dig it up," Margaret said, as she helped Rebecca settle into bed with her foot propped on a pillow.

"Absolutely not. You know it's dangerous to walk around. Did Thomas not tell you to never go out by yourself?"

"He told me." Margaret's tone was sullen. "But what if someone comes and sees where we were digging and gets the treasure out while we're not there?"

"If they do then they are stealing, and a thief will be punished by God."

"But I don't want to wait for God to punish him, and I don't want him to get our treasure."

"You just have to be patient, Margaret." The truth was that she wanted to send word to Thomas that her ankle was healed, wanted to run out there on her sore ankle and see the treasure for herself, but that would delay her ankle's healing. The treasure was safe where it was, as no one knew about it except the Westbrooks, herself, and her mother and sister.

God, please let my ankle be healed by tomorrow morning.

~ ~ ~

Thomas slept very little the next two nights after they found the treasure chest. Early each morning he and Benjamin quietly walked over to make sure it was still there, hiding their shovel under a fallen tree and dead leaves.

"Hasn't Rebecca's ankle recovered yet?" Benjamin asked every morning.

And every morning Caroline went to call on Rebecca and came back saying her ankle was very little better. "She is being very careful. Probably tomorrow morning it will be all well."

The third night Thomas went to bed early, leaving his window open, as it was an unusually warm night and the fire had been stoked too high.

He opened his eyes. He was in his bed, but something had awakened him.

A gunshot.

The sound came from the window, which opened toward Heywood House.

Thomas leapt out of bed, drew on his clothes, grabbed his hunting rifle, and ran out of the room.

CHAPTER NINETEEN

Rebecca was startled awake by a noise. Someone was in her room.

Her heart pounded as she stared hard into the darkness. Finally, she saw a shadowy figure moving toward her.

Her pistol, which was loaded and ready to shoot, was in the drawer of the table next to her bed. If she reached for it, would the person attack her?

"Give me your map," the raspy voice said.

"Get out of my room."

The figure stopped moving. "You have the map and I want it."

Her heart pounding, she quickly opened the drawer and took hold of the pistol. Once she was pointing it in the direction of the intruder, she said, "Get out. I have a gun and I will shoot you." She pushed herself into a sitting position on the bed.

"You will not shoot me. I want the map. Give it to

me now and I won't kill you."

How did this man know about the treasure map? Thomas had the map that showed in closer detail where the treasure was buried, did he not? But she would not tell this man that. He might go to Thomas's house and steal it.

"Get out of my room," she repeated. "If you leave now, I won't shoot you."

"I want that map. I won't leave until I get it."

The man's voice sounded familiar. Then he took a step toward her, bumping into the foot of her bed.

"If you come any closer, I will shoot you."

The man took another step. "You will not shoot me. But if you don't give me that map, I'll make you regret it."

Rebecca braced her arms, aiming for his right shoulder. "Stop. Don't come any closer." She remembered Thomas's words not to miss if she shot at an intruder, because she would have to reload the gun, and in that time the intruder could take the gun away from her.

The man lunged toward her, his hand raised in the air.

Rebecca squeezed the trigger.

The sound was deafening, roaring in her ears even as she forced herself not to blink.

The man's body was thrown backward, then he fell hard and didn't move.

O God! Did I kill him? Her heart seemed to stop beating.

She scrambled out of bed just as the housekeeper, Mrs. Atwater, came into the open doorway with a candle.

The large man was lying on the floor, starting to make whimpering sounds.

"He was in my room, so I shot him." Rebecca's hands were shaking, and she put the gun down on her bed.

As Mrs. Atwater came closer with the candle, they both leaned over him. His face was unmistakably that of the constable, Mr. Fogg.

"I didn't mean to kill him. I tried to shoot him in the shoulder."

"He's not dead," the housekeeper said. "He's moaning."

Indeed, his eyes were closed but he was making the sounds of someone in pain.

What a horrid man, to invade her room while she was sleeping, to demand that she give him her map! But she didn't wish to kill him.

"What should we do?" Her heart was pounding against her chest now, and the scent of blood mingled with the smell of gunpowder, stinging her nostrils.

Soon, more voices were heard coming closer.

"Rebecca! What happened?" Margaret came running into the room in her nightgown, reminding Rebecca that she herself was only wearing her nightdress. She should go get her wrapper, but it was hanging in the wardrobe on the other side of the constable's body.

Servants swarmed into the corridor, standing in the doorway gazing in.

"Go fetch some bandages, hot water, and my medical bag," Mrs. Atwater ordered. "Be quick."

"Rebecca, did you shoot him? Who is it?" Margaret stood next to the body, gazing down with her mouth open.

Rebecca tried to think. She should send for someone. But it was the constable she would normally send for.

A servant brought some bandages. Mrs. Atwater opened the man's coat and began pressing the rolled-up cloth into the bleeding wound.

"Oh," Mr. Fogg called out. "Am I dying?"

"No, you're not," Mrs. Atwater said, sounding as if she wished he was.

Then Rebecca saw the large knife near Mr. Fogg's body. He must have been holding it when he fell.

"Who are you working for?" Rebecca demanded, as heat rose into her cheeks and forehead. How dare this man invade her room and threaten her with a knife?

"What?" he said, blinking up at her as if dazed.

"You heard me. Who sent you to threaten me with a knife? Tell me, because I can reload this gun and shoot you again." She picked up the gun off the bed and pointed it at him. It wasn't loaded, now that she'd shot at him, but she just might hit him with it.

"Strader," Fogg said in a strained voice. "He's gotten me killed, and I won't let him get away with it."

"The Justice of the Peace? Strader?" Rebecca asked.

"He knew about the treasure trove, but he sent me to do all the work."

"And the coroner, Mr. Pursglove? Does he know?"

Fogg looked confused for a moment. "Pursglove knows nothing. Ah, you have killed me." Tears swam in the big man's eyes. "Won't you even send for the surgeon?"

"No." Mrs. Atwater was pressing hard into the man's shoulder with the rolled-up bandages, which she kept having to change as they became saturated with dark red blood. "You don't deserve a surgeon. And how did you get in here? Who let you in?"

"I'm coming up the stairs!" a voice called from downstairs. It sounded like Thomas Westbrook.

Her heart leapt inside her. Could Thomas have heard the gunshot all the way from Wyghtworth?

Heavy steps sounded on the stairs, as if he was taking them two or three at a time.

"We're in here," Rebecca called.

Just then, Mother moved in closer, carrying a large candelabra with several candles, illuminating the room.

"Thank God you are not hurt," she said in a breathy voice.

The servants lingering in the doorway moved out of the way as Thomas came in.

"What happened?" he said, striding toward her, his eyes roving over her. "You are well?"

"Yes."

Then he saw who was lying on the floor. "Fogg, you blackguard."

"Westbrook. This is all a mistake. This is Strader's doing, and now I'm shot."

"You deserve to be shot." Thomas's tone was without a jot of sympathy.

While he was talking, he pulled off his coat and put it around Rebecca's shoulders.

She put her arms in the sleeves and the coat seemed to swallow her up. How kind he was, and though her nightgown was her winter one, and so more substantial, she was grateful not to have to walk across the room to retrieve her wrapper. And his coat was quite warm from his body heat and smelled of the outdoors and his bergamot cologne, which once again smelled so good it made her knees weak.

"I wish I could have shot you myself," Thomas went on at Fogg. "You tell us everything, now, or we will let you bleed to death."

"It was Strader, I tell you. He forced me to do it. He said he would divide the treasure with me, and we wouldn't tell Pursglove."

It was the coroner's responsibility to hold any treasure troves that were found until the authorities could determine who was the rightful owner.

"That was a pretty plan," Thomas said wryly, squatting beside Fogg. "Why did he think there was treasure buried here? Where did he come to hear of such a ludicrous thing? Talk."

"Ah! I'm dying, Westbrook. Have you no compassion? Not even enough to send for a surgeon?"

"Keep talking and we shall see."

"Strader's grandfather was a sailor. He used to tell his grandson tales of his time on Captain Heywood's ship and how they captured the pirate's treasure. He said he helped bury the captain's share, but he couldn't be sure where it was buried, as the captain blindfolded him and the other men who helped him carry it there. But he told him it was beside a big rock. We found a rock, and he made me dig for it."

"You shot Arthur Heywood when he caught you digging."

"I had no choice. Strader told me I had to. If Arthur Heywood saw me, I had to shoot him."

"You keep saying Strader made you, forced you. How? How did he force you?"

"He . . . he has authority over me. He's the Justice of the Peace."

"Yes, but why did you not report him to a higher authority, to the Lord Chancellor?"

"I can't tell you." He sounded sullen.

"Then I can't send for the surgeon."

He moaned. "Can't you see I'm dying?"

"You deserved what you got," Mrs. Atwater mumbled. "Coming into our good lady's room with a knife. I'm glad she shot you."

The housekeeper's words went down into Rebecca's heart and filled her with warmth. She'd often wondered how the servants felt about her, after having Arthur's mother as their mistress for so long. Perhaps they liked her after all.

"I suppose Strader had information about you that you didn't want anyone to know about. Is that it?"

"Yes." Mr. Fogg was starting to look around him. No one seemed to be paying him much attention. They were all talking amongst themselves, and even Mrs. Atwater had ceased applying pressure to his wound. She'd placed a bandage over the wound and let him hold it in place.

Margaret started chattering excitedly to her mother. "I cannot wait to tell everyone that my sister shot an intruder."

Then Rebecca noticed Thomas Westbrook smiling at her.

"You did well," he said quietly.

"All due to you showing me how to shoot."

"But you had the courage to shoot him."

"I thought you said you would send for the surgeon." Mr. Fogg's lips twisted as he started crying, actual tears spilling from his eyes.

Thomas called to a footman, who was standing in the hallway, then went out of the room. Rebecca heard him say, "Do the grooms know where to go to fetch the surgeon?"

A few moments later, Thomas came back into the room, with the two footmen following him. "Take him out of here. Mrs. Atwater? Where would you like them to take him?"

"I shouldn't be moved," Mr. Fogg blubbered.

"They can put him in the servants' sick room next to the kitchen. There's a cot in there."

The footmen hauled him to his feet, in the midst of his alternating groans and sobs.

After they took him out, Thomas asked, "Did anyone see how he got into the house?"

The servants shook their heads and said, "No, sir."

He looked at Mrs. Atwater. "When I arrived, the door was unlocked and I walked right in."

Mrs. Atwater said, "I thought I heard someone on the stairs. I couldn't sleep, so I went to see if one of the servants was where they shouldn't be. I came as quick as I could when I heard the gunshot. But someone must have let him inside and then left the door unlocked. The doors are always locked and bolted at night."

"Is Adler here?" Rebecca asked.

"Who is Adler?" Thomas asked.

"The butler."

The servants who were standing in the corridor looked around, then said, "He's not here."

"Mrs. Atwater? Do you know something of Mr. Adler's whereabouts?" Thomas asked.

"No, but I remember him saying a few months

ago that he was hoping to be able to cease working in a few months and go live with his son in Dorchester. I asked him how he would be able to do that and he wouldn't answer me."

"We should go ask Fogg about whether Mr. Adler had a hand in all this," Thomas said quietly.

"Forgive me," Mrs. Atwater said. "That was only gossip. Mr. Adler could be completely innocent."

"No, you were being helpful," Thomas said. "Thank you. And we shall wait until we have evidence or a confession before accusing anyone."

"Do you need me anymore, Mrs. Heywood?" The housekeeper turned to Rebecca.

"No, but . . . where is Mrs. Heywood, my mother-in-law?"

"I have not seen her. But she often takes her sleeping tonic, as she calls it, when she goes to bed."

"Could she sleep through a gunshot?" Rebecca could hardly imagine it.

"I believe she could, when she takes the tonic. It's mostly laudanum."

"I see. Thank you, Mrs. Atwater. If you will send one of the servants to take care of Mr. Fogg until the surgeon comes, you may retire to bed. Thank you again."

"Of course. And I'm very glad you are unharmed, Mrs. Heywood." She nodded to them both and left the room.

"We should send word to someone," Rebecca said, glancing at the gun she had used to defend herself. "But we can't send for the Justice of the Peace."

Thomas said. "No. Strader is behind all of this, according to Fogg. But I happen to know the Lord Lieutenant of the county. He's not terribly far away, an old friend. I'll send for him."

"Oh, thank you." Rebecca rubbed her temple, feeling a headache coming on.

"Your ankle," he said, looking down at her bare feet. "You shouldn't be standing on it, should you?"

"I forgot all about it." She noticed now that it was hurting, but not as much as the day before. "It seems to be getting better."

She suddenly realized they were alone in her bedroom.

"You should go back to bed," he said. "I'll go down and question Mr. Fogg and—"

A scream split the quiet.

"That came from downstairs." Rebecca's gaze fastened on his.

"I must go and see—"

"Take me with you." This was her household, after all.

"Shall I carry you?"

"I can walk, if you let me lean on you."

They each put an arm around the other and she limp-walked as fast as she could down the stairs.

Once again, a crowd of servants had gathered, this time outside the doorway of the little sick room off the kitchen.

"What is the matter?" Rebecca called out, and the servants parted to let them through.

"He's dead." A servant girl named Hattie was standing beside the constable, her hands clasped in front of her. "He was dead when I got here."

"Where are the men who brought him down here?" Thomas asked.

"We're here," the two footmen said.

"What happened?"

"We half carried him down here and helped him onto the bed," one of the footmen said.

"He was alive when we left him," the other one said.

"He couldn't have been alone more than five minutes," Mrs. Atwater said.

"Did he bleed to death?" Rebecca asked, looking at Thomas.

They both moved toward the bed. Mr. Fogg was lying on his back, his eyes and mouth open, his hands palm out, as if trying to defend himself. Rebecca felt sick at the sight of his face, frozen in an expression of terror.

"The bleeding had stopped," Mrs. Atwater said.

"I don't think he bled to death." Thomas's tone was grim. He looked at one of the footmen. "Fetch Mr. Adler."

The man hurried away. When he returned, he said, "Mr. Adler is not in his room."

"Go check the stable and see if there are any horses missing," Thomas said.

Hattie, the servant who had found him, was visibly shaking, her face pale. Rebecca gently squeezed Hattie's arm. "I am sorry you had to see that, to be the first to find him, but all will be well. Try to sleep."

"Thank you, mum. You're very kind." Her lips trembled as she spoke, and a tear slid down her cheek. She turned and fled the room.

Rebecca wished she could do the same, but she had to stay strong and figure out what to do. *Thank you, God, for sending Thomas Westbrook to me tonight.*

CHAPTER TWENTY

Thomas yet again noted Rebecca Heywood's admirable behavior. Instead of dissolving in hysterics or fainting dead away, as some women seemed prone to do, she behaved as he imagined his sister Caroline would.

"If anyone saw anything suspicious," she said to the servants, "please let me or Mr. Westbrook know. But unless you have information, please, go back to bed. There is nothing any of you can do now. We will send for the authorities."

The servants slowly started to disperse.

"Go get some sleep and try not to worry."

She was so kind to everyone. He'd never heard her speak a sharp word to any of her servants.

When all the servants were leaving, the footman came hurrying back. "One of the horses is missing, Mr. Arthur's favorite gelding."

"Thank you," Thomas said. "Can you go to Wyghtworth?"

"Yes, sir."

"Go and tell my groom, Logan, to come here on a fast horse. I need to send him on an important errand."

"Yes, sir." The footman hurried away.

"I can hardly believe this is happening," Rebecca whispered when they were alone, except for the dead body. "He looks as if he was trying to fend someone off, like he was being attacked."

"Let me get you back upstairs. You need to rest your ankle."

"Thank you. I am surprised it isn't hurting very much."

"It will be if you don't rest it."

"I'm thinking it's almost healed." Her voice trailed off, as if her thoughts had wandered to something else.

They put their arms around each other again and started up the stairs. Moving slowly but steadily, neither of them talked. He could become accustomed to having her arm around him, leaning on him, depending on him. He couldn't imagine ever getting tired of her soft voice and her quiet but determined way of speaking and acting.

When they were just entering her bedroom, she broke the silence.

"What do you think happened to Mr. Fogg?" Rebecca whispered.

"Someone killed him."

"I can't stop thinking that *I* killed him." Rebecca's voice hitched.

He stopped her and moved to look her in the eye. "You did not kill him. You shot him in the perfect spot, away from his heart and other organs, even missing his bones. Besides that, you were defending yourself. He chose to come into your house at night without your permission and come into your bedroom with a knife, demanding something that did not belong to him. You did the right thing by shooting him, and I'm very proud of you, partially because I am the one who taught you how to shoot."

"You did, didn't you?"

"Yes. You did nothing wrong."

"Mrs. Atwater must have sent someone to clean up the blood." She was staring down at the floor where Fogg had lain bleeding.

She gazed up at him. Her eyes were so big and innocent, shimmering in the candlelight of all the candles that had been brought into the room. The faint smell of lemon and gardenia was all around him, making him feel dizzy.

His heart was beating fast as he reached out and cupped her cheek in his hand.

He groaned inwardly, knowing he shouldn't touch her, shouldn't kiss her, but wanting to just the same.

She is Arthur Heywood's widow, a voice inside his head accused. *Do you want Arthur's wife?*

Arthur didn't deserve her, and now he's dead, he argued.

But it was improper for him to be there, in her bedroom, at night. Alone with her. He quickly let his hand drop.

"I should go."

"Don't go yet." She put her arms around him and buried her face in his shirt.

She was still wearing his coat, and he could feel

her warm breath on his neck, as he hadn't taken the time to put on a cravat.

He held her close, loving the way she felt in his arms, so warm and soft and real, loving her nearness and her perfume, filling his head with daydreams.

If you married her, you could hold her like this every day.

It was an intoxicating thought, almost as intoxicating as her breath on his bare skin. But he had to keep his head about him. He could not behave like a scoundrel.

He could think of her as a sister, needing comfort after a very trying and upsetting event.

He couldn't fool himself that easily. His feelings for Rebecca were nothing like his feelings for his sister. But he also didn't want to make her uncomfortable or cause her servants to question her reputation.

But she didn't seem uncomfortable at all. Her arms were quite tight around him, and she made no move to pull away from him.

They stood there, not moving, and he felt as if he could stay there forever. Who needed sleep? This . . . this was what he needed.

Priscilla had been his fiancée first before allowing Arthur Heywood to seduce her. She'd chosen Arthur over him. But he'd never met Rebecca before she married Arthur—and Arthur must have seen her as a virtuous woman to have married her. She'd also said herself that she'd been unhappy married to Arthur. No doubt he had hurt her, had broken her heart over and over again.

What if she chose Thomas now? Why should he care that she had married Arthur first? It was inconsequential, besides the fact that it showed she'd trusted Arthur, believed in him, and he'd betrayed her.

She began to gently pull away, slowly, lifting her head.

The top of her head was at the level of his eyes, and he took in how soft her hair looked. He wasn't used to seeing it long and flowing over her shoulders and down her back, but it was beautiful, and if possible, made her even more lovely, the way the soft waves touched her temples.

"You are so beautiful," he said, then sucked in a breath. He hadn't meant to say that. "Forgive me."

She leaned her head back. Her eyes were half closed, and they were staring at his mouth. She wanted him to kiss her.

Was he insane for thinking so? Her lips were parted and he could hear her breaths coming in quick gasps. Her hand moved to his shoulder.

He leaned down. Would she kiss him if he moved closer? One small kiss couldn't hurt anything, and he could see she wanted to.

She stood on her toes and touched her lips to his. He waited to see if she would pull away. She didn't. He pulled her closer and she was suddenly kissing him like he was a soldier who had just returned from war.

His blood was pumping so hard it made a rushing sound in his ears.

Rebecca suddenly pulled away. He loosened his hold and she stepped away from him. Then he heard it—footsteps on the stairs.

She was looking into his eyes, but as the footsteps pounded up to the top of the stairs, a male voice said, "Mrs. Heywood? I'm looking for Mr. Westbrook."

Thomas inhaled, trying to calm his wayward breathing, and hurried into the hallway.

"Logan, you're here. Good man." He'd completely forgotten about sending for his groom. He had to act calm and not suspicious—not like he had just been kissing the widowed mistress of Heywood House.

"I need you to go to Derby to fetch the Lord Lieutenant, Rawson. Tell him our constable is dead here at Heywood House and I need him right away." He gave him the direction to the Lord Lieutenant's house, then said, "Be quick but safe."

The Justice of the Peace was supposed to decide whether to call in the coroner, but since their JP was obviously corrupt, he would let Rawson decide whether to send for Pursglove.

Fogg was dead, and there was nothing left to do except take his leave of the beautiful woman with whom he'd just shared a most amazing kiss.

He went back to her doorway and found her standing just inside. She'd taken off his coat and was wearing a thin, gauzy thing that covered her nightgown from her chin to her feet.

"Thank you for the use of your coat," she said, a soft smile on her lips as she handed him the garment.

"You're welcome." What should he say? Perhaps he should ask her to marry him on the spot. But she had initiated the kiss. He had to think about this. Besides, if he were to decide he wanted to marry her, he'd want a more romantic place and time for the proposal, not right after a man had been murdered in her house.

"And thank you for teaching me how to shoot. You may have saved my life."

"I am at your service." He threw his coat over his

arm, then took her hand and lifted it to his lips.

Her gaze never left his as he kissed her hand, her lips parted and her chest rapidly rising and falling.

How he wanted to kiss her lips again. It took everything in him not to pull her into his arms and do just that.

"I don't like the thought of leaving you here alone, not when we do not know who killed Fogg. Do you have a deadbolt on your door?"

"Yes."

"Bolt your door and, if I have your permission, I will sleep on the sofa in the drawing room."

"I would feel safer having you here, but you will not be very comfortable on the sofa."

"I shall be well enough. I can sleep anywhere. And I shall ask Mrs. Atwater for blankets and a pillow."

"Of course."

In spite of everything, his heart was leaping inside his chest. He'd have to sort out his thoughts and feelings later. For now, he only knew that the loveliest woman of his acquaintance had embraced and kissed him, and that was all he needed to know.

~ ~ ~

Rebecca's heart was still beating so hard it stole her breath, and he was still holding her hand. He kissed it again with those wonderful lips before turning and walking away.

She closed her door and locked it, then bolted it, doing the same with the door that adjoined Arthur's old bedroom. All the while she was thinking of Thomas drawing attention to the fact that he was spending the night in the drawing room by asking the housekeeper for blankets and a pillow, and thinking of him sleeping all night on the sofa. Because he wanted to keep her safe.

She clasped her arms around herself, sighing and whispering, "Thank you, God. Thank you." But speaking to God made her wonder if she had done wrong by kissing Thomas.

She hadn't planned to do it. But in that moment, feeling so shaken by what had just happened, having shot a man and then seeing that man dead, at least in part by her own hand, she couldn't bear to let Thomas leave her, not at that moment. She needed his comfort. Her mother and sister were nearby, but he was the one she wanted to hold her.

How shameless she was. But she didn't care. And Thomas hadn't seemed to mind. She recalled how tightly he had held her, his hands on her back, his arms strong and unyielding. He made her feel safe and protected. When was the last time she'd felt safe and protected?

And his kiss . . . so gentle and yet so sure and firm. It had made her stomach turn inside out.

Then, after she wrapped her arms around him, the way he'd looked at her . . . How could she have resisted kissing him? And he hadn't seemed to mind that either. He kissed her back and she'd reveled in it.

What might have happened if his servant hadn't come up the stairs when he did? She both regretted his intrusion and was relieved by it.

But what kind of woman kisses someone who had never made her a declaration, to whom she wasn't engaged, and, what was worse, less than an hour after a man had died in her home?

She stared at the floor where Mr. Fogg had lain bleeding from her gunshot. She could still see the faint stain and shuddered, remembering her terror at realizing there was a man in her room. And then the sound of the gunshot and the heavy thudding sound of him falling to the floor. She could still hear his whimpers and moans.

But how dare he come into her room? Anger warred with horror and regret.

"O God, thank you that I am safe, but please forgive me, if it was a sin to shoot him." She didn't believe it was, but the thought of it overwhelmed her. And her shooting him had made him vulnerable to the murderer who subsequently killed him.

Was it Adler? Had Adler agreed to help Fogg in order that he might get a share of the treasure and thereby be able to retire? Had her butler murdered Fogg to keep him from telling of his hand in the business?

She would never want to falsely accuse anyone, but if Adler was gone, if he had fled from the house, would that not prove his guilt? And though Mrs. Atwater had claimed Mrs. Heywood took a sleeping draught most nights, it seemed strange that she had slept through all the commotion.

Rebecca's teeth were starting to chatter from the cold, so she climbed into bed with her wrapper still on and pulled the covers up to her chin. She pressed the back of her hand where Thomas had kissed her up to her cheek and closed her eyes, trying to remember every sensation of his kiss.

Such a strange, terrible, and yet wonderful night.

CHAPTER TWENTY-ONE

Thomas lay awake most of the night, and just after daybreak, his old friend Rawson arrived.

Fogg's body was still where they had left it, lying on the narrow bed in the little sick room off the kitchen. Thomas did his best to tell him everything as Rawson examined the body.

"It certainly looks as if someone did him in after the gunshot." Rawson winced at the expression on Fogg's face, frozen in place, as it were, for all time. "And you were with Mrs. Heywood when this happened?"

"Yes."

"Was anyone else with you?"

"Not the entire time. I was taking Mrs. Heywood to her room. She recently injured her ankle and needed assistance up the stairs."

Rawson gave him a look, his brows arching, along with a wry smile. Thomas said nothing, for the servants were in the next room preparing food for the household.

He and Rawson discussed what happened to Fogg and what Fogg had said, then they looked through the absent butler's room.

"It certainly seems as if the butler did it." Rawson looked up from inspecting the man's small and tidy room—tidy except for the small cabinet where he kept his clothes. It hung open, with items of clothing hanging half out and strewed on the floor.

"I will make certain to tell the Lord Chancellor the particulars. I believe he will send the Bow Street runners here to investigate, and Strader, as well as Adler the butler, will be apprehended."

When Rebecca came downstairs, she invited Rawson and himself to break their fast with her.

He couldn't imagine she'd slept much the night before. Even so, she looked as pretty as ever, her dark blue eyes shining every time she looked his way. Was she thinking of their kiss as much as he was?

When they were finished with their morning meal, Rebecca began to describe the events of the night before for Mr. Rawson. She had barely begun when they heard Mrs. Heywood's grating voice coming down the stairs.

"What has happened? What has happened?" she kept saying. When she finally entered the breakfast room, her eyes were wide and her mouth slack. "I am astonished. My servant has told me the constable is dead and Rebecca shot him during the night. I demand to know what has happened?"

Rebecca introduced Rawson, then she began again to explain everything that happened. It was unfortunate that Mrs. Heywood was there, as she kept interrupting and making little remarks, barely veiled contempt for Rebecca in every one. But Rebecca carried on until she'd finished, and he marveled at her patience.

Rawson did not tarry, no doubt eager to get away from Mrs. Heywood.

Wishing he could have had even a moment alone with Rebecca—and knowing that was probably not wise, simultaneously—he left with Rawson, but not before his eyes met Rebecca's and he imagined he saw a bit of longing in them, mirroring his own.

~ ~ ~

It was the day before the ball, and Rebecca leaned on her walking stick as she and Thomas escorted the coroner Pursglove, with Benjamin, Caroline, Margaret, and Mrs. Heywood into the woods to see what they had found.

Pursglove had examined the letter written by Arthur Heywood's grandfather and commented that it looked legitimate. He said little else as they walked through the garden and into the trees.

Now that they were able to carry two shovels with them and did not have to keep their find a secret, Thomas and Benjamin worked together to move the dirt and uncover the chest.

Their shovels made a sound of metal on wood, and Rebecca's heart fluttered. They used their hands to brush away the last of the dirt and reveal the top of the chest.

"There was no lock on it," Thomas commented, and he and Benjamin grasped the lid and lifted it.

Everyone leaned in, the men crouching on their knees. Benjamin stuck his hand down into the dark chest and brought it up full of gold coins.

"It's real," he said. "The pirate treasure is real."

The coroner took one of the coins and held it up to catch a ray of sunlight coming through the leaves of the trees.

"It appears to be a gold doubloon. If the chest is full of them, this treasure will be worth a great deal."

Pursglove stood back and allowed them to dig through the coins. Margaret examined several coins with wide, bright eyes. Thomas, Benjamin, and Caroline each took a turn digging in the chest, finding a few silver coins out of all the gold ones.

"This treasure belongs to the Heywood family," Mrs. Heywood said in her most imperious tone. "It does not belong to anyone else, as you can plainly see from old Captain Heywood's letter. The Heywood family are the rightful owners."

"As I have said before, and as is well known, I will have to hold an inquest with a jury, who will decide who the rightful owner is of this treasure trove. It is the way things are done, and no one can change that." He gave a cold stare to Mrs. Heywood. "Two men have died over this chest of gold, and from now on, things will be done decently and in order."

Rebecca could assert that the estate belonged to her, and since it was found on the estate, it rightfully belonged to her. But she wanted to do what was right. Captain Heywood's descendants could also have rightful claim to the treasure, but when Arthur was killed, there were no more direct descendants. He was the last.

Pursglove had brought a couple of strong men with him, and with the help of the grooms, they began getting the chest ready to lift from the hole using thick tree limbs, ropes, and a strange-looking contraption that they called a winch.

Thomas moved toward Rebecca. His eyes were so warm and kind. Was he thinking of their kiss? Her cheeks grew warm. *Stop thinking about it,* she scolded herself.

He drew near and said softly, "Pursglove will have to take the treasure back with him until the inquest is finished. May I escort you home?"

She hesitated, desperately wanting to spend whatever time with him she could. "I would like that. Thank you."

Benjamin was more interested in the treasure than in her, thankfully. He hadn't glanced in her direction since they opened the chest.

They started walking toward the house and he asked, "How is your ankle faring? I hope it is not paining you."

"It is nearly well, but I am trying not to put my weight on it, which is why I'm using the walking stick."

Her heart fluttered, partially because he was so kind and thoughtful, but also because she wondered if he would kiss her again, if they found themselves alone.

"I am coming with you," Mrs. Heywood called out from behind them.

Rebecca's heart sank.

They waited for Mrs. Heywood. She was already breathing hard after hurrying to catch up with them, and then they resumed their walk back to the house.

"I suppose you were snooping in Captain Heywood's room, in his private papers and things, to find that map and that letter." Mrs. Heywood was speaking between huffed breaths. "But if you had not found them, I suppose we'd never have found the Heywood family's treasure. And I suppose it has occurred to you that if you marry Gilbert Heywood, you shall secure both the treasure and this house, in addition to his grand estate. But do not think that I blame you. I'm sure any young woman would do the same."

Not only her heart, but her stomach sank at Thomas Westbrook being forced to listen to Mrs. Heywood's ugly assumptions.

What had she ever done to make that woman hate her so?

In the early months of her marriage, Mrs. Heywood had been cordial to her, much of the time, anyway. But she'd become less cordial in her attitude the more Arthur ignored her and betrayed her with other women. It was as if she couldn't get angry at her son, and since he was doing things that embarrassed her, she had to blame his behavior on someone else. Rebecca was the only scapegoat around.

For the longest time, Rebecca had yearned for the days when her mother-in-law had been amiable, or at least had veiled her contempt and criticism so that it wasn't so obvious. But now she had no expectations of the woman ever being more than barely civil. For now she had no choice but to endure the woman's blatant hatred. At least she could be under no illusions anymore about what the woman thought of her. She felt sick, though, as she wondered what Thomas thought of the woman's accusations.

"I have never had any intention of marrying Gilbert Heywood." Rebecca tried to keep her voice calm and emotionless. Certainly, it had enraged Mrs. Heywood that her son had left the estate to his wife instead of his mother, though he had made ample provision for her. But again, Mrs. Heywood couldn't direct her anger at her precious son.

"Well, and I had no intention of marrying Mr. Heywood until he asked my father for my hand. Leastways, now we know who killed my Arthur. I am only too sorry that that rotten butler of ours had to kill the constable before he was brought to bear for his sin—murdering a landowning gentleman on his own land. Sickening. If he were alive, and if I were a man, I'd beat him until he was sorry he'd ever been born, and then I'd slit his throat."

Rebecca shuddered inwardly.

"Perhaps if you had not shot the man, he could have been apprehended properly and locked away. Then he would have had to face the King's Court and all could have been done decently and in order."

Her repetition of the coroner's own words made Rebecca wonder if he thought she was to blame for shooting the constable.

"What was he doing in your room?" Mrs. Heywood abruptly asked.

"He wanted the treasure map. He demanded I give it to him, several times. When he came toward me, I shot him." She resented feeling the need to explain this again to Mrs. Heywood. The woman made her feel like a chastised child, causing her to feel that she should explain it to Mrs. Heywood all over again.

"And you could not have shared the knowledge of the treasure map with me? It belonged to me more than to you, as you've only been in this family for two years and I have been in it for thirty. Mr. Westbrook, I still don't understand how you became involved in all of this. You and Arthur were not friends."

Thomas said nothing for a few seconds, and Mrs. Heywood went on.

"I suppose Rebecca confided in you instead of me. But so might I, if I were young and unmarried. Well, here we are. I am going up to my room, and I shall write the news to my brother. He shall know how to advise—well, good day." She hurried away up the stairs.

"I would apologize for her," Rebecca said softly, "but I feel no responsibility for her behavior."

"As well you shouldn't," Thomas said. He reached for her hand, but just then, a servant passed through the hallway behind them. He let his hand drop.

"Atwater!" Mrs. Heywood called, as her footsteps could be heard coming down the stairs. "I must speak with the cook about the dinner tonight." As she came into view again, she asked, "Will Mr. Westbrook and Caroline be staying for dinner?"

Rebecca could feel herself bristling, her shoulders and neck growing tense at Mrs. Heywood's rudeness and the fact that she felt free to take charge of the servants and such household matters as dinner, duties Rebecca had been carrying out since Mrs. Heywood had left on her visit to her brother's home.

"We will not be staying," Thomas said.

Rebecca liked it better when Mrs. Heywood refused to speak to Thomas Westbrook.

Mrs. Heywood walked in the direction of the kitchen while she continued to talk, something about dinner and servants not taking direction and how hard it was to get a good cook.

When she was out of earshot, Thomas's gaze met hers and he gave her a gentle smile. Her heart stuttered.

"I should get back, to see if they need my help."

"Of course."

He wasn't going to kiss her. She stepped away from him. *I never should have kissed him, never should have embraced him or had thoughts of attraction and marriage.* Hadn't attraction to Arthur Heywood, and marriage, ruined her happiness? She'd always been a rather peaceful and joyful person until she'd married him. And how much did she really know about Thomas Westbrook?

Fear gripped her throat like a fist.

"How is your ankle feeling after the walk?"

"Not bad."

"Do you think you will be able to go to the ball tomorrow night?"

"I do."

"Did Caroline ask you? She and Mother want you to ride with us to the ball. They greatly enjoy your company and did not like the thought of you having to ride with . . ." He cut his eyes in the direction Mrs. Heywood had just gone.

In spite of her sudden feelings of fear, she felt a burst of gratitude for Caroline and Mrs. Westbrook.

"I thank you. I would be happy to accept the invitation to ride with your family."

"Very good. We shall call for you tomorrow."

"Thank you."

As she stood at the door and watched him walk across the garden, her eyes filled with tears and her chest ached. *He seems to be such a good man and has treated me with nothing but kindness and selflessness. He's nothing like Arthur.*

But what if she was wrong?

CHAPTER TWENTY-TWO

The next morning, Rebecca said farewell to her mother and sister as they left for London. They'd already extended their stay a week, but Mother insisted she had to get back to help Father.

"Any issue with the servants or the management of the household and he is all out of sorts. And he does have a great deal of work to do. Business demands nearly all of his attention. But you will write and tell us all about the ball and what happens with the pirate treasure."

"Of course. And you will write to me when you are able."

"Yes, my dear." Mother kissed and patted her cheek, as was her wont, and Rebecca embraced her and Margaret one last time.

"I'm so glad you are able to go to the ball," Margaret said.

"Yes, my ankle feels well again." Rebecca lifted her

ankle. The swelling was completely gone.

"You should be careful and not dance too much or the swelling may come back," Mother said as she allowed herself to be handed into the carriage.

They waved at each other as the carriage pulled away, and Rebecca went inside the house, a heaviness filling her heart as she remembered she was alone again with Mrs. Heywood.

Thankfully, though the woman was attending the ball, she was traveling in her own carriage and staying overnight with someone else who was attending the ball, though Rebecca had yet to learn with whom.

At least she had the ball to look forward to, and the ride to Beaumont with her dear friends, the Westbrooks.

Even though she happily anticipated spending time with them, and dancing with Thomas, the very same thoughts also caused trepidation. Would Thomas ultimately reject her, since he could have any woman he wanted? Or would she discover that he wasn't the good sort of man she'd thought him to be?

The thought of marrying again was terrifying, and yet, she couldn't stop thinking about their kiss, his gentle touch and warm voice.

When she was married and Arthur was avoiding her—or off on one of his trysts—the longing to feel loved, to give and receive love and affection, would sometimes overwhelm her, especially at night when she was alone. She thought those feelings would dissipate now that she had no husband, now that the possibility of love seemed out of reach, but . . . Thomas Westbrook seemed to have perpetuated those feelings and made them even stronger, but in a slightly different way.

But what if kissing him had been a terrible mistake? Certainly the kiss had been imprudent and impulsive, and those two things were bad and led to terrible outcomes. What had she been thinking? She still could hardly believe she'd kissed him.

It had been a wild night, full of terror and horror, and she'd been overwhelmed with the effects of it, when they'd suddenly found themselves alone together. She simply hadn't been able to resist putting her arms around him and asking for his comfort.

She sighed as she went up to her room. She still had to prepare for the ball, to decide what to wear and speak with her maidservant about how to arrange her hair for the ball.

Surely the ball would help to clarify things for her.

~ ~ ~

Thomas found himself thinking more about Rebecca's kiss than about the treasure, the murder, or the treacherous events of the past week.

Perhaps this ball would help him untangle his thoughts about Rebecca Heywood.

His sister's and even his mother's spirits seemed high as they entered the carriage and started on the short way to Rebecca Heywood's home. His brother's spirits, on the contrary, were more subdued. He barely spoke all day except to ask his sister's opinion on what he should wear and how he should tie his cravat, an oddity that had Caroline exclaiming, "You want *my* help?" His brother had very strong opinions about everything, even clothing, so it was not surprising that Caroline would react thusly.

But all was quiet as they rode to Heywood House.

And when they arrived, he expected Benjamin to jump out and call for Rebecca, taking the opportunity to hand her into the carriage, but he made no move. So Thomas went to the door. But before he could knock, Rebecca appeared.

How lovely she was, wearing a lacy ball gown and a genuine smile that stretched her lips and showed her teeth. There were many ladies who never smiled like this, with warmth, genuinely and without artifice.

She took his hand and he led her down the steps.

"Thank you for inviting me to accompany your family in your carriage," she said.

"You are most welcome, as you know."

Ignoring a vow one had made, even when the vow was to oneself, was no small thing. He was still of two minds, however, but he'd prayed for God to give him a sign at the ball tonight. Should he follow his more foolish feelings of attachment and love? Or should he adhere to his original vow, never to get involved with anyone who was attached to Arthur Heywood?

Tonight he would let his fate be decided.

He and Benjamin were seated across from the ladies, with Rebecca between his mother and sister, who both looked quite happy to have her there.

Benjamin was quiet as the ladies chattered away together like magpies, talking of how much Rebecca must miss her mother and sister now that they were gone, talking of who would be at the ball and with whom they hoped to dance.

"Mother, you should dance tonight. Truly, you should," Caroline said.

"Oh, no, I think my dancing days are over. I only used to dance with your father, if you remember."

"Yes, but it's all right now." Caroline spoke softly. "You should dance and enjoy yourself. You're still alive."

"I am aware." Mother gave her a cheeky half smile. "And I hope to see Rebecca dance with every eligible man at the ball."

Rebecca's cheeks seemed to turn pink as she stared open-mouthed at Caroline. "I think that would be a good thing for you, Caroline, but I am newly widowed. It would not be proper."

"You are so young," Caroline said, undeterred. "You deserve to be happy after . . . Well, you deserve to be happy. No one would begrudge your enjoyment of a ball. No good-hearted person, that is."

"I do not wish to have everyone talk and say that I made a spectacle of myself, but I confess, I do hope to dance tonight, at least a few dances." Again, her cheeks grew rosy at the confession.

"I daresay the host, Gilbert Heywood, will want to dance with you," Mother said.

"Yes!" Caroline said. "He came all this way to call on you twice."

"That was only because he wanted to purchase Heywood House."

"You don't know that."

"And you should consider why he might want to purchase Heywood House," Benjamin said, arching his brows. "Perhaps he knew about the treasure and wanted it for himself."

"Benjamin," Mother said in a scolding tone.

"It's true. Who else is more likely to have heard the rumors about Captain Heywood's treasure than someone in the family?"

"But darling, you don't want to falsely accuse anyone. It isn't kind, and what if you're wrong?"

"All I'm saying is that it's a possibility that we should consider."

"Benjamin is right," Thomas said. "We should at least consider it."

"But everyone now knows, do they not, that the treasure was found?" Rebecca's brows were drawn together in obvious concern.

Everyone expressed an opinion about how quickly the news would have spread, especially since the Bow Street Runners had been called in to investigate. But they all agreed that "everyone who doesn't know will hear about it within minutes of arriving at the ball."

"And we all think it most likely," Caroline said, "that you will be awarded the treasure."

"Do you not think it will be divided among Captain Heywood's rightful heirs?" Rebecca looked surprised.

"I think not," Benjamin said. As if he were wise beyond his seventeen years, which he wasn't. "The treasure was found on your property—you are the sole owner—and you had made no attempt to hide the treasure yourself and knew nothing of it when you came into ownership. I believe the inquest will find in favor of you."

Mother and Caroline nodded.

"You will certainly have very many eligible gentlemen vying for your attention," Caroline said with a sly smile.

"Not that you would not have had many suitors before they knew about the treasure," Mother said.

"But you will have many more now, and so must

be on your guard," Thomas said.

Everyone stared at him.

"It is true, and you all know it." Thomas looked out the window rather than defending his statement further.

"There are unscrupulous men in the world, to be sure," Mother said.

"What will you do with the treasure?" Caroline asked, changing the topic of conversation. "It is a great deal of money, quite a fortune in gold."

"It is probably foolish to spend it before it is even mine," Rebecca said, "or plan for it when it has not yet been given to me and may be distributed elsewhere. But if it is given to me, I should like to share it with my brothers and sisters, to lay by a dowry for each sister, and a sum for each brother to set up housekeeping when they decide to marry."

"That is so very generous and kind," his mother and sister said.

"But I also don't wish to give only to my family, as that seems a bit selfish."

"What do you mean?" Caroline asked.

"I wish to give to the poor as well, as we are instructed in the Scriptures."

"It is not wrong to keep some for yourself," Caroline insisted.

"Yes, but hoarding wealth is surely wrong, as in the Bible story of the man who tore down his barns to build bigger ones to store his wealth but was not rich toward God. We never know when our last day will be."

Thomas was reminded of how charitable Rebecca had always been, taking food and medicines to the poor, especially among her tenants, but even outside of them.

His heart seemed to go out of his chest in desire for her.

Was this his sign?

~ ~ ~

Rebecca didn't like to think that Thomas and Benjamin were falsely accusing Gilbert Heywood in their hearts. Were they letting their attachment for her cloud their judgment and make them jealous?

Thomas and Benjamin were both good men. They would not take it too far. After all, there was no evidence to link Gilbert Heywood to any of the nefarious events of the past several weeks. The constable had accused the Justice of the Peace, who, they had been told, had been apprehended and jailed, although he might not remain in jail long, as they had no evidence beyond Mr. Fogg's confession—Mr. Fogg who was dead. But whoever were the guilty ones, the Bow Street Runners would no doubt uncover the truth of it all, for which they were famous.

The conversation went silent for a moment, possibly due to the fact that they had been asked not to speak of any of the details of the constable's possible murder and how they found the treasure, the map, or any other details. After all, if they questioned someone and that person knew more than they should, it would be a good indication that they were guilty.

Rebecca took the quiet moment to say another silent prayer that there would be no quarrel or upset feelings between Benjamin and Thomas at the ball tonight. She felt strange even praying that—a bit narcissistic, truthfully—but it was obvious that Benjamin had felt a bit of an attachment for her, although she hoped he had overcome those feelings.

She also said a prayer that her own feelings of attachment for Thomas would not be crushed tonight. As it was, he had not made any declaration for her, had not indicated he was in love with her or wished to marry her, even though they had kissed. She'd seen the tenderness in his expression and manner that night, but since then, she had not seen a return of that tender feeling —though they hadn't had any opportunity to be alone since then.

She might need to accept the fact that he was not in love with her and might never wish to marry her.

That thought sent a pang, like the jab of a knife, through her chest. *Do not borrow trouble,* she reminded herself. This was a ball and she should enjoy herself, though discreetly and with propriety, as a new widow should.

But deep in her heart, though she would never admit it to anyone, she hoped tonight Thomas would take the opportunity to tell her, in a quiet corner or in the garden, that he loved her and hoped to set a date to marry her, when an appropriate amount of time had passed.

CHAPTER TWENTY-THREE

The ballroom glowed with the warmth of candle-light.

Rebecca felt strange being there. It was as if her husband's death was a wound that was still raw, her feelings still connected in a tangible way to that terrible, sudden, life-altering event, which lent a rawness to her feelings. And yet, the beauty and liveliness of the evening healed her, at least a bit.

Gilbert Heywood appeared by her side, startling her as he grabbed her hand.

"I am so pleased you are come," he said. "Might I beg to dance with you the first two dances?"

Rebecca stared at the man, casting about in her mind for an appropriate refusal. "Forgive me, but may I accept for only one dance? As you know, I am a new widow. I must consider my reputation and how some people might talk. But I thank you, I shall be glad to stand up with you for the first dance. You are my husband's cousin, after all."

Gilbert's expression changed more than once during her hurried speech, and finally he said, "The first dance, then?"

She nodded and hurried away, allowing him to greet the Westbrooks, who were just behind her.

She sighed in relief at her escape. If she'd danced the first two dances with him, people might have thought they had an understanding, or at least that Gilbert Heywood was hoping to form an attachment to her. Indeed, she suspected that very thing.

She greeted some acquaintances, who expressed their condolences on the death of her husband. She thanked them and hurried away before they should ask her about the treasure, as she could almost see their questions on their faces. Would she be avoiding those questions all night?

She joined Mrs. Westbrook and Caroline as they proceeded to the refreshments. Moments later, a young man asked Caroline for the first dance and she accepted.

"Who was that?" Rebecca whispered.

"Nash Golding, who is the Earl of Barrentine, since his father died recently. He's handsome but rather shy. I suspect his mother urged him to ask me to dance."

"Why do you think so?"

"I have heard her push him to ask a lady to dance before, and she has always liked me. There she is now." Caroline smiled and nodded at a lady sitting down with the other dowagers.

"It is a great compliment to you. I wouldn't imagine there are very many earls here."

"No, I suspect he is the only one. But the last time I danced with him, he hardly said a word, so I will not be hoping for a second dance."

"Well, enjoy it as best you can. I shall be dancing with Gilbert Heywood."

"He didn't ask you for the first two dances did he?"

"He did, but I convinced him it would endanger my reputation to accept, so I am only dancing the first dance with him."

"Clever girl." Caroline smirked and squeezed her arm.

Soon the first dance was announced. Rebecca put on her most sober face as Gilbert led her to the dance floor and they began to dance. She had to look the part of the grieved widow, which was not difficult to do. She'd had many occasions for tears and sad expressions over the course of her two-year marriage.

Gilbert was almost as awkward at dancing as he was at conversation. But he managed to get through the dance without stepping on her toes or bumping into her.

"You are a most elegant dancer, Mrs. Heywood," he said as he walked her to where Mrs. Westbrook was sitting. "Thank you for the dance, and I hope I may have this pleasure later in the evening, when the gossips have forgotten this one." He winked at her.

"Perhaps. I thank you."

Rebecca had thought Caroline faired considerably better with her partner, the handsome Earl of Barrentine.

"You looked quite fetching dancing with Lord Barrentine," Rebecca greeted her.

"His dancing is slightly awkward, but not terribly so, and he is handsome," Caroline said. "But he always seems as if he's thinking of something else. I like my partner to look at me and talk about me, not about the last novel he read."

"He talked of novels?"

"He talked very little, only saying he read a novel that he liked and asked if I'd read it."

"What was it?"

"I don't remember."

Rebecca stifled a laugh and shook her head.

"No, wait, I do remember. It was Northanger Abbey. He said it was a satire on gothic novels. I said, 'I like gothic novels.' And he made no reply." Rebecca raised her eyebrows and frowned. "I don't think I could marry a man who enjoys satires."

"Whyever not?"

"It means he laughs at things I enjoy, and I would not like that." Caroline was sipping her lemonade and simultaneously glancing around the room, the Earl of Barrentine already forgotten.

Personally, Rebecca thought it indicated he had an intellectual bent and enjoyed amusing stories, which did not seem like bad things. But she didn't wish to argue with her friend.

Gilbert Heywood asked Caroline for the next dance, though he smiled at Rebecca while he asked her —a strange, flat-line smile that made Rebecca glad to sit down with Mrs. Westbrook and make pleasant conversation about the loveliness of the ladies and their gowns and the decorations of spring greenery and flowers.

Thomas came over during the middle of the dance and talked with them.

"Why aren't you dancing?" Mrs. Westbrook asked him.

"I am coming around to it." He turned to Rebecca. "Will you do me the honor of the next dance?"

"Of course." Rebecca was quite eager to dance with him, and she knew she needn't pretend she wasn't. Thomas and Mrs. Westbrook would not judge her or call her improper.

Thomas talked with them until it was time for the next dance to begin. He took her hand and led her to the dance floor.

Her heart rejoiced at being near him again and the touch of his hand, even though they were surrounded by people. He seemed to hold her hand a bit longer than necessary, which lifted her heart right out of her chest.

"Perhaps I shouldn't smile so," she said quietly.

"Why should you not?"

"I was only thinking of my reputation as a widow. You know how people talk."

"They will only talk if they cannot find someone else they think is more scandalous. You needn't care for everyone's good opinion."

"That is true. And I suppose I don't care."

The dance began.

"Are you enjoying the evening?" she asked him.

"Yes, now that I'm dancing with you."

His words were so unexpected, for a moment she could think of nothing to say. When she was recovered, she said, "And I am very glad you asked me."

He was looking intently into her eyes, his expression making her heart skip. What would this night bring? Perhaps another secret kiss? Her chest constricted, her breathing shallow in anticipation.

Thank goodness no one here could read her

thoughts or they would declare her shameless, having such feelings only a few weeks after her husband was killed.

She'd never been a bold or shameless girl. Indeed, she'd had little experience with men before Arthur asked her to marry him. She remembered he once laughed and said, "You are so innocent. I shall have to take you as my wife before anyone else realizes what a jewel you are."

Her heart had swelled as if his words were the greatest praise. But now she saw them in an entirely different light. He'd laughed at her innocence instead of appreciating it. And he'd decided to marry her so no one else could have her, not so he could love her and cherish her and enjoy their life together.

How foolish she had been, and how she despised his duplicity and cold-hearted ways.

"Is everything all right?" Thomas asked.

"Of course." She smiled up at Thomas. "Forgive me. I'm afraid my thoughts took me elsewhere for a moment."

The dance continued, and she was careful to keep her thoughts on her partner. Truly, he was a polite gentleman, and she'd never heard him speak of other women or look at them in that predatory way she sometimes saw in Arthur. He was nothing like Arthur.

"You look very lovely tonight, your hair and your gown." Thomas said.

"Thank you."

"You seem to be glowing."

"Thank you. You are very kind." Her heart was beating fast at the genuine-sounding praise. These were no backhanded compliments intended to fool her into thinking he meant something other than what he said.

"I admire the way you are so kind to my mother and sister," he said.

"They are my friends, and they are as kind to me, and more so, for I needed their friendship more than they needed mine."

He was smiling. "I also admire how courageous you were when the constable entered your room in the middle of the night, then shot him."

"I was only defending myself. I am surprised you admire me for that."

"You were brave and did not shrink in fear from an evil man trying to harm you. Of course I admire you for that."

"Truly, you make me blush. I am grateful for your kind words. And you cannot imagine how grateful I am for your friendship. It was you who taught me how to shoot, your words and faith that gave me the courage to defend myself."

The dance ended with Rebecca's breath coming fast, but not due to the exercise. It had more to do with her words, as she'd just spoken more plainly than ever before, and with his intense blue eyes gazing back at her.

They gave each other the customary bow, then he led her back to her seat beside his mother.

"You both look so graceful and confident when you dance," Mrs. Westbrook said. "I declare, I enjoyed watching you dance together immensely. And Benjamin and Caroline both looked quite handsome with their partners as well." She seemed to add the latter sentiment as an afterthought, perhaps to keep from embarrassing them.

"I was so pleased to see Benjamin dancing." Rebecca could still see him talking with his dance partner and her mother. The girl was pretty and looked quite young.

"That is Mattie Springfield," Mrs. Westbrook said. "She is such a sweet girl, and her mother and I are old school friends."

Caroline rushed to join them and whispered, "Just look at Benjamin's smile!" then giggled.

"Don't let him hear you say such things," Thomas said. "If he thinks you want him to like the girl, he will decide against her."

"Yes, we know not to say a word to him about her," Mrs. Westbrook said.

Caroline pressed a finger to her lips to indicate her silence.

So, Benjamin's family were as eager as she was to see Benjamin show interest in someone other than Rebecca. What a blessing it was that she had not angered them with her disinterest in their son and brother.

Thomas asked if he could get them any refreshment, but as they had all already drank and nibbled a bit before the dancing started, they declined his offer. He went to get himself something, and was joined by two other gentlemen. He was in conversation with them when the next dance started.

Rebecca was quite content to sit with Mrs. Westbrook the rest of the night and hold Thomas's compliments close to her heart and memorize them. And while she sat there, it was less likely she'd be asked to dance. But when the next dance started, Caroline went to dance with another young man, Thomas remained talking with his friends, and a gentleman, someone she knew as a friend of Arthur's, came to speak to her.

"Please allow me to express my condolences on the death of your husband, Mrs. Heywood," he said.

What was his name? Rebecca couldn't remember, though she'd heard Arthur speak of him several times.

"I thank you. You are very kind."

She hoped he would move away, but he seemed determined to hold a conversation with her and Mrs. Westbrook. Then she saw Mrs. Heywood sitting on the other side of the room glaring at her. She'd almost forgotten Arthur's mother was attending the ball.

"I do hope your wife is in good health, Mr. . . . ."

"Ludlow," Mrs. Westbrook whispered close to her ear.

"Mr. Ludlow." Of course. Now she remembered.

"I am not married. Arthur and I were school-fellows. Would you do me the honor of standing up with me for the next dance?"

"Of course." Perhaps Rebecca should have been embarrassed at forgetting the man's name and forgetting that he was unmarried, but he asked her to dance so quickly that she didn't think he was offended.

Feeling quite strange at dancing with one of Arthur's friends, she stood up with him as they announced the next dance. There was something about his manner, as well as the way he walked so close to her, that made her even more uncomfortable.

"I have heard that Arthur was murdered by treasure seekers," he said at a lull in the dance. "That must have been a shock to you."

"Yes, it was." Surely he wouldn't want to talk about that while they danced. She cast about in her mind for something to say but her thoughts seemed sluggish.

"And finding a treasure trove buried in your woods. That must also have been surprising. I wonder that Arthur never mentioned it."

"Apparently even the family members who had heard of it did not believe it existed. But this is a dance. You will hardly want to talk of the thing that caused two murders."

"It is a very interesting development, you must admit, Mrs. Heywood. You shot and killed an intruder, I also heard."

"Truly, I do not wish to speak of it tonight. This is a ball." *Not an inquisition,* she nearly added. But she was trying to be polite.

"Of course. Forgive me. But I'm sure you must be getting a great deal of questions about it."

"No, Mr. Ludlow. Yours are the first."

Thankfully, the dance ended at that moment. She gave him a little bow and hurried away, not even waiting for him to walk her back to her chair.

Before she could seat herself, Gilbert Heywood appeared at her elbow.

"May I have this dance?" He was smiling and holding out his hand.

Without thinking, Rebecca took it and let him lead her to the dance floor.

This is my last dance, she vowed. The next person who asked her, she would tell them she did not intend to dance any more. She could say that she did not wish to re-injure her ankle, which was true.

She did her best to enjoy the dance with Gilbert Heywood, though he made two missteps during the course of the dance. And the way he was staring at her reminded her of a cat that the grooms used to keep around the stable for catching mice. She'd once watched it stalk a field rat, and Gilbert's face inexplicably reminded her of that feline's predatory stare.

On the way back to her chair, she said, "I do not intend to dance any more tonight."

"Oh?" For a moment he looked confused, but then a smile spread over his face. "I understand."

What did he mean?

"I have some hosting duties to attend to, but I shall come to you later." He winked and hurried away.

Rebecca couldn't fathom why Gilbert Heywood would wink at her. Did he have something in his eye? It certainly seemed as if he was insinuating something that he assumed she understood. But she had no wish for him to "come to her later."

Thomas was standing next to Caroline a few feet away, staring at her. He bent and whispered something in his sister's ear.

Rebecca sat beside Mrs. Westbrook, thankful that women were so much less complicated and difficult to understand than men.

Caroline came toward Rebecca. Her eyes were big and her manner was quite animated and she sat down on her other side and whispered in her ear, "My brother wishes to speak to you on the terrace overlooking the garden." Her eyes and smile were bigger than Rebecca had ever seen them. When Rebecca did not reply, she whispered, "I think he means to propose marriage."

Rebecca's heart beat a strange tattoo in her chest. Could it be? But why would he not simply wait until they were back at home? There were plenty of opportunities to declare himself there, every day if he wished.

No, he must wish to speak with her about something else.

"I will walk with you to the door," Caroline said in a tone of excitement, "but we should probably wait a moment, so no one will notice we are following him."

They sat watching the dancers for a few moments, then they both stood and walked slowly toward the door that led out to the garden. As soon as they reached it, Caroline squeezed her arm and left her.

The terrace was lit by several lanterns, as well as the light of a full moon and the light coming through the windows. A dark figure several feet away came toward her. It was Thomas.

"I just wanted to remind you to be wary of trusting Gilbert Heywood." Thomas stopped two feet away from her without reaching for her hand or even smiling.

"I am not sure in what way you think I will trust him."

"I only wished to remind you to be on your guard. He seems very eager to dance with you and be near you." He still kept his distance from her.

Was this truly all he wanted to say to her? A pang stabbed her heart.

"As I said, I'm not sure what you thought I would do . . . that I would pledge to sell my house to him? Or perhaps that I would fall in love with him and forfeit the treasure to him?"

"I am sure you may fall in love with whomever you wish." His words were clipped. "I only thought to put you on your guard, as I just received a note from Mr. Pursglove that said—"

"There you are, Rebecca. I saw you—" Gilbert

Heywood stopped in mid-step as he strode through the door and across the terrace toward her. "Mr. Westbrook. I didn't know you were . . ." Gilbert Heywood's countenance changed into a dark scowl, an expression she'd never seen on his face before.

"I came out to get some air. Such a beautiful night," Rebecca said quickly, trying to diffuse the tension that seemed to be mounting. "Shall we return to the ball?"

Her stomach sank at the way Thomas and Gilbert were glaring at each other.

"I have a private word to speak with Mrs. Heywood, if you don't mind." Thomas's voice did not exude the usual warmth. In fact, she felt as if she didn't know him at this moment.

"Very well," Gilbert said with equal coolness. "I shall be inside if you need me." He directed this comment to Rebecca, bowing to her before going back inside.

"I don't think you should be allowing that man to get so close to you," Thomas said.

Rebecca stared at him, open-mouthed. This was a side of him she had not seen—a petty, jealous side. Well, it was good that she was seeing it now, before any promises had been made.

"I don't understand," she said, heat rising inside her. "There is no reason to suspect Gilbert Heywood of anything nefarious. Is it so difficult to believe that he simply likes me for myself, not for my fortune?"

This was her fear coming true, not only that no one could care for her, as her first husband certainly had not cared, even enough to stay home with her, but also that she would fall in love with another man who would mistreat her, making her sad and miserable.

Thomas did not reply right away. She saw his chest rise and fall rapidly, his eyes narrowing.

"You may believe what you will, of course. Far be it from me to dissuade you from defending Gilbert Heywood, but I was trying to tell you that the coroner, Mr. Pursglove, reports that upon questioning him, Mr. Strader, the Justice of the Peace, implicated Gilbert Heywood in the matter of the treasure. Strader says it was Heywood's idea to search for it, and it was he who enlisted the butler's help in discovering the existence of a treasure map."

"These are the allegations of the Justice of the Peace?"

"Yes. I am sorry to cast a shadow on your new suitor, but . . . I will trouble you no further. Good evening, Mrs. Heywood." Thomas walked past her without a glance in her direction.

Rebecca felt sick. What had she done?

Thomas was angry with her. That was clear from his manner. But why should he be? She didn't know that he had information from Mr. Pursglove casting suspicion on Gilbert Heywood. He could not be angry with her when she did not know.

But she had sounded quite petty herself, had she not? Accusing him of—*O God, what did I say?*

She'd said something about him thinking she would fall in love with Gilbert Heywood and give him her fortune. Had she truly said that?

She could feel her face growing hot. But he had said she could fall in love with anyone she wished, and . . . what else had he said?

This was just like the fights she had with Arthur,

when she was so upset that she couldn't remember what they had said to each other when it was over.

Well, if this was what marriage to Thomas West-brook would be like, she wanted no part of it. She was better off alone and on her own. She had her own fortune and did not need a man.

She held her head high and walked back through the door into the ballroom.

CHAPTER TWENTY-FOUR

Thomas rode home from Gilbert Heywood's ball with his eyes closed, pretending to be asleep.

He'd only been trying to help her, since she'd been so friendly with the man since they arrived, choosing to ignore Benjamin's and his advice that Gilbert Heywood was likely not to be trusted. But if she wished to flirt with Gilbert Heywood, why should he care? She'd kissed *him*, not the other way around.

He'd been right to make a vow to himself about staying away from Arthur Heywood's widow. Any woman who could marry Arthur Heywood was not very discerning, to say the least. And here was proof —she was dancing and flirting with Gilbert Heywood, who only wanted her for the treasure that was buried on her estate.

What was worse was that she was so quick to lash out at him when he was only trying to tell her, discreetly, what he had learned from the note Pursglove had sent, which had been placed in his hand personally by Pursglove's courier.

He had spent the rest of the evening away from the ballroom, mostly talking with the other men in the card room, which was why he now reeked of smoke. He'd never been fond of the smoking habit himself.

The ladies spoke quietly when they did speak. Mostly they were quiet, for the first half of the trip home, until they persuaded Benjamin to talk. And then he couldn't seem to stop talking about Miss Mattie Springfield, the girl he'd danced with four times. If he weren't pretending to be asleep, he might warn Benjamin that it was unwise to dance with a lady more than once, and certainly not more than twice, unless he was engaged to her. But his advice had been spurned once tonight, and he would not give it again.

Besides, Benjamin already had been told not to dance so much with a woman he was not engaged to. His brother thought he knew more than Thomas.

He refolded his arms over his stomach without opening his eyes.

The ladies were so quiet that Thomas began to wonder if Rebecca had told them what had occurred between them. His curiosity about whether she had danced any more that night and with whom also began to torment him. But he would never let her know that.

When they stopped at her door, he continued to feign sleep so that Benjamin would get out with her and walk her to her door. Perhaps that was beneath him, but he was still too angry to be perfectly civil toward her and not betray his feelings.

The sooner he could forget about Rebecca Heywood, the better.

~ ~ ~

How foolish she had been to kiss Thomas Westbrook!

Rebecca recalled how he had completely ignored her after their exchange on the terrace. Meanwhile, she had told every gentleman who asked her to dance that she was resting her ankle. But while she watched the other couples dancing, she was remembering her dance with Thomas Westbrook, every time he touched her hand, and the kind compliments he had paid her.

She needed to stop thinking about him. He obviously was not the man she thought he was, as he turned out to be easily offended and quick to judge her.

Truth be told, she was not proud of her own behavior, as she had also been quick to accuse him. She wished it had never happened, but perhaps it was for the best. Perhaps this was God's way of protecting her from a loveless match.

She slept very little after arriving home just before sunrise from the ball. Despite staying in bed late, the day seemed to go by slowly. She tried knitting, but her neck began to ache. She tried reading, but her mind kept wandering, so that she'd barely read a page in half an hour. Her thoughts kept going to the ball, to the treasure, to the constable, the Justice of the Peace, the coroner, and especially to Thomas Westbrook.

A carriage was coming up the lane toward the house. Was Mrs. Heywood home already? She'd hoped she would stay a few days with her friends who lived near Gilbert Heywood.

As it drew closer, she realized it wasn't Mrs. Heywood at all. She watched until the carriage door opened and out came Gilbert Heywood.

Her breath caught in her throat. What was he doing here? If he was under suspicion of being part of the scheme to steal the buried treasure, why hadn't he been apprehended?

She had no wish to face the man. Could she have her servant tell him she wasn't at home? She'd never lied like that before, or asked a servant to lie, and it did not sit well with her. But if the man had been scheming against her, it couldn't be safe to be in his company.

God, help me.

She hurried down the stairs as Gilbert Heywood rang the bell. When the servant came to her, she said, "Show him into the sitting room."

Perhaps the Justice of the Peace had lied about Gilbert Heywood being involved in their scheme to find the treasure for themselves. Perhaps he was only trying to save himself by blaming a landowning gentleman. Although she wasn't quite sure how that would help him.

"Mrs. Heywood." Gilbert bowed to her, a smile on his lips.

"Mr. Heywood, what a nice surprise to see you. Did you enjoy the ball?"

"It is a surprise, no doubt, but I had something particular to propose to you."

"I suppose you wish to purchase this property, which belonged to your cousin, but I am not interested in selling it to you, I'm afraid. I'm very sorry to disappoint you."

"Oh, no. I am not here to renew my offers for Heywood House. Forgive me if I am startling you or intruding on your sensibilities." His face seemed to freeze, as though remembering something. "How is your ankle? I trust you are not feeling any ill effects from the few times you danced on it last night?"

"No, thankfully it seems to be well today. I suppose it was because I took care not to dance too frequently."

"Yes, of course." There was a slight pause, then Mr. Heywood fell to one knee and clasped his hands together. "Mrs. Rebecca Heywood, I pray you will take pity on my desperate state and say you will accept me as your husband, for I find I cannot be happy unless we two are one."

His eyes reminded her of a frog's, bulging, as sweat beaded on his pale forehead.

Rebecca's stomach felt sick, as it had the night before, when Thomas walked past her on the terrace, coldly refusing to look at her.

"Mr. Heywood, please forgive me, but I'm afraid I cannot accept your proposal of a marriage between us. I am truly sorry to give you pain, and I pray you will not be overly hurt by my refusal."

Perhaps she should have postponed her answer, saying she needed time to think it over. After all, if he was found to be involved in criminal activity concerning the buried treasure and the constable's death, he would soon be in jail. But the thought of marrying him was so abhorrent to her, she felt it was better to tell the truth.

Rather than appearing hurt by her refusal, his expression turned dark. In fact, his eyes, which she had thought were blue, suddenly seemed to turn black.

"You dare to refuse me?"

"Pardon me, but did you just ask me if I dared refuse you?" Her thoughts went to her gun, the one she had used to shoot Mr. Fogg. But it was upstairs in her bedside table drawer.

Gilbert Heywood made a strange noise through his teeth, as if trying to speak but unable to come up with the right word.

"I am sorry you are disappointed, Mr. Heywood, but I think it best if—"

"But you danced with me two times. You gave me every encouragement that you would accept my suit. And now you refuse me, and with such finality? This estate was my uncle's. It rightfully belongs in the Heywood family. This is Heywood House. What were you before you married my cousin? Nothing but a tradesman's daughter with no fortune and no connections."

"Mr. Heywood, I must ask you to leave." Rebecca reached for the bell to call a servant.

"Stop." Gilbert Heywood leapt at her and grabbed her wrist.

"Unhand me." Rebecca purposely raised her voice and tried to pull her hand free.

Gilbert only tightened his grip, driving his thumb into the middle of her wrist, sending a horrible aching pain through her hand.

"Let go of me!" Her voice sounded high-pitched, almost hysterical.

Finally, he let go, and she quickly moved away from him and rang the bell.

"I am going. But if there is anything I can do about it, you will neither inherit this estate nor be granted the treasure that my great-uncle buried here." He stalked quickly from the room before the servant could arrive, his boot heels ringing on the marble floor as he exited the house.

Rebecca's breaths were coming fast but shallow.

She hurried to the window, standing away from it so he wouldn't see her, as she watched Gilbert Heywood leap into his carriage and start down the lane from whence he had come.

Rebecca's hands shook as she gingerly touched her wrist where the odious man had just grabbed her, squeezing so hard it still ached. How had he dared to accost her so in her own home?

Truly, she could have screamed and her servants would have come running, but she was as frightened, now that it was over, as she had been when Mr. Fogg had come into her room in the middle of the night. To think of marrying a man such as that, a man who would accost a lady in her own home. It made her stomach twist and a shudder go through her.

She could easily believe he was the man who was ultimately responsible for both Arthur's and Mr. Fogg's murders.

Fearing her knees would no longer hold her, she sank down in a chair and put her head in her hands.

After a few moments, she heard the rumble of carriage wheels on the lane outside. Had Gilbert Heywood returned? She jumped up and hurried to the window. Should she run upstairs and get her gun? Or send for the grooms and the other male servants? Her heart pounded as the carriage turned the corner, then saw it was Mrs. Heywood returning.

Rebecca turned and fled from the room and up the stairs. She could no more face Mrs. Heywood than she could fly through the air like a bird.

Once she was safe in her room, she dressed—as quickly as she could with shaking hands—into her riding habit. There was only one place she could think to go, and that was to the Westbrooks' home. She suddenly longed to be there.

When she was relatively certain that Mrs. Heywood had gone to her bedroom, Rebecca left her room, treading lightly down the stairs, and then out to the stable. She had the groom saddle her horse, and she rode toward the Westbrooks' home.

~ ~ ~

Thomas watched through his bedroom window as Gilbert Heywood stepped out of his carriage.

He had half a mind to yell through his open window and tell the man to go home. What could he mean, coming to Wyghtworth? He must not yet realize that Strader had accused him to the authorities. Either way, Thomas was in no mood to entertain the man.

Still, he couldn't let his mother and sister be alone with him.

As he went down the stairs, he heard his mother's voice. Gilbert Heywood was already in the sitting room.

"Good day. I hope you are well," Gilbert was saying.

Thomas strode into the room. "To what do we owe this unexpected call?"

"Darling, don't be rude," Mother said quietly. "Won't you sit down, Mr. Heywood? I was just about to ring for tea."

Mother did just that, and Thomas had time to study Gilbert. He was also glancing pointedly at Thomas every few moments. And if Thomas had to guess, he would say something had occurred that Gilbert was none too pleased with. Had he been visited by the Bow Street Runners?

"I have been to call on Mrs. Rebecca Heywood," he

said.

Thomas raised his brows as if to say, "And how does that concern me?"

"That woman utterly refused to sell Heywood House to me," Gilbert Heywood said.

Mother looked startled, leaning away from the man.

"It is understandable that you look perplexed," Gilbert Heywood said. "To think of an interloper such as she, who was only married to my cousin for two years, refusing to sell to the rightful owners. She probably thinks that chest of gold, which was taken by my great-uncle in the course of duty as a sea captain in the king's navy, should be given to her as well."

"Sir, you mistake me if you think I take your side against Rebecca Heywood," Mother said. "She is a dear friend of our family and I will not have you speaking against her."

"Did you know that she gave me every encouragement and yet refused me when I asked for her hand in marriage? It was a perfectly good situation for her, who is only a tradesman's daughter, and yet she refused."

"Sir, I think it is time for you to take your leave," Thomas said, rising from his chair.

Gilbert Heywood hesitated, then stood to his feet. "I see she had taken you in, but no doubt it is due to the feud between you and my cousin. You could not bear to be bested by Arthur, who took your fiancé from you, who as it turned out was a hoyden, and worse."

Thomas took a step toward Gilbert Heywood. "Get out. Now."

"Oh my." Mother was turning pale.

At that moment, he noticed Rebecca and Caroline

standing in the doorway. Rebecca jumped back as Gilbert Heywood came toward her.

"I am leaving, but Heywood House shall be mine." He shook his finger at Rebecca. "And I shall make sure this woman's reputation is ruined."

"Get out," Thomas ordered. Coming up behind the man and taking him by the shoulder, he pushed him toward the door.

Gilbert turned and held up his forearms in a defensive posture. "How dare you, sir?" He cleared his throat, raised his chin in the air, and walked out.

Rebecca looked quite shaken as she held onto Caroline.

"That man accosted Rebecca!" Caroline cried. "She was telling me about it when we came inside and heard his voice."

"My dear!" Mother said. "Come and sit down."

"What did he do?" Thomas felt the heat rising into his forehead.

"He only grabbed my wrist and held it."

Caroline took hold of her wrist as if it were made of porcelain. "There are bruises here! Look at what he did!"

A red fog covered Thomas's vision as he strode the short way through the entrance hall and out the door.

CHAPTER TWENTY-FIVE

Rebecca felt her cheeks begin to burn as Caroline called attention to the bruises on her skin. Indeed, she hadn't known there were bruises until Caroline pointed them out.

Truly, she didn't know why she felt the sting of shame. It wasn't as if she'd done anything wrong, but she felt as if she had. And she hardly knew what to think when Thomas Westbrook strode away and out of the front door without a word.

"Oh, my dear." Mrs. Westbrook put her arms around Rebecca's shoulders, and Caroline did the same on her other side.

It must have been their compassion, coupled with the memory of Gilbert Heywood grabbing her, but tears started to fall from her eyes.

She kept her head down so they wouldn't see. She didn't want to be like Mrs. Heywood, making everyone around her uncomfortable with her displays of extreme emotion, trying to force people to feel sorry for her.

Thomas had been right all along to warn her about Gilbert Heywood. She should have listened to him instead of getting offended. But how could she have known?

She wiped the tears from beneath her eyes with her fingers.

"That man will be brought to bear for what he has done," Caroline said hotly. "The king's court will not look lightly upon his actions—assaulting a lady."

"I doubt it will be necessary to bring that into court, to force Rebecca to speak of it publicly," Mrs. Westbrook said. "He is facing far worse allegations, if he is responsible for the constable's actions, as well as for his death."

Yes. He would be held responsible for both Arthur's murder and the constable's.

She took a deep breath and let it out at the thought that she would not have to bring her own accusations to light. Perhaps it was weak of her to be glad of that, but she was.

She heard someone come in the front door, probably Thomas. She looked up and her gaze was caught by Thomas's as he stopped in front of her.

"I hope you put your fist through his face." Caroline said.

"Caroline!" Mrs. Westbrook gasped.

"I wanted to, but no. I also wanted to taunt him about being tried in court for murder, but instead, I told him if he ever laid a hand on a lady again, he would not walk away without some bruises of his own."

"I hope he wet himself."

"Caroline, please!"

"Well, I do. He's a craven little worm."

"He's a murderer, if Strader told the truth, and he will pay for his crimes."

"I should have listened to you," Rebecca said, looking him in the eye, "when you tried to warn me about him. Forgive me."

"You only wished not to falsely accuse anyone, which is good. I am of an overly suspicious nature, and that is not good."

She smiled at his answer, which was not petty at all.

"Let us take some tea," Mrs. Westbrook said. "That will make us all feel better."

They followed her into the sitting room. Rebecca still felt a bit teary-eyed, but she managed to hold back any tears. Thankfully, her hands had stopped shaking when she accepted the cup of tea from Mrs. Westbrook.

They talked of pleasant things, and when the sun started to go down, Caroline said, "Please stay the night with us."

"To be honest, I am loathe to return home."

"With Mrs. Heywood there, I shouldn't wonder."

Rebecca waited for the gentle word of scolding from Caroline's mother, but none came.

Thomas stayed with them, talking, until Benjamin came in.

"You all look very dull," he said. "I have been out hunting and killed five pheasants."

"I suppose you think nothing of great consequence has gone on here today," Caroline said with a smirk.

"What? What has gone on? Has the clock had to be rewound? Or perhaps you missed a stitch in your knitting."

"You don't deserve to hear it, but I shall tell you that you missed Gilbert Heywood coming here after he went to Rebecca's home and accosted her, bruising her wrist. Can you imagine? Thomas—"

"I hope you beat him with a stick." Benjamin looked at Thomas. "I hope you broke his jaw and his nose."

"His punishment is coming," Thomas said calmly.

Benjamin stared at him with his mouth hanging open.

"The man is a mouse. He cowered so before me that I couldn't hit him. I could only send him on his way, knowing that he would probably be apprehended as soon as he arrived home and would be held behind locks and bars."

Benjamin shook his head. "At any rate, I should have liked to have seen you threaten him, and him cowering before you."

"Such talk," Mrs. Westbrook said quietly.

"Forgive me, Mother."

She only waved a hand at him.

Soon they retired to dine, then to play and sing for an hour, everyone so sufficiently cheered that they were all laughing by the time they parted to retire to bed. And all the while Rebecca could not stop thinking about how she wished she could further explain to Thomas that she was sorry for what she had said at the ball.

But when Caroline showed her to her bedroom, she'd not had a moment alone with him.

Caroline went in with her. "If you need anything, you can ring the bell."

"Of course. Thank you for being so kind as to ask me to stay. I know it is silly, but I was dreading going home."

"Not silly at all. I am so glad you stayed. You know you always make us, all of us Westbrooks, very happy."

"I am not at all sure that is true."

"You told me you and Thomas quarreled at the ball, but all seems well now."

"Yes, I think all is well."

"I confess, Mother and I hoped that you and Thomas would form an attachment, that we would be blessed to have you as a sister and daughter."

"Well, I do not know if that will ever happen. And perhaps it is for the best. I thought marriage would bring me happiness, but . . . I was so miserable, Caroline."

Thankfully, it was dark in the room, with no light except from the fire in the grate, for Rebecca could feel the tears welling up. Her heart ached just as it had when she'd heard, for the first time, that Arthur was spending his nights with a paramour, hidden away in London for a week. How deeply it hurt! Like a knife in her heart, knowing he was with another woman, knowing he did not love Rebecca enough to stay with her, that he had broken his vows to her.

The tears flowed down her cheeks. "I'm sorry. I don't wish to make you uncomfortable."

"You can talk to me, dear Rebecca. What is it you are thinking about?"

"I was remembering the pain of Arthur's betrayals and rejection. Marriage did not make me happy at all. After a year or so, I realized the best I could hope for was a child. I thought if I had a child, I could find a measure of happiness as a mother. I could give all my love to my child and forget my pain. But as you know, I had no child." The tears flowed afresh.

"Oh, Rebecca, I'm so sorry." Caroline took her hand and squeezed it.

"I think I just needed to realize that neither marriage nor motherhood, indeed, no other person, can make me happy. I must be happy on my own. I was wrong to put my hope in a husband or a child. Does not the Bible say that God should be our everything, that we should not have any other gods before him?"

"Yes, but it also says that it is not good for man to be alone, which is why God made us male and female, so we could help each other, or something like that."

"Yes." She had read that before.

"And there's that passage that I've heard at weddings, that two are better than one because they have someone to help them up if they fall, and a threefold cord is not easily broken. It isn't bad to love someone or to marry, or to wish to marry. Marriage is not supposed to bring you pain and misery. It isn't meant to be that way, and it won't be, when you marry a good man."

She'd berated herself for her feelings for Thomas Westbrook, and especially for kissing him. She'd called herself foolish and impulsive, and perhaps she was, a bit. But should she be thinking of it another way? Perhaps she should see herself as a woman with natural feelings, a woman whose husband had betrayed her so thoroughly that she was afraid to trust again.

And yet, she was a woman who longed to love and to feel loved. But perhaps that was how God intended it. She wasn't meant to be alone. She was meant to give love. And to receive it. From a human person, not just from God.

"I think you're right." She squeezed Caroline's hand, finding that her tears had dried.

"Of course I'm right. But I also understand that your feelings are probably very close to the surface. That's how Mother and I felt for months after Father died. And as much as it shocked and wounded us when he died, it must be much worse having your husband murdered. I can hardly imagine it. So be kind to yourself."

Rebecca nodded, grateful for her friend's compassionate words.

"And if my brother has said anything amiss to you, I shall go and reprimand him sternly this very minute."

"No, no, please don't. I'm afraid I was to blame more than he was. I didn't want to listen to him. Instead of being offended by his words, I should have thanked him for his concern."

"I know he can be very opinionated and can take too much upon himself when he should mind his own business. He sometimes goes too far."

"No, no, he did nothing wrong. Do not trouble yourself."

"Very well. Shall I send for some warm milk to help you sleep?"

"No, thank you. I am so tired, I shall sleep very soundly, I think."

They wished each other a good night.

Rebecca considered Caroline's words, about marriage and about her brother. When she thought about Thomas Westbrook, how kind he'd been to her, the way he spoke, the gentleness in his manner and in his eyes, she just wanted to see more of him, to know him better, to hear his thoughts. She marveled at how quickly she'd forgotten her anger toward him and the way he'd behaved at the ball. Perhaps he had been a bit heavy-handed in continuing to warn her to stay away from Gilbert Heywood, but she had also reacted badly to his advice. If only she could talk with him about it privately.

She said her prayers, thanking God for keeping her safe from Gilbert Heywood. She also asked for guidance and wisdom, before drifting into sleep.

~ ~ ~

Thomas stayed close all morning and was ready when Rebecca told his mother and sister, "Thank you, but I believe I must go home now."

"I shall ride back with you," Thomas said, knowing she had ridden her horse there the day before.

"Thank you." She smiled at him and his heart beat faster.

No one questioned why he would need to ride back with her, thankfully, but at this point he would hardly have cared. He'd been waiting two days to get a few moments alone with her.

When they entered the woods between their two houses, he said, "Do you mind if we stop here a moment?"

"Not at all."

They stopped their horses and dismounted, letting their horses drink from the spring that bubbled up from the ground here, the origin of the little stream that cut through his own property.

"I wanted to tell you how sorry I am for plaguing you so at the ball. I should not have been so dogged. I could have waited to tell you of Mr. Pursglove's note after the ball was over."

"No, you were perfectly right in warning me. And I have been wanting to say how very sorry I am for allowing myself to be offended when you were only trying to help."

"The fault is mine, for the truth is, I was jealous, seeing you dancing a second time with Gilbert Heywood."

Rebecca had been reaching for a leaf on a tree, but she stopped and turned toward him. She was deliciously near. He could see her every eyelash, framing her pretty blue eyes. And her lips were slightly parted as she tilted her head up toward him.

"You were jealous? But you couldn't think I would have feelings for . . . for anyone besides you."

"Forgive me." He took another step toward her, so that he could easily take her hand in his. "I am afraid I'm much too mistrusting. I realize, however, just because I was betrayed by my first love, the woman I chose to marry, as well as my best childhood friend, that doesn't mean I should never trust anyone again, does it?"

"No, it doesn't." Her voice was breathy and soft, and she seemed to lean toward him. "And just because my first marriage was nothing but misery and pain, that doesn't mean my second marriage would be miserable and painful."

"No, indeed." He took her hand and turned it over, staring down at the dark blue bruises on her otherwise perfect skin. He lifted her wrist to his lips and kissed the offending evidence of a cruel man's fingers, softly brushing his lips against her wrist.

He heard the sound of her breath hitching in her throat. His heart started to beat double time, and he continued to kiss her wrist slowly, letting his mouth linger on her skin.

When he lifted his head, her eyes were half closed but staring at his mouth. He leaned in, pulling her to him, and kissed her lips.

Her arms went around his back and he kissed her again, holding her close, kissing her as if his life depended on convincing her that she would enjoy kissing him every day for the rest of her life.

When he pulled away, her eyes were still closed.

"On the contrary," he said, speaking slowly and deliberately, "I think your second marriage will be very happy."

When she finally opened her eyes, she gazed back at him and placed her hand on his cheek. "How do you know?"

"Because I plan to spend most of my time making you happy."

Her bottom lip trembled. Then she drew in a ragged breath and said, "I love you."

He hugged her tightly to his chest and said, "I love you, Rebecca. Will you marry me?"

"Yes."

His heart soared, and he suddenly felt as if everything was right in the world.

CHAPTER TWENTY-SIX

Rebecca and Thomas took their time in the small clearing in the woods, talking and kissing. How absolutely wonderful it felt to commune with the best and most wonderful man she knew, kissing his lips, her arms around him, and his arms around her.

When he'd started kissing the bruises on her wrist, she completely lost her breath, her knees going weak at the tender, intimate gesture, and at how warm and gentle his kisses were. And when he asked her to marry him, and kissed her lips, she couldn't imagine anything more heavenly.

When they had got back on their horses and were almost to Heywood House, she asked him, "Can you look at me and see that we've been kissing?" She could still feel his lips on hers.

"No." He smiled. "You are incredibly lovely, though, and adorable."

"My heart is so full, I don't know that I will be

able, but I think we should conceal our engagement for a while, probably until the inquest has decided who should get the treasure, and until after the trials of Gilbert Heywood and Mr. Strader. And then we should wait until everyone has ceased to talk about the treasure, and —"

"Will you have us wait until we are too old to have children?" His brows were low and drawn together.

"No. But we should wait an appropriate amount of time."

"Appropriate according to who?"

"I don't know. How long do you think we should wait?"

"I don't want to wait. I would marry you tomorrow. Say the word and we shall be on our way to Gretna Green."

She laughed. "This is a side of you I haven't seen."

"You haven't seen me impatient?"

"No, I haven't."

He rode his horse so close to hers that their boots were touching in the stirrups, and he leaned over and kissed her again.

They rode on until the house was in sight.

"I think I might be able to wait six months, but no longer," he told her.

"Six months? I don't know if anything will be decided that soon."

"Decided or not, I want my bride."

She giggled and shook her head. "Very well." She stared at him, feeling rather impatient to be married as well.

"If you keep giving me that sly look, I may just take you back to the little glade by the spring."

Her breath hitched in her throat.

Unfortunately, a groom was already coming toward them to take their horses.

They dismounted and he seemed to be struggling to behave, as he did not even take her hand as they walked to the house.

She looked over at him and her heart seemed to lift out of her chest. This was the man she would begin a family with, have children with, and grow old with. It seemed she would not have to be alone after all.

~ ~ ~

The next day Rebecca and Thomas wasted no time in telling Mrs. Westbrook, Benjamin, and Caroline about their engagement. Mrs. Westbrook and Caroline reacted as they'd expected.

Caroline squealed. "This is the best news in the world! Oh, Thomas! Thank you for ensuring I have Rebecca as my sister forever!"

Thomas shook his head. "All for you, of course," he said sarcastically but with a smile as Rebecca embraced her new soon-to-be sister-in-law.

Mrs. Westbrook cried, "Oh, my darlings. You've made me so happy." Her eyes filled with tears, and she took out her handkerchief and dabbed her eyes.

Benjamin, whose reaction they most worried about, was a bit less enthusiastic, but even he smiled and wished them joy. "I hope you will try to deserve her," he told Thomas.

"I shall try." He looked at Rebecca and winked.

Rebecca's heart was so full. "I don't know how I will keep this a secret from anyone. I can't stop smiling."

"Must you keep it a secret?" Caroline asked.

"Rebecca believes we must wait until after the inquest into the treasure is over, after the trials of Strader and Gilbert Heywood are over, and after she's sure no one will gossip about her."

"There's no need to wait for all that," Caroline said.

"People will always talk. You cannot concern yourselves with that," Mrs. Westbrook said.

"I just want to make sure I do the right thing." Rebecca was already starting to doubt her desire to wait.

The next day when Thomas came early to call on her, they went for a walk in the garden and beyond but were forced inside by the rain. They were in the sitting room, talking and laughing, when Mrs. Heywood appeared in the door.

"I thought the house was being invaded by a mob, from the noise coming from this room." She glanced around, then said, "Did the rest of your family not accompany you here?" she asked Thomas with a tone of exaggerated surprise.

"No, I am alone today," Thomas said.

Mrs. Heywood stared back at them for so long that Rebecca wondered if she had finally been rendered speechless.

"I suppose this time spent alone means that you're engaged."

Thomas looked at Rebecca, allowing her to decide whether they would tell her.

"We are engaged," Rebecca said.

"To be married?" Mrs. Heywood said.

"Yes, to be married," Thomas said.

"I knew it," Mrs. Heywood said in a low voice. "I knew you would be married soon enough after my poor son was barely in his grave. You could not even wait a decent amount of time, could you? Greedy, grasping . . . Well, I won't . . . You . . ." She stammered a moment longer before silently walking away.

"Greedy and grasping," Thomas said mildly. "Does she mean me? Or you, do you think?"

"I think she means me." Rebecca almost laughed at how lightly Thomas seemed to take her insulting words.

"Do you think she will finally move out to the dowager cottage?"

"Let us hope so."

~ ~ ~

Two weeks later, they received word that the inquest had begun and jurors were being selected. A week after that, the jury had decided that the treasure belonged to Rebecca Heywood as the finder of a treasure that had been abandoned and forgotten on property that belonged solely to her.

"I cannot believe it," Mrs. Heywood said, when they were informed together. "You must have bribed someone, for this is an injustice that even a babe in arms could see."

"If you object so much as to accuse me of bribing the judge in the King's Court, then I would think you would not wish to stay in the same house with me." Rebecca gave her former mother-in-law stare for stare, trying not to show how shocked she was at her own courage to say what she'd been wanting to say for months.

Mrs. Heywood's face became a mask of cold anger. "If you think a tradesman's daughter can make me cower down, you are mistaken," she said, hissing the last word.

She stormed away and did indeed move her things into the dowager cottage, taking most of the servants into her service for the better part of two days to help her with the move.

~ ~ ~

One week later . . .

While it was lovely to have the house all to themselves, it did give them a degree of freedom that, to Rebecca's way of thinking, was causing another problem.

After receiving him into the sitting room, she told Thomas "I don't think we should wait six months to get married."

He grinned. "Does this have to do with what happened yesterday?"

He was of course referring to the heated kissing that they had been engaged in, only to look up and see three servants watching them from the doorway.

The servants immediately scattered, but Rebecca could feel her cheeks burning.

"Yes, and I just don't want to wait."

He kissed the tip of her nose. "Very well. We can have the banns read this Sunday and be married three weeks after that."

Rebecca took a deep breath and let it out. "I think it is best."

"Well, don't look as if it is something unpleasant."

"Forgive me. I have too much fear, I know, and it has nothing to do with you." She embraced him, burying her face in his shoulder. "I know we will be very, very happy."

"I know you are afraid, but think of it this way. If I don't treat you well—which I will, but just hypothetically—then my mother, sister, and brother will champion your cause and I'd have little choice but to mend my ways."

"Actually, that is true . . . and comforting."

Thomas looked askance at her. She smiled and kissed him.

~ ~ ~

Two weeks later . . .

Rebecca arrived early at Wyghtworth and joined the family in the breakfast room.

"I received a letter," she said, and handed it to Thomas to read, which he did.

"This is an offer to purchase Heywood House."

"It is."

"Will you accept it?"

"It is from a distant relative of Arthur's. I believe I met him briefly at Arthur's funeral. He has made a fortune in London in trade—won't Mrs. Heywood be horrified? And he wishes to settle in the country. And since I am marrying you, I don't need Heywood House, and since it will enable me to cut all ties with Mrs. Heywood, I think, yes, I will sell it to him."

"That is wonderful," Mrs. Westbrook and Caroline both said.

"This offering price is less than the estate is worth, I would think. Will you ask for more?" Thomas looked at her rather blandly, as if the matter hardly concerned him.

"I should be glad if you would advise me," she said, smiling in a way that she hoped was beguiling.

"Are you sure you wish me to interfere in your business matter?"

"Yes, I would like you to interfere, if that's what you wish to call it."

She had no idea how much Heywood House was worth or how to go about negotiating the price, but she knew he would.

"But I wish to sell it, even if he doesn't give me a fair and reasonable price."

"Very well. But we shall not tell him or his solicitor that."

Thomas went to write a letter to the solicitor while Rebecca, Mrs. Westbrook, and Caroline went to see the miraculous roses in the garden.

"I have never seen such large roses, or such an abundance of them," Mrs. Westbrook told Rebecca as she tucked her hand in hers. "Truly, I know you and Thomas will be very happy here at Wyghtworth for many years to come."

And Rebecca was sure of that too, if only she and Thomas could both prevent themselves from reacting to each other out of fear, born of things that had wounded them in the past. And knowing what a good heart Thomas possessed, and knowing the depth of her love for him, she was certain they would succeed.

~ ~ ~

Three and a half weeks later . . .

Rebecca and Thomas stood before the rector of their parish church and vowed to love each other until death should part them.

The rector recited from Scripture, "'Two are better than one; because they have a good reward for their labour. For if they fall, the one will lift up his fellow: but woe to him that is alone when he falleth; for he hath not another to help him up. Again, if two lie together, then they have heat: but how can one be warm alone? And if one prevail against him, two shall withstand him; and a threefold cord is not quickly broken.'

"What God hath joined together, let not man put asunder. Amen."

Once they were in the carriage and on their way to the seaside for their wedding trip, Thomas kissed her quite thoroughly. As she sat beside him looking dreamily into his handsome face, he asked, "How does it feel to be a wealthy woman, having money set aside for your mother, your sisters, your brothers, and your future children? Not only that, but having investments in a variety of businesses and ventures, both here and in America?"

"It feels good," she said, as he nuzzled her ear. "But today I don't care about any of that. Today I only care that you love me."

She kissed him, losing her train of thought, if she even had one before the kiss.

"This must be what the poets all felt when they wrote their love poems and sonnets." Thomas kissed her temple, then her cheek, then her chin, then her lips.

"I'm so glad you married me."

"Why is that?"

"Because I finally know how it feels to be loved, and to be in love."

"In love?"

"Yes. I think being in love is different from loving. Being in love means you admire the other person's character, besides the fact that you've chosen to love them. Being in love means you couldn't help loving them, even if you tried."

"Then I am in love with you too."

Though they did not yet know the outcome of the trials and investigation behind who had killed Arthur and Mr. Fogg, they did not let any of that trouble them, for this was their day, and they were sure that even in the future, no matter what troubles might come, they would have someone beside them who was trustworthy and true, a spouse who would help them, fight for them, and never leave them.

The End

Book 3, A Deadly Secret

Coming Soon!

Lillian Courtney's husband's criticizing and bullying ways culminate with him physically striking her, and she runs away to the Isle of Wight, taking her young daughter with her. Her husband follows her there—and is found dead the next day. Her mother-in-law accuses her of killing her husband, then tries to take her child away from her. Lillian is devastated at the prospect of losing her daughter.

Nash Golding, Earl of Barrentine, was not looking for trouble. He was only trying to keep his secret safe—the secret that he is a novelist publishing amusing satires under the pen name Perceval Hastings. His family would be aghast if his secret were made public. As an earl and a member of the House of Lords, working as an author of satirical novels is beneath him. Early one morning, after sending his latest manuscript to his publisher, he emerges from a tiny village post office to witness a man, obviously up to no good, stalking a young lady. Nash follows them and is forced to be of service to the lady—in saving her life.

Nash strives to keep the pretty widow safe from her late husband's devious family members, who wish to gain control of her daughter. But while he is protecting them, will his own secret be revealed? His position in society and in Parliament will be irreparably damaged when it is discovered that, not only is he the notorious satirist, Perceval Hastings, but he is also harboring a poor widow suspected of murdering her husband.

Lillian is falling in love with the handsome earl, despite her fear and lack of trust. Nash, in turn, finds that neither his reputation nor his heart is safe when the lovely Lillian is near.

Other Books By Melanie Dickerson

IMPERILED YOUNG WIDOWS
A Perilous Plan
A Treacherous Treasure
A Deadly Secret (coming soon)

REGENCY SPIES OF LONDON
A Spy's Devotion
A Viscount's Proposal
A Dangerous Engagement

THE DERICOTT TALES
Court of Swans
Castle of Refuge
Veil of Winter (coming June, 2022)
Fortress of Snow (coming December, 2022)

MEDIEVAL FAIRY TALES (THORNBECK SERIES)
The Huntress of Thornbeck Forest
The Beautiful Pretender
The Noble Servant

FAIRY TALE ROMANCE (HAGENHEIM SERIES)
The Healer's Apprentice
The Merchant's Daughter
The Fairest Beauty
The Captive Maiden
The Princess Spy
The Golden Braid
The Silent Songbird
The Orphan's Wish
The Warrior Maiden
The Piper's Pursuit
The Peasant's Dream

SOUTHERN SEASONS
Magnolia Summer

Acknowledgements

I want to thank all the people who have been walking this "indie publishing" journey with me. First of all, I want to thank my daughters, Grace and Faith, and my husband, Aaron, who are always willing to help me brainstorm and let me talk out my stories with them, and that is so very helpful.

Second of all, I want to thank my writing accountability partners, Kristin Billerbeck, Cheryl Hodde, Tina Radcliffe, and Josee Telfer. I never could have imagined how much writing on video chat with other writers at a certain time each day could change my life and make me so much more productive! It has been miraculous, and I'm so thankful for it.

I want to thank and acknowledge Nancy Mayers for her help in answering my research questions. I found her to be a fount of knowledge on Regency England's complicated system of constables, coroners, Justices of the Peace, and other law enforcement officials. Nancy was so kind to help me figure out the roles of each office, but any research mistakes are mine alone.

I also have to thank my agent, Natasha Kern, for encouraging me to self-publish this series. She is truly a godsend, unselfish, and ahead of her time, always.

Thanks especially to everyone who prays for me, buys my books, reads my books, tells other people about my books, and writes reviews for my books. I am so grateful for you! God bless you.

Want To Stay In The Know?

To stay up to date about new books and book news, sign up for my newsletter here, https://bit.ly/3dUsh7B or on my website, www.MelanieDickerson.com.

You can also follow me on social media, particularly on Instagram @melaniedickerson123 https://www.instagram.com/melaniedickerson123/ and Facebook, www.facebook.com/MelanieDickersonBooks

If you would like to get an email notification whenever I have a new book comes out:

Follow me on BookBub, www.Bookbub.com/authors/melanie-dickerson

And/or on Amazon, www.amazon.com/Melanie-Dickerson/e/BOO3BAAJG6/

Thanks so much!

Discussion Questions

1. Who did Rebecca originally think murdered her husband? Why?

2. What would you do if your husband was unfaithful to you?

3. Why did Rebecca not consider divorcing her husband? How are things different now than they were in Regency England?

4. What do you think of the customs surrounding death and funerals in Regency times?

5. How did Rebecca deal with her mother-in-law's treatment of her? How do you tend to deal with people who don't treat you well?

6. Did you think Thomas Westbrook was a trustworthy man? What made you think so?

7. How did Rebecca's and Thomas's pasts make them more fearful and suspicious?

8. What events or relationships in your past have affected your thinking, and how?

9. If you were to find a treasure worth a lot of money, what would you do with it?

10. Margaret advised Caroline, "She should look for the man who has everything, because she is worth a good man who is handsome,

wealthy, and most importantly, possesses good character and ideals." Do you agree with Margaret's marriage advice? Why or why not?

11. What did you think of the sibling relationships between Thomas, Caroline, and Benjamin? Did their interactions remind you of any of your relationships with siblings, cousins, or friends?

12. Do you think Rebecca was justified in shooting Mr. Fogg? Why or why not? Should she have felt responsible for his death? Why or why not?

13. The passage in Ecclesiastes says "two are better than one." Do you agree? If so, in what ways has that proven true—and what ways do you anticipate that proving true—in your life?

ABOUT THE AUTHOR

Melanie Dickerson

Melanie Dickerson is the New York Times bestselling author of Regency romantic suspense and Medieval fairy tale retellings. Her novels have won the Christy Award, National Reader's Choice Award, Golden Quill Contest, Book Buyer's Best Award, and more.

Since she was a kid, Melanie has been writing stories involving a hero and heroine, lots of adventure, and a happily ever after ending. She's been a romantic for as long as she can remember. Now you'll find her in North Alabama hanging out and watching movies with her handsome hero husband and her oddly calm Jack Russell terrier—when she's not sprint-writing on video chat with writer friends or daydreaming about the characters for her next book.